KT-872-459

FALLING IN LOVE

Donna Leon was named by *The Times* as one of the 50 Greatest Crime Writers. She is an award-winning crime novelist, celebrated for the bestselling Brunetti series. Donna has lived in Venice for thirty years and previously lived in Switzerland, Saudi Arabia, Iran and China, where she worked as a teacher. Donna's books have been translated into 35 languages and have been published around the world.

Her previous novels featuring Commissario Brunetti have all been highly acclaimed; including *Friends in High Places*, which won the CWA Macallan Silver Dagger for Fiction, *Fatal Remedies*, *Doctored Evidence*, *A Sea of Troubles* and *Beastly Things*.

Praise for Donna Leon and *Falling in Love*

'Donna Leon's deft and descriptive words do for Venice what Canaletto did for this serenest of cities with his brushes and paint palette and bring it to life in all its reach and colourful gaiety . . . [An] intriguing tense thriller. The ending is to die for.' *Daily Express*

'Donna Leon is a truly fine novelist, period, and should be acclaimed as such' *Times Literary Supplement*

C333910341

Also by Donna Leon

Death at La Fenice
Death in a Strange Country
The Anonymous Venetian
A Venetian Reckoning
Acqua Alta
The Death of Faith
A Noble Radiance
Fatal Remedies
Friends in High Places
A Sea of Troubles
Wilful Behaviour
Doctored Evidence
Blood from a Stone
Through a Glass, Darkly
Suffer the Little Children
The Girl of His Dreams
About Face
A Question of Belief
Drawing Conclusions
Beastly Things
The Jewels of Paradise
The Golden Egg
By Its Cover

Donna Leon

FALLING IN LOVE

arrow books

3 5 7 9 10 8 6 4 2

Arrow Books
20 Vauxhall Bridge Road
London SW1V 2SA

Arrow is part of the Penguin Random House group of companies whose
addresses can be found at global.penguinrandomhouse.com.

Copyright © Donna Leon and Diogenes Verlag 2015

Donna Leon has asserted her right to be identified as the author of this
Work in accordance with the Copyright, Designs and Patents Act 1988.

This is a work of fiction. Names and characters are the product of the
author's imagination and any resemblance to actual persons, living or
dead, is entirely coincidental.

First published by William Heinemann in 2015
This edition published by Arrow Books in 2016

www.randomhouse.co.uk

A CIP catalogue record for this book is available from the British Library.

ISBN 9781784750749
ISBN 9781784750756 (Export edition)

Map © ML Design

Typeset in Palatino by Palimpsest Book Production Ltd,
Falkirk, Stirlingshire
Printed and bound in Great Britain by Clays Ltd, St Ives Plc

MIX
Paper from
responsible sources
FSC
www.fsc.org   FSC® C018179

Penguin Random House is committed to a sustainable
future for our business, our readers and our planet.
This book is made from Forest Stewardship
Council® certified paper.

For Ada Pesch

Le voci di virtù
Non cura amante cor, o pur non sente.

A loving heart pays no attention to the voice of virtue,
or cannot hear it.

Rodelinda
Handel

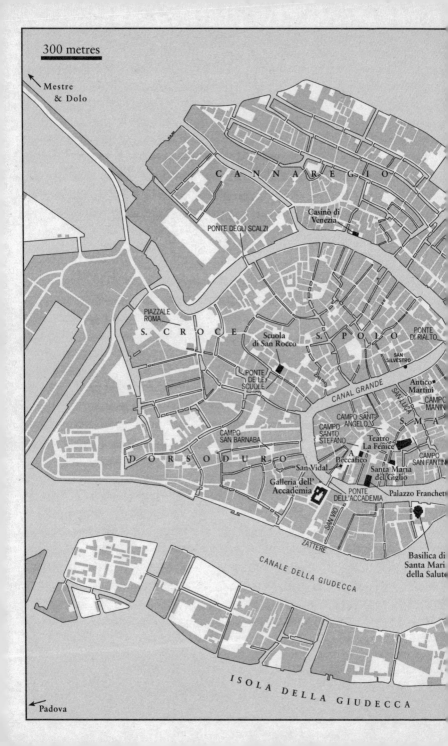

300 metres

Mestre & Dolo

CANNAREGIO

Casino di Venezia

PONTE DEGLI SCALZI

PIAZZALE ROMA

S. CROCE

Scuola di San Rocco

S. POLO

PONTE DI RIALTO

SAN SILVESTRO

CANAL GRANDE

Antico Martini

PONTE DE LE SCUOLE

CAMPO MANIN

SAN LUCA

S M A

CAMPO SANT ANGELO

CAMPO SANTO STEFANO

CAMPO SAN BARNABA

Teatro La Fenice

CAMPO SAN FANTIN

DORSODURO

A Beccafico

San Vidal

Santa Maria del Giglio

Galleria dell' Accademia

PONTE DELL'ACCADEMIA

Palazzo Franchet

SAN VIO

ZATTERE

Basilica di Santa Mari della Salute

CANALE DELLA GIUDECCA

Padova

ISOLA DELLA GIUDECCA

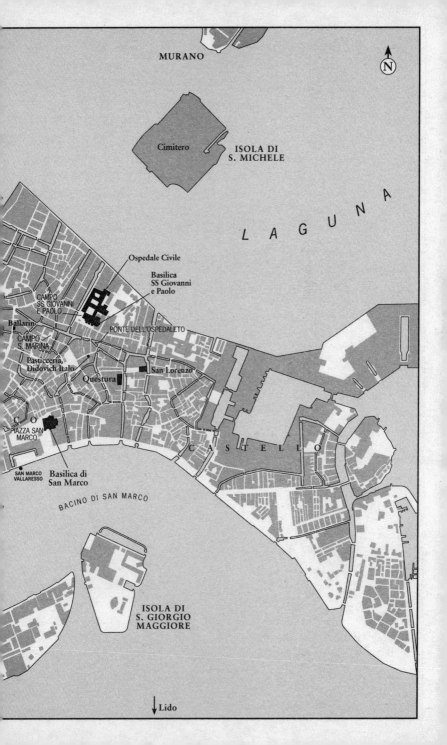

1

The woman knelt over her lover, her face, her entire body, stiff with terror, staring at the blood on her hand. He lay on his back, one arm flung out, palm upturned as if begging her to place something into it; his life, perhaps. She had touched his chest, urging him to get up so they could get out of there, but he hadn't moved, so she had shaken him, the same old sleepy-head who never wanted to get out of bed.

Her hand had come away red and, without thinking, she pressed it to her mouth to stifle her scream, knowing she must make no noise, not let them know she was there. Then horror overcame her caution, and she screamed his name again and again, telling herself he was dead, and it was all over; like this, in blood.

She looked at where her hand had been and saw the red blotches: how had so much blood come from them, so small, so small? She rubbed her clean hand across her mouth, and it came away coloured with the blood on her face. Panicked, seeing the blood, she spoke his name. All over, all over. She said his name again, this time louder, but he could no longer hear or answer her, or anyone. Unthinking, she leaned forward to kiss him, grabbed at his shoulders in a vain attempt to shake some life into him, but there was to be no more life, for either one of them.

A loud cry from the leader of the gang that had killed him came from her left, and she pressed her hand to her breast. Fear drove out speech, and she could only grunt 'Ah, ah', like an animal in pain. She turned her head and saw them, heard their shouting but had no idea what they were saying: all she knew was terror and, suddenly, fear for herself, now that he was dead, and for what they wanted to do to her.

She pushed herself to her feet and moved away from him: no looking back. He was dead, and it was all gone: all hope, all promise spent and dry.

The men, four of them on the left, then five more from the right, came out on to the littered rooftop where the murder had taken place. The leader of the pack shouted something, but she was beyond hearing him or hearing anyone or anything. She knew only the need to escape, but they had her blocked in from both sides. She turned and saw behind her the edge of the roof, no other building in sight: no place to go, no place to hide.

There was choice, but there was really no choice: death was better than any of this, either what had just happened or what was sure to happen once they got their hands on her. She stumbled once, twice, as she ran towards the ledge, stepped up on to it with unexpected grace and turned back to look at the men who were running towards her. 'O Scarpia, avanti a Dio,' she cried, turned, and leaped.

The music crashed out and then continued to boom around a bit, as it always did at the end of this shabby little shocker,

2

and then there was a long moment of stunned silence as the audience realized what they had just heard and seen. Not since Callas – and that had been half a century ago – had anything like this *Tosca* been seen or heard. Tosca had really killed Scarpia, the chief of police, hadn't she? And her lover really had been shot by those creeps in uniform? And she'd really jumped into the Tiber. By God, the woman could act and, even better, she could sing. It's completely real: the murder, the fake execution that turned out to be real, and her final leap when there was nothing left and nothing to lose. It's romantic balderdash, the whole thing is beyond parody, but then why was the audience sitting there clapping the skin off their hands and shouting like banshees?

The curtains slowly parted at the centre, and Flavia Petrelli slipped through the narrow space. She wore red, redder than red, and a tiara that had apparently survived her plummet into the river. She looked out at the audience, and stunned delight slowly lit up her face. For me? All that noise for *me*? Her smile grew, and one of her hands – somehow magically free of blood or whatever had been used to resemble it – rose to the exposed flesh above her breasts and pressed at her heart, as if to force it to remain in place in the midst of all this excitement.

She took her hand away and opened one arm as if to embrace them all, then the other, exposing her entire body to the assault of the applause. Then both hands again found their way to her breast, and she sank in a graceful motion, half bow, half genuflection. The applause increased, and voices, both male and female, shouted out '*Brava*', or, for those who were either blind or not Italian, '*Bravo*'. She didn't seem to mind, so long as they shouted. Another bow, and then she raised her face as if to bathe it in the cascade of applause.

3

The first rose, long-stemmed and yellow as the sun, fell just in front of her. Her foot pulled back from it involuntarily, as if she were afraid of doing it an injury, or it her, and then she bent, so slowly as to make her motion seem studied, almost practised, to pick it up. She pressed it to her bosom and crossed her hands upon it. Her smile had faltered when she saw it – 'This is for me? For *me*?' – but the face she raised to the upper balconies gleamed with joy.

As if summoned by her reaction, the roses continued to fall: first two, then three more, tossed individually from the right side, and then more and more, until dozens of them lay at her feet, turning her into a Joan of Arc, brushwood rising to her ankles, and above.

Flavia smiled into the thunder of the applause, bowed again, stepped back from the roses, and slipped through the curtains. A few moments later, she emerged, holding her no-longer-dead lover by the hand. Like the shouts of Scarpia's henchmen, the applause mounted at the sight of him, heading towards that delirium that so often rose at the sight of a handsome young tenor who had all the high notes and used them generously. Both of them looked nervously below them, trying to avoid stepping on the carpet of roses, then they abandoned the attempt and crushed them underfoot.

Responding instinctively to some note in the applause that told her it was for him, Flavia took a step backwards and joined in, raising her hands high as she clapped with the audience. Just at the moment when the applause started to diminish, she stepped up beside him, took his arm and leaned into his side, then kissed him briefly on the cheek, the companionable peck one gives a brother or a good colleague. He, in his turn, grabbed her hand and thrust their joined hands above their heads, as if announcing the winner of a contest.

4

The tenor took one step back to make room for her, crushing more roses, and she slipped in front of him and through the curtains; he followed her. After a moment, the resurrected Scarpia, the front of his brocade jacket still incarnadined, stepped through the curtains and moved to the right, avoiding most of the roses. He bowed, bowed again, and crossed his hands on his bloody chest to show his thanks, then, returning to the opening in the curtain, he reached in and withdrew Flavia, whose other hand was attached to the hand of the young tenor. Scarpia led the conga line of three no-longer-dead people to the right, crushing the blossoms, the hem of Flavia's gown sweeping them aside. They raised their linked hands, bowing together, their faces equally radiant and transformed by pleasure and gratitude at the audience's appreciation.

Flavia unhooked herself from the two men and slipped behind the curtain again, this time to emerge hand in hand with the conductor. He was the youngest person on the stage, but his self-possession matched that of his older colleagues. He walked forward, not even noticing the roses, and scanned the audience. He smiled and bowed, then waved the orchestra to its feet for their share of the applause. The conductor bowed again, then stepped back and placed himself between Flavia and the tenor. The four of them moved forward and bowed, then again, always pleased and grateful. The level of applause diminished minimally; sensitive to this, Flavia waved happily to the audience, as if she were about to board a train or a ship, and led her male colleagues behind the curtain. The applause tapered, and when the singers did not appear again, trickled to a halt, until one male voice rose up from the first balcony, shouting, '*Evviva Flavia,*' a cry which evoked some wild clapping, and then silence and only the sound of murmurs and low talk as the audience wormed its way towards the exits.

2

Behind the curtain, the acting stopped. Flavia walked away from the three men without a word and made towards her dressing room. The tenor looked after her with the same sort of look that had animated Cavaradossi's face when he thought of her '*dolci baci, o languide carezze*', the loss of which would be worse than death. Scarpia pulled out his *telefonino* to call his wife and tell her he'd be at the restaurant in twenty minutes. The conductor, who had no interest in Flavia save that she obey his *tempi* and sing well, left his colleagues with a silent nod and headed for his own dressing room.

Halfway down the corridor, Flavia caught the heel of her shoe in the hem of her scarlet gown and lurched forward, managing to save herself from falling only by lunging towards one of the costume assistants. The young woman proved surprisingly strong, as well as quick-thinking: she wrapped her arms around the singer and managed to support her weight and thrust without being knocked to the ground.

As soon as Flavia was steady on her feet, she pulled herself free of the younger woman, asking, 'Are you all right?'

'It's nothing, Signora,' the assistant said, reaching across her body to rub at her shoulder.

Flavia placed a hand on the woman's forearm. 'Thank you for catching me,' she said.

'I didn't really think about it: I just grabbed you.' Then, after a moment, 'One fall is enough for tonight, don't you think?'

Flavia nodded, thanked her again, and continued down the corridor to her dressing room. She started to open the door but paused, shaking in delayed reaction to her near-fall and with the adrenalin rush that always followed performances. Feeling slightly faint, she rested her other hand against the jamb and closed her eyes. Moments passed, and then the sound of voices at the other end of the corridor energized her, and she opened the door and went in.

Roses here, roses there, roses, roses everywhere. She caught her breath at the sight of the flowers, every surface covered with vases filled with dozens of them. She stepped into the room and closed the door. Motionless, she studied the sea of yellow, growing even more uneasy when she noticed that the vases were not the usual catch-alls that most theatres kept for such occasions: chipped, even paint-smeared, some of them obviously taken from the prop room to be put to less visible use.

'*Oddio*,' she muttered, going back through the open door. Her usual dresser stood to the left, a dark-haired woman old enough to be the mother of the costume assistant who had saved her from falling. As she had after every performance, she'd come to take Flavia's costume and wig back to the storeroom.

'Marina,' Flavia ventured, 'did you see who brought these flowers?' She waved vaguely and stepped back to let her into the room.

'*Oh, che belle,*' Marina exclaimed when she saw them. 'How much they must have cost. There's dozens and dozens.' Suddenly she, too, noticed the vases and asked, 'Where'd those come from?'

'Don't they belong to the theatre?'

Marina shook her head. 'No. We don't have anything like that. They're real.' Seeing Flavia's confusion, she pointed to a tall vase of alternating white and transparent stripes. 'Glass, I mean. That one's Venini,' she said. 'Lucio used to work there. I can tell.'

'I don't understand,' Flavia said, wondering how the conversation had led to this. She turned her back on the woman and said, 'Can you unzip me?'

She raised her arms, and Marina helped her step out of the shoes and then the costume. Flavia pulled her dressing gown from the back of a chair and sat in front of the mirror and, almost without thinking, began to wipe at the thick makeup. Marina hung the dress on the back of the door and stood behind Flavia to help her remove her wig. She slipped her fingers under the back and prised it from Flavia's head, then peeled away the tight rubber cap that covered her hair. As soon as her head was free, Flavia dug her fingers into her hair and scratched her head for a full minute, sighing with relief and pleasure.

'Everybody says that's the worst part,' Marina said. 'The wig. I don't know how all of you stand it.'

Flavia spread her fingers and ran them through her hair repeatedly, knowing it would dry quickly in the over-heated room. It was as short as a boy's, one of the reasons she was so seldom recognized on the street, her fans having in mind the long-haired beauty they saw on stage, not this woman with a short cap of curly hair in which there were already faint traces of grey. She rubbed harder, enjoying the continued relief as her hair dried.

The phone rang; with some reluctance, she answered with her name.

'Signora, could you tell me how much longer you'll be?' a man's voice asked.

'Five minutes,' she answered, the response she always gave, whether she would be that amount of time or half an hour longer. They'd wait.

'Dario,' she said before he could hang up. 'Who brought those flowers?'

'They came on a boat.'

Well, since they were in Venice, it was unlikely they'd come any other way, but she said only, 'Do you know who sent them? Whose boat it was?'

'I don't know, Signora. There were two men, and they brought everything to the door here.' Then, after a moment, he added, 'I didn't see the boat.'

'Did they give a name?'

'No, Signora. I thought that . . . well, I thought that, with so many flowers, you'd know who they came from.'

Ignoring this, Flavia repeated, 'Five minutes,' and replaced the phone. Marina had gone, taking the gown and the wig with her, leaving Flavia to the silence and solitude of the dressing room.

She stared at her reflection, grabbed a handful of tissues and wiped her face until most of the makeup was gone. Remembering that there would be people waiting for her at the exit, she lined her eyes with mascara and smoothed some makeup over the signs of tiredness under her eyes. She picked a lipstick from the table and applied it carefully. A wave of tiredness swept over her, and she closed her eyes to wait for the adrenalin to fight it away and

9

buoy her up again. She opened her eyes and studied the objects on the table, then took the cotton shoulder bag from the drawer and swept everything – makeup, comb, brush, handkerchief – into it. She no longer carried anything of value into the theatre – into any theatre. Once, in Covent Garden, her coat had been stolen; at the Palais Garnier, it had been her address book, the only thing taken from the purse she had left in a drawer. Who in God's name would want her address book, and given the fact that she had had it for ages, who would be able to decipher the hodgepodge of cancelled names and addresses, updated email addresses and phone numbers that kept her in touch with other members of this strange geographically liquid profession of hers? Luckily, most of the addresses and numbers were also in her computer, but it had taken her weeks to get some of the others back. Then, unable to find an address book she liked, she decided to trust to her computer and prayed that no virus or crash would sneak in and erase them all.

It was only the third performance in the run, so there were sure to be people waiting. She pulled on a pair of black tights and put on the skirt and sweater she had worn to the theatre. Slipping on her shoes, she took her coat from the closet and wrapped a woollen scarf – red as her dress had been – around her neck: Flavia often referred to her scarves as her hijab: she could never leave the house without wearing one.

At the door, she paused and looked back into the room: was this the reality that came to replace the dream of success? she wondered. A small, impersonal room, used for a time by one person, the next month by another; a single wardrobe; a mirror surrounded – just as in the movies – by light bulbs; no carpet on the floor; a small bathroom with shower and sink. And that was it: if you had this, you were a star, she supposed. She had it, so she must be a star. But she didn't feel like one, only like a woman in her forties – she forced herself to say – who had just worked like a dog for more than two hours and now had to go and smile at nameless people who wanted a part of her, wanted to be her friend, her confidant; for all she knew, her lover.

And all she wanted to do was go to a restaurant and eat and drink something and then go home, call both of her children to see how they were and to say goodnight to them, and when the rush of performance began to dissipate and normal life started slipping back, go to bed and see if she could sleep. During productions where she knew or liked her colleagues, she looked forward to the conviviality of dinner after the show, of jokes and stories about agents and managers and theatre directors, of being in the company of those with whom she had just experienced the miracle of making music. But here, in Venice, a city where she had spent a great deal of time and where she should know a lot of people, she had no desire to mingle with her colleagues: a baritone who spoke only of his success, a conductor who disliked her and found the feeling hard to disguise, and a tenor who seemed to have fallen in love with her – and she looked herself in the eye when she maintained this silently – with certainly no encouragement from her. Not only was he little more than a decade older than her son; he was far too innocent to interest her as a person.

As she stood there, it occurred to her that she had effectively blocked out the flowers. And the vases. Should the man who had sent them be at the exit, she should at least be seen leaving the theatre with one of the bouquets. 'To hell with him,' she said to the woman in the mirror, who nodded back at her in sage agreement.

11

It had happened first in London, two months before, after the last performance of *Nozze*, when the single yellow rose had rained down on her at the first curtain call, and during each successive one. Then at a solo recital in St Petersburg, they had fallen amidst quite a number of more traditional bouquets. She had been charmed by the way some of the Russians, most of them women, had walked to the front of the theatre after the performance and handed the bouquets up to her on stage. Flavia liked seeing the eyes of the person who gave her flowers or said something nice to her: it was more human, somehow.

Then it happened here, the opening night, scores of them falling like yellow rain, but she had found none in the dressing room after that performance. Yet they had appeared again tonight. No name, no information, no note to explain such an excessive gesture.

She was stalling: she didn't want to have to decide about the flowers, and she didn't want to have to go and sign programmes and exchange small talk with strangers or, sometimes worse, with those fans who came to many performances and believed that frequency earned familiarity.

She slipped the cotton bag over her shoulder and ran her hand through her hair again; it was dry. Outside, she saw the dresser at the end of the corridor. 'Marina,' she called.

'*Sì*, Signora,' the woman answered, approaching her.

'If you'd like, take the roses home with you: you and the other dressers. Anyone who wants them.'

She didn't answer at once, which surprised Flavia. How often were women given dozens of roses? But then Marina's face brightened in obvious delight. 'That's very kind of you, Signora, but don't you want to take some of them?' She waved her arm towards the room, where the flowers glowed like artificial daylight.

Flavia shook the idea away. 'No, you can take them all.'

'But your vases?' Marina asked. 'Will they be safe if we leave them here?'

'They aren't mine. You can have them, as well, if you like,' Flavia said, patting her arm. In a softer voice, she added, 'You take the Venini, all right?' She turned away towards the elevator that would take her to her waiting fans.

3

Flavia was aware of how long it had taken her to change and hoped that the long delay would have discouraged some of the people waiting for her. She was tired and hungry: after five hours in a crowded theatre, surrounded by people behind, on, and in front of the stage, she wanted only to find a quiet place to eat in peace and solitude.

She stepped from the elevator and started down the long corridor that led to the porter's office and the space in front of it where guests could wait. The applause started while she was still ten metres from them, and she flashed her most delighted smile, the one she kept for her fans. Seeing them, she was glad that she had made the attempt to disguise how very tired she was. She quickened her step, the singer eager to see and hear her fans, sign their programmes, thank them for having waited all this time for her.

At the beginning of her career, these meetings had been a source of triumphant joy to her: they cared enough to wait to see her, wanted her acknowledgement, her attention, some sign that their praise was important to her. It was then, and it was now: she was honest enough to admit that she still needed their praise. If only, if only they could be faster about it: say they enjoyed the opera, or her performance, and then shake her hand and leave.

She saw the first two, a married couple – elderly now, both of them shorter than when she had first seen them, years ago. They lived in Milano and came to many of her performances, then came backstage only to thank her and shake her hand. She had seen them all these years but still she didn't know their names. Behind them stood another couple, younger and less willing to thank her and leave. Bernardo, the one with the beard – she remembered because both words began with 'B' – always started with praise for a single phrase or, occasionally, a single note, clearly meant as evidence that he knew as much about music as she did. The other, Gilberto, stood to one side and took their picture as she signed their programme, then shook her hand and gave her generic thanks, Bernardo having taken care of the details.

When they left, their place was taken by a tall man with a light overcoat draped over his shoulders. Flavia noticed that the collar was velvet and tried to recall the last time she had seen that: probably after an opening night or gala concert. His white hair contrasted with his deeply tanned face. He bent to kiss the hand she offered him, said he had seen the role sung by Callas at Covent Garden half a century ago, and thanked her without causing the embarrassment any comparison would make, a delicacy she appreciated.

Next was a soft-faced young woman with brown hair and badly chosen lipstick. In fact, Flavia suspected she had put it on especially to meet her, so strongly did it clash with her pale skin. Flavia took her outstretched hand and started to look behind her to see how many people were still there. When the young woman – she wasn't much more than twenty – said how much she had enjoyed the opera, she said these simple words in the most beautiful speaking voice Flavia could remember hearing. It was a deep, luscious contralto, its depth and richness in wild contrast to the girl's evident youth. The thrill it caused Flavia was almost sensual, like having her face stroked by a cashmere scarf. Or a human hand.

'Are you a singer?' Flavia asked automatically.

'A student, Signora,' she answered, and the simple response struck Flavia like a cello's lowest note.

'Where?'

'The Conservatory of Paris, Signora. I'm in my final year.' She could see that the girl was sweating with nervousness, but her voice was as steady as a battleship in a tranquil sea. As they continued to speak, Flavia sensed the growing restlessness of the people standing behind the girl.

'Good luck to you, then,' she said, and shook the girl's hand again. If she sang with that same voice – something that was often not the case – in a couple of years she'd be on the other side of this crowd, measuring out pleasantries and thanks to grateful fans, going out to dinner with other singers, not standing awkwardly in front of them.

Valiantly, Flavia shook hands, smiled, spoke to people and thanked them for their compliments and good will, said how happy she was that they had stayed behind to say hello. She signed programmes and CDs, careful always to ask the name or names of the people to whom to write the dedication. Never once did she show impatience or reluctance to listen to fans' stories. She might as well have had a sign saying 'Talk to Me' printed on her forehead, so much did the people believe she wanted to hear what they had to say. All that made her worthy of their trust and affection, she kept telling herself, was her ability to sing. And, she thought, her ability to act. Her eyes closed, and she raised one hand to wipe at them, as if something had flown into one of them. Then she blinked a few times, and beamed at the crowd.

She noticed, in the midst of the remaining people, a middle-aged man at the back of the group: brown-haired, head lowered to listen to something the woman next to him was saying. The woman was more interesting: natural blonde, powerful nose, light eyes, probably older than she looked. She smiled at whatever the man had said and batted her head a few times against his shoulder, then stood back and looked up at him. The man wrapped an arm around her and pulled her towards him before turning to look at what was happening at the head of the queue.

She recognized him then, though it had been years since she'd last seen him. There was more grey in his hair; his face was thinner, and there was a crease running from the left corner of his mouth down to his chin that she didn't remember from before.

'Signora Petrelli,' a young man who had somehow got hold of her hand said, 'I can only tell you it was wonderful. It's my first time at the opera.' Did he blush at saying that? Surely, admitting it seemed difficult for him.

She returned the pressure of his hand. 'Good,' she said, '*Tosca*'s a wonderful way to begin.' He nodded, eyes wide with the magic of it. 'I hope it made you want to see another,' Flavia added.

'Oh, yes. I had no idea it could be so . . .' He shrugged at his inability to express his meaning, grabbed at her hand again, and for a moment she feared he was going

17

to pull it to his mouth and kiss it. But he let it go and said, 'Thank you', and was gone.

There were four more, and then the man and the blonde woman were in front of her. He put out his hand and said, 'Signora, I told you my wife and I would like to hear you sing.' With a smile that deepened the wrinkles in his face, he added, 'It was worth the wait.'

'And I told you,' she said, ignoring the compliment and extending her hand to the woman, 'that I wanted to invite you both to a performance.' After the two women shook hands, Flavia said, 'You should have got in touch with me. I would have left tickets. I promised you.'

'That's very kind of you,' the blonde woman said. 'But my father has an *abbonamento*, and he gave us the tickets.' As if to ward off the suspicion that they might have come only because her parents didn't want to, she added, 'We would have come anyway, but my parents are busy tonight.'

Flavia nodded, then looked over their shoulders to see if there were more people, but there were none. Suddenly she didn't know how this meeting was meant to conclude. She had reason to be grateful to this man, who had saved her from awful . . . she didn't know what, exactly, because his help had been so quick and so complete. He had saved her twice, not once, and the second time he had also saved the person most dear to her at the time. After that, she had met him once for coffee, and then he had disappeared; or she had, swept up by a career in the ascendant, singing in other cities, other theatres, leaving behind this provincial city and this very provincial theatre. Life, horizons, talent had all expanded, and she had not thought about him for years.

'It was thrilling,' the woman said. 'It's not an opera I usually like, but tonight it was real, and moving. I understand why so many people love it.' Turning to her husband, she added, 'Though it's not a very complimentary picture of a policeman, is it?'

'Just another day at the office, my dear, doing those things we do so well,' he said amiably. 'Sexual blackmail, attempted rape, murder, abuse of office.' Then, to Flavia, 'It made me feel right at home.'

She laughed outright and remembered then that he was a man who took himself with a certain lack of seriousness. Should she invite them to dinner? They would be easy, amusing company, but she didn't know if she wanted company at all, not after the performance and not after the sight of those flowers.

He saw her hesitation and made the decision for them. 'That's where we have to go now,' he said. 'Home.' He didn't make an excuse or offer an explanation, and she appreciated that.

Awkwardness fell upon them, and all Flavia could think to say was, 'I'm here for another week or so. Perhaps you'd like' – she used the plural – 'to have a drink.'

The woman surprised her by asking, 'Are you free for dinner Sunday evening?'

Over the years, Flavia had developed, and often used, the tactic of delay and would speak of another pending invitation when she was unsure about whether she wanted to accept an offer or needed time to consider it. But then she thought of the roses and that she might tell him about them and said, 'Yes, I am.' Not wanting them to think she was lonely and abandoned in the city, she added, 'I'm busy tomorrow night – so Sunday would be perfect.'

'Would you mind coming to my parents'?' In quick explanation, the woman added, 'They leave for London next week, so it's our only chance to see them before they go.'

'But can you just invite . . .' Flavia began, careful to use

19

the formal '*Lei*' with her, though she had used the familiar '*tu*' with her husband.

'Of course,' the woman answered even before Flavia had a chance to ask the question. 'In fact, both of them would be delighted if you could come. My father's been a fan for years, and my mother still talks about your Violetta.'

'In that case,' Flavia said, 'I'd be delighted.'

'If you'd like to bring someone,' the man said but left the sentence unfinished.

'That's very kind,' she said blandly, 'but I'll come alone.'

'Ah,' he answered, and she registered his response.

'It's in Dorsoduro, just off Campo San Barnaba,' his wife said, then slipped into the familiar '*tu*'. 'You go down the *calle* to the left of the church, on the other side of the canal. It's the last door on the left. Falier.'

'What time?' asked Flavia, who had already visualized the location.

'Eight-thirty,' she answered, whereupon her husband pulled out his *telefonino* and initiated the business of exchanging numbers.

'Fine,' Flavia said after entering both their numbers, 'and thank you for the invitation.' Still curious about the flowers, she said, 'I have to have a word with the porter.'

When they had shaken hands again, Flavia Petrelli went towards the porter's window, and Paola Falier and Guido Brunetti left the theatre.

4

When Flavia reached the window of the porter's office, he was gone, perhaps to make a round of the theatre or more likely to go home. She wanted him to tell her in more detail how the roses had arrived and about the men who brought them. Which florist had they used? Her favourite, Biancat, had closed: she had found that out the day after she arrived, when she had gone to get some flowers for the apartment and had discovered that the bright abundance of the florist had been replaced by two shops selling shoddy made-in-China purses and wallets. The colours of the handbags in the window reminded Flavia of the cheap sweets her children had loved to eat when they were very young: vicious reds, violent greens, vulgar everything else. The bags were made from some sort of material that failed, no matter how hard its attempt or garish its colours, to look like anything but plastic.

Talking to the porter could wait a day, she decided, and left the theatre. She started towards the apartment, half of a *secondo piano nobile* in Dorsoduro, not far from the Accademia Bridge. Since she had arrived, a month ago, her Venetian colleagues had talked of little but the decline of the city and its gradual transformation into Disneyland on the Adriatic. To walk anywhere in the centre at midday was to push through shoals of people; to ride a vaporetto was sometimes impossible, often unpleasant. Biancat was gone: but why should she care? Though she was a northerner, she wasn't Venetian, and so why, or to whom, the Venetians chose to sell their patrimony was none of her business. Wasn't there something in the Bible about a man who sold his birthright for – a phrase that had fascinated her when she'd first heard it in catechism class decades ago – 'a mess of pottage'? The words reminded her how hungry she was.

She stopped in Campo Santo Stefano and had a pasta at Beccafico, though she paid little attention to what she ate, and drank only half of the glass of Teroldego. Less, and she would not sleep; more, and she would not sleep. Then across the bridge, to the left, over the bridge at San Vio, down to the first left, key in the door, and into the cavernous entrance hall of the *palazzo*.

Flavia paused at the bottom of the stairs, not from tiredness so much as from habit. After every performance, unless the time difference was disruptive, she tried to call both of her children, but to do that she had to come to peace with the performance she had just given. She played her memory of the first act, found nothing much to criticize. Same with the second. Third, and the young tenor did go a bit wobbly, but he'd had little enough support from the conductor, who made no attempt to disguise his low opinion of anything except his high notes. Her performance had been good. Undistinguished, but good. It wasn't much of an opera, truth to tell, only a few bits where her voice could shine, but she had worked with the stage director enough times for him to give her free rein, so the dramatic scenes had worked to her advantage.

She shared the stage director's opinion of the baritone singing Scarpia but was far better than he in disguising it. The director had decided to have Tosca stab him in the stomach, not the chest; and repeatedly. When the baritone had begun to object to such an indignity, the director had explained that the brutality of Tosca's behaviour must be provoked by equal brutality on his part in the first two acts: thus he would have the opportunity to create a dramatic and vocal monster and push his dramatic skills even further than they had been tested in the past.

Flavia had seen the smug expression on the baritone's face when he realized that the director was creating a chance for him to upstage Tosca, but she had also seen the wink the director gave her behind Scarpia's back as he embraced the idea with both word and action. She hadn't killed many people on stage, but to murder him, and then to look forward to killing him three more times, was honey and nectar both.

Cheered by these thoughts, she started to climb the steps, ignoring the handrail and appreciating the breadth of the staircase, perhaps created to allow wide-skirted women to pass one another going up and down or to walk arm in arm. She reached the landing and turned right towards the apartment.

Her mouth fell open. In front of the door lay the largest bouquet of flowers she had ever seen: yellow roses, of course – though why did she think that? – five or six dozen arranged in an enormous glowing mass that, instead of providing the delight such beauty should create, filled Flavia with something close to terror.

She looked at her watch: it was after midnight. She was

staying alone in the apartment; whoever had left the flowers had entered through the downstairs door. They could be anywhere. She stood and breathed deeply until she felt her heart return to its normal rhythm.

She pulled out her *telefonino* and found the number of the friend who was lending her this apartment. He lived on the floor above, but she had enough presence of mind to realize that a phone call would be less threatening at this hour than the ringing of the doorbell.

'*Pronto?*' a man's voice answered on the fourth ring.

'Freddy?' she asked.

'Yes. Is that you, Flavia?'

'Yes.'

'You locked out?' he asked. His voice was warm, almost paternal: there was no hint of reproof.

'Are you still up?' she asked instead of answering his question.

'Yes.'

'Could you come down?'

After the briefest of hesitation, he said, 'Of course. One minute. Let me tell Silvana,' and replaced his phone.

Flavia backed across to the wall farthest from the door and from those flowers. She busied herself by trying to think of something to which the size of the bouquet could be compared. A hula hoop came to mind, but that was too big. A beach ball was too small. The tyre of a car: that had the proper circumference. The flowers were massed together into one mushroom-shaped bouquet, but a mushroom gone mad, like something in a horror film, blasted out of control by atomic radiation, the sort of film she used to see in the cinema and that, still today, she remembered with glee.

No sound from upstairs. Which was more menacing, that still bouquet, beauty gone perverse because of setting, or the atomic mushrooms? Absorbed in these stupidities,

24

she did not have to think about the meaning of the roses or ask herself how someone had managed to enter the *palazzo*. Or about what in hell was going on.

She heard a noise from above and then voices, a man's and a woman's. Steps descending the stairs. She glanced through the banister and saw the slippered feet, the pyjama bottoms, the hem and then the belt of a red silk dressing gown, a hand from which dangled a set of keys, and then the comfortable, bearded face of Marchese Federico d'Istria. Her friend Freddy was her former lover, reluctant best man at her wedding, reluctant not from jealousy, she was later to discover, but because he knew the groom too well but, honour-bound, could say nothing to her – and curse his silence.

He stopped on the last stair and looked from her to the enormous bouquet lying at the bottom of the steps. 'You bring them home?'

'No, they were here. Did you let anyone in?'

'No. Silvana neither. No one's come.'

'The people upstairs?' she asked, raising a finger and pointing, as if he might not know where 'upstairs' was.

'They live in London.'

'So no one came?'

'Not that I know of; Silvana and I are the only people here at the moment.'

Freddy moved down from the final step and approached the flowers. As if they were a drunk asleep on his doorstep or a suspicious parcel lying there, he prodded at them with his foot. Nothing happened. He looked at Flavia and shrugged, then bent and picked them up. He was all but invisible behind them.

'Yellow roses,' he said unnecessarily.

'My favourite.' As she spoke, Flavia realized this was no longer true.

'Do you want me to take them inside?' he asked.

'No,' she said fiercely. 'I don't want them in the house. Give them to Silvana. Or put them out in the *calle*.' She heard the note of panic rising in her voice and leaned back against the wall.

'Wait here,' Freddy said, passed in front of her and started down the stairs. She listened to his diminishing steps, then a different sound as he crossed the entrance hall, the door opening, closing, and then his returning steps.

'Will you come in with me?' she asked. Seeing his surprise she added, 'And have a look around. I want to be sure . . .'

'That the downstairs door was the only one they opened?'

She nodded.

'Has this happened before, Flavia?' he asked.

'A few times, but in theatres. Flowers tossed on to the stage, and tonight dozens of bouquets in my dressing room.'

He looked at her empty arms. 'You left them there?'

'I didn't want them. Don't want them,' she said and heard the horror in her own voice. She looked at him, motionless, considering, and she exploded. 'For God's sake, help me, Freddy.'

He walked across the landing and put an arm around her shoulders, and then both arms, and then she was leaning into his chest and sobbing. 'Freddy, how did he get in here? How does he know where I live? Who is he?'

He had no answers to give her, but the familiar feel of her body against his brought back the turmoil of emotions he had once felt for her: love, jealousy, anger, passion, as well as the ones that had not been burned up by her abandonment of him: respect, friendship, protectiveness, trust. He both loved his wife and was in love with her, but he had never lost the power to think about anything but her. Now Flavia had two almost-adult children, and he had three, as well as a wife: their well-being was the central focus of his life.

He pulled back a little, careful to keep one arm around her. 'Give me a minute, Flavia, and I'll go in and check,' he said, then added, 'If the flowers were outside the door, it's not likely anyone's inside, is it?' He smiled at her and shrugged. The bodyguard in the silk bathrobe, she told herself: perhaps he can take a slipper off and hit them with that.

She moved back from him, and he found the right key and turned it four times, hearing the bolts pull back from the steel frame. If someone were inside, then he'd locked himself in, she thought. Freddy pushed the door open and reached in to switch on the lights. He took two steps into the hallway and stopped. Flavia went in behind him.

'I thought you wanted me to look,' he said, almost as if he feared her presence would compromise his courage.

'It's my problem,' she said.

'It's my house,' Freddy answered, long familiarity with the feeling of the apartment telling him there was no one there.

Flavia surprised him by starting to laugh. 'We're together again five minutes, and we have a fight,' she said.

Freddy turned to face her, as if wondering if this was another example of her dramatic skill. But there were still tears on her face and she still had the frozen look of a person who has had a shock. 'Stay here,' he said, 'and don't close the door.'

He went from room to room, even ducking down to look under all of the beds in the three bedrooms. He opened the closets, looked into the guest shower, and opened the door to the terrace. There was no one, nor was there any sense of the presence of another person.

When he returned to the hallway, he found her leaning against the wall beside the door, head back, eyes closed. 'Flavia,' he said, 'there's no one here.'

She tried, but failed, to smile. 'Thank you, Freddy, and I'm sorry I shouted.'

'You have every right to shout, Flavia. Now come upstairs with me and talk to us for a while and have something to drink.'

'And then what?'

'Then you come back down here and go to sleep.'

'Why? Don't you want me sleeping in your apartment?'

His glance remained warm, affectionate, and he shook his head in feigned exasperation. 'I expect better than that from you, Flavia. You have to come back down here to sleep or you won't be able to sleep here again.' He walked to the door and pointed to the lock. 'If you lock it from inside, even the firemen couldn't get in, and they can open almost any lock in the city.' Before she could speak, he barrelled ahead. 'And there's no way anyone can get to the terrace. Not unless they want to rappel down from ours, and I don't think that's very likely.'

Flavia knew everything he said was true, knew she was overreacting because she was exhausted by the stress of performance and by the savage rush of fear she'd felt when she saw those flowers lying there. She'd known fear in the past, but there had been a logic in what she feared: she'd known what it was about. These flowers made no sense: they should have been a compliment to her talent, sent in appreciation of a good performance. Instead, she felt in them menace and something even stronger than that, something approaching madness, though she had no idea why she thought this.

She took a deep breath and looked at Freddy. 'I'd forgotten what a good man you are, and patient,' she said, putting her hand on his arm. 'Thanks for the invitation, but I think I'd like to go to sleep now. It's been too much: first the performance and the flowers at the end, then seeing all those people, and now this.'

She ran her hands across her face, and when she took them away she looked even more exhausted. 'All right,' he said. You've got my number. Put the phone by your bed and call me if you want. Any time. If you hear something or think you do, call me. All right?'

Flavia kissed him on the cheek, the way old friends kiss one another. 'Thank you, Freddy.'

He turned to the door. In a voice entirely devoid of drama, he said, 'Lock it when I'm gone.' He patted her arm. 'Go to bed.'

She did, pausing only to get undressed and pull on an old T-shirt she'd stolen from her son. She and Mickey Mouse were almost asleep when she remembered she had failed, for the first time after a performance, to phone her children. That guilt remained with her as she plummeted into sleep.

5

Flavia woke with what felt like a hangover, or with the feeling she associated with having drunk too much, though this had not happened for years. Her head ached, her eyes felt gummy when she tried to open them. Her back and shoulders were stiff and tight when she stretched her body under the covers. She had no idea that stress could do this, until she remembered the jump and fall she had made from the roof of Castel Sant'Angelo the previous night: hurling herself forward on to a pile of foam mattresses, where she had landed tilted to one side rather than on her stomach. She'd felt the asymmetry at the moment she landed, but the rush of applause from the other side of the curtain had driven it from her mind.

Hoping that heat would drive whatever it was from her body, she took a long shower, as hot as she could bear it, letting the water batter at her head and then at her back. Wrapped in an immense towel, another turbaned around her hair, she went into the kitchen and made coffee, which she drank black and without sugar. Barefoot, sipping at her second espresso, she wandered into the living room and over to the windows that opened on to the balcony. In the front rooms, she could hear passing vaporetti, although they were barely audible at the back of the apartment, where the bedrooms were. Another limp grey day glowered back at her, and she suspected that, if she opened the windows, stepped out on to the terrace and stuck her hand out over the water, she would be able to grab a handful of moisture and bring it back inside with her.

She stood at the window for a long time, watching the boats chug along in both directions. From where she stood, she could see the *imbarcadero* of Santa Maria del Giglio down to the right on the other side of the canal; she stayed there long enough to watch two boats dock. If only her mind had just two directions, she caught herself thinking, and went back into the bedroom to see what time it was.

The clock next to her bed told her it was almost eleven; the phone next to the clock told her that Freddy had sent her three messages, the last one saying that, if he didn't hear from her by noon, Silvana would come down and ring the doorbell, he being in his office and unable to do so.

She tapped in an SMS, asking him to call off the dogs, then backed up and erased the message, replacing it with one saying that she had slept until just now and felt worlds better. Though a *telefonino* was hardly the proper medium, she thanked him for his help and patience the night before and told him he was a friend beyond price.

Within moments, his reply appeared. 'So are you, my dear.' Nothing more, but it cheered her immeasurably. She dressed quickly, pulling on a brown dress that she had had for years and refused to part with and a pair of low brown shoes comfortable enough to wear for hours of standing through a practice session.

She stopped at the bar on the left of the *calle* leading to the bridge and ordered a brioche and a coffee, no sooner ordering them than asking herself if she were mad, trying to sabotage the practice session by arriving there with a caffeine and sugar high. She called to the barman and changed her order to a *tramezzino* with prosciutto and mozzarella and a glass of orange juice. Someone had left a copy of *Il Gazzettino* on the counter, and she paged through it idly as she ate, enjoying neither the newspaper nor the sandwich but proud of herself for having resisted sugar and more coffee.

When Flavia got to the theatre, she found the porter in his glassed-in cubicle and asked him to tell her more about the men who brought the flowers, but he could recall only that there were two of them. In response to her question, he said that, yes, they were Venetians, though he couldn't remember either of them ever having delivered flowers to the theatre before.

As Flavia turned away, the porter called after her and asked if what Marina had told him was true: she didn't want the vases or the flowers. In that case, could he have some to take to his daughter, please? No, his wife had left him and gone to live with someone else, but his daughter – she was only fifteen – had insisted on staying with him – no, she didn't want to live with her mother and the new man, and the judge had said she could stay with her father. She loved beautiful things, and he'd asked Marina if he could take her one of the vases and some flowers, and Marina had said only if the Signora said it was all right because she'd said they were for the dressers, but only two of them worked with the Signora, so perhaps she could keep them until the Signora told her she could give them to him.

Again, Flavia wondered what quality people saw in her

that made them want to talk, or was it merely that any sign of interest or curiosity brought forth this torrent of information, regardless of who the listener was?

She smiled and looked at the clock above his desk and gave great evidence of surprise at seeing how late it was. 'Tell Marina you spoke to me, and I said you can have whichever you like.'

'Your pianist isn't here yet, Signora,' he said as a return courtesy. 'He lives in Dolo, so he's late a lot of the time.'

'But Dolo's just there,' she said, making a vague pointing gesture in what she thought was the direction of the mainland.

'It's only about twenty kilometres, Signora. But he doesn't have a car.'

How did she get sucked into these things? 'But, surely, there's the train, or a bus.'

'Of course. But the trains don't really run much any more, at least not in the morning. And the bus takes more than an hour.'

More than an hour? Had she been transported to Burkina Faso in her sleep? 'Well, I hope he gets here,' she said. Pulling free of the conversational quicksand, she turned towards the elevator.

Upstairs, she found one of the cleaners, who told her that most of the flowers and vases had been given away, though two vases were still downstairs in Marina's locker. Before the cleaner could begin to tell her more, Flavia gave her watch the same wide-eyed glance she'd given to the porter's clock and said she was late for a meeting with her pianist.

To avoid giving the impression that she was escaping, Flavia walked downstairs slowly, running her memory over the two arias she and the pianist had agreed to work on that day.

From verismo to bel canto in one month. Finish the run here, spend a week on vacation with the kids in Sicily, then to Barcelona to work with a mezzo whom she admired but with whom she had never sung. It would be her first appearance in Spain since her divorce, her ex-husband being Spanish and wealthy but also violent and well-connected. It was only his remarriage and transfer to Argentina that had opened the doors of both the Liceu and the Teatro Real, where she'd be able to sing roles she had longed to sing for years: Donizetti's Maria Stuarda and Anna Bolena, both of whom lose their heads, though for different reasons and to different music.

La Fenice had given her a rehearsal room in which to prepare these roles, a generous concession on the part of the theatre, since she'd be singing both parts in another opera house. Her room was the last door along the corridor on the right side.

As she passed the first door, she heard a piano from behind it giving the chirpy introduction to an aria she recognized but could not identify. Plunky, plunky, plunk: it sounded like the cheeriest of airs, yet her musical memory told her it was quite another thing, the light-heartedness entirely false. No sooner came the thought than the music turned ominous. The low female voice entered, singing, *'Se l'inganno sortisce felice, io detesto per sempre virtù.'* As the singer began to elaborate on that thought, Flavia remembered the aria. What in heaven's name was Handel, and – even more incredibly – Ariodante's enemy Polinesso, doing here? The voice soared off into coloratura whirligigs that made Flavia marvel that she was listening to a contralto, for the agility of these leaps by rights should belong to a soprano, but a soprano with a dark, musk-rich bottom register to go home to.

34

She leaned against the wall of the corridor and closed her eyes. Flavia understood every word: consonants bitten off cleanly, vowels as open as they were meant to be, and no more. 'If the deception works, I will detest virtue for ever.' The melody slowed minimally, and Polinesso's voice grew more menacing: *'Chi non vuol se non quello, che lice, vive sempre infelice quaggiù.'* Flavia gave herself over to the pleasure of contrast: the melody skipped along, beside itself with joy, as Polinesso declaimed the truth that anyone who always does the right thing will always be unlucky in this world.

Then back to the A section and off she went, coloratura chasing the notes all over the place, laying a light hand upon each one of them, and then again as if in a game of hide-and-seek. Flavia had seen *Ariodante* two years before in Paris, when a friend sang the rather thankless role of Lurcanio: she remembered three of the singers, but not the Polinesso, who could only dream of singing like this. The vocal flourishes grew ever more demented, shooting up only to slip down to the lowest range of the contralto voice. The final sweep up and down the scale left Flavia limp with physical delight and more than a little relieved that she would never have to compete with this singer, whoever she was.

Just as she reached this conclusion, a man's voice came to her from her right: 'Flavia, I'm here.'

She turned, but so strong was the spell of the music that it took her a moment to recognize Riccardo, the *ripetitore* with whom she had worked on *Tosca* and who had offered to help her prepare the Donizetti opera. Short, stocky, bearded, nose askew, Riccardo could easily be mistaken for a person given to aggression, and yet his playing was sensitive and luminous, especially in the soft introductions to arias, to which, he insisted, too many singers failed to pay sufficient attention. In the weeks they'd worked on the Puccini opera together, he had shown her more than a few nuances in the music she had not seen when reading the score, nor heard when singing it on her own. His playing had made them audible, halting after passages he thought required dramatic emphasis. It was only after the successful first performance, when his work was effectively over, that he admitted to Flavia how much he disliked *Tosca*. For him, opera had stopped with Mozart.

They kissed, he told her how wonderful her performance had been the night before, but she interrupted him to ask, 'Do you know who's in there?' pointing to the door opposite her.

'No,' Riccardo answered. 'Let's find out,' he added and knocked on the door. Flavia was too slow to stop him.

A man's voice called out '*Momento*', a woman's voice said something, and then the door was pulled open by a tall man holding a few sheets of music. '*Cosa c'è?*' he said as he stepped into the corridor, but when he recognized his colleague, and then Flavia, he stopped and raised the score in front of his chest as if he wanted to hide behind it.

'Signora Petrelli,' he said, unable to contain his surprise, or to say more. Behind him Flavia saw the girl who had waited at the stage door after the performance the night before, the one with the beautiful speaking voice and nervous manner. She looked much better today, hair brushed back from her face and no attempt at makeup. Without the badly chosen lipstick, she had quite a pretty face. She too held sheets of music in her hand, and Flavia saw in her the glow of someone who has just sung well and knows it.

'They teach you very well in Paris, my dear,' Flavia

said, entering the room without asking permission and walking over to the girl. Flavia leaned forward and kissed her on both cheeks, patted her arm, smiled, and patted her arm again. 'I'm amazed you'd try a role like that.' Before the girl could speak in defence or explanation, Flavia went on, 'But you're perfect for it, even at your age. What else are you preparing?'

The girl opened her mouth to answer but seemed unable to speak. 'I . . . I . . .' she began, then flipped the papers and pointed to one.

'"Ottavia's Lament",' Flavia read. 'It's a heartbreaker, isn't it?' she asked the girl, who nodded but still proved incapable of speech. 'I've always wanted to sing it, but it's far too low for me.'

Flavia gave herself a sudden shake and said, addressing both the girl and the pianist, 'I'm sorry to interrupt.'

'We were just finishing,' the man said. 'The session is an hour, and we've been here more than that already.'

Flavia glanced at the girl, who seemed to have calmed down a bit.

'Did you really like it, Signora?' she managed to ask.

This time Flavia laughed outright. 'It was beautifully sung. That's why I came in: to tell you that.'

The girl's face flushed again and she bit her lips as if fighting back tears.

'What's your name?' Flavia asked.

'Francesca Santello,' she said.

'She's my daughter, Signora,' the piano player said. He stepped forward and offered his hand. 'Ludovico Santello.'

Flavia shook it and then offered hers formally to the girl. 'Let me get to work myself,' she said, smiling at both of them and turning to Riccardo, who stood in the doorway.

Flavia, with a friendly nod to the girl, left the room and

walked down the hallway. The door behind them closed and they heard the sound of voices within. A few people, talking among themselves, came down the hall towards them, and as they passed, Flavia said to Riccardo, 'That girl's got a marvellous voice. She's going to be a fine singer, I think.'

Riccardo took the key to the room from his pocket and said, 'If you'll permit me to say this, she already is.' He opened the door and held it for her.

Still speaking, she entered the room. 'It's not often that people that young are so . . .' The sentence was chopped off by the sight of the flowers: a single bouquet of them, in a simple glass vase. They stood on the top of the piano, a small white envelope propped against the vase.

Flavia walked to the piano and picked up the envelope. Without thinking, she handed it to Riccardo, saying, 'Would you open this and read it to me, please?'

If he found her request strange, he gave no sign of it. He slipped his thumbnail under the flap, opened the envelope, and pulled out a simple white card. Turning to her, he read, 'I'm disappointed that you gave away the roses. I hope you won't do it again.'

'Is there a signature?' she asked.

Riccardo turned the card over, picked up the envelope and looked at the back; he set them on top of the piano. 'No. Nothing.'

He glanced at her and asked, 'What's wrong?'

'Nothing.' She placed her folder of sheet music on the music stand and took the vase of flowers and put it out in the corridor. 'I think we were working on the end of the second act,' she said.

6

Brunetti and Paola talked about the performance on the way home, each having enjoyed it in a different way. Brunetti had seen Flavia sing Violetta only once, and that had been on television, during the years when the producers at RAI still considered opera sufficiently important to merit broadcasting. Since then, it had disappeared from television, as it had from any serious consideration in the press. Of course, the occasional opera-related story did appear, but more space was dedicated to a singer's marital status, or lack, or substitute, or change thereof than to their work as an artist.

It was impossible to believe that so much time had passed since he had last seen Flavia sing *La Traviata* and watched her die, his heart tight with the desire to step in and save her. He had known then, in the same way he knew that Paolo and Francesca would spend eternity chasing one another through the winds of Hell, that Violetta would cry out her joy at the return of life and vigour and then crash down, dead as only dead can be. It was just a story. So although Tosca had killed Scarpia and was set for the drop, he'd known she'd be back on stage in a matter of minutes, smiling and waving at the audience. But that could not change the reality of the murder or of her suicide. Fact was meaningless: only art was real.

Paola had grown fonder of opera in recent years and had admired Flavia's performance without reservation, though she judged the plot ridiculous. 'I'd like to see her in an interesting opera,' she said, just as they reached the top of the Rialto Bridge.

'But you told me you liked it.' He started down the steps, suddenly tired and wanting only to have a drink and go to bed.

'She was thrilling at times,' Paola agreed. 'But I cry when Bambi's mother is killed: you know that.' She shrugged.

'And so?' he asked.

'And so I'll never be carried away by opera the way you are; I'll always have reservations about how serious it is.' She patted his arm as she spoke, then latched hers in his as they reached the bottom of the stairs and started along the *riva*. More thoughtfully, she added, 'Maybe it comes of your reading so much history.'

'Excuse me?' he said, completely lost.

'Most history – at least the sort you read – is filled with lies: Caesar forced to accept power against his will, Nero playing the lyre while Rome burns, Xerxes having the waters of the Hellespont thrashed. So much of what gets passed off as truth in those books is just rumour and gossip.'

Brunetti stopped and turned to face her. 'I've no idea what point you're trying to make, Paola. I thought we were talking about opera.'

Speaking slowly, she said, 'I'm merely suggesting that

you've acquired the gift of listening.' By the way she slowed both her speech and her pace as she said the last words, Brunetti knew she was not finished with the thought, so he said nothing. 'In your work, much of what you hear is lies, so you've learned to pay attention to everything that's said to you.'

'Is that good or bad?'

'Paying attention to words is always good,' she answered immediately. She resumed walking but had to pull at his arm to get him moving again.

Brunetti thought of the newspapers and magazines he read, the reports of crimes written by his colleagues, government reports. She was right: most of them were as much fiction as fact, and he read them with that knowledge. 'I think you're right,' he said. 'It's often impossible to tell the difference.'

'That's what art's all about,' she said. '*Tosca* is a bunch of lies, but what happens to Tosca isn't.'

How prophetic those words were Brunetti was to learn two nights later when they met Flavia for dinner at Paola's parents' home. He and Paola arrived at eight-thirty and found il Conte e la Contessa in the main salon, the one that looked across to the *palazzi* on the other side of the Canal Grande. There was no sign of Flavia Petrelli.

He was surprised by how casually his parents-in-law were dressed until he realized this meant the Conte's tie was wool and not silk, while the Contessa was wearing black silk slacks and not a dress. Brunetti saw, slipping out from the sleeve of her jacket, the bracelet the Conte had brought back for her from a business trip to South Africa some years before. Well, he brought her chocolates from Zurich, did he not? And so diamonds from South Africa were only fitting.

The four of them sat on facing sofas and talked about the children and their schools and their hopes, and their own hopes for them: the sort of things families always talked about. Raffi's girlfriend, Sara Paganuzzi, was studying in Paris for a year, but Raffi had not yet gone to visit her, which led the four adults to endless speculation about what might be going on between them. Or not. Chiara seemed still resistant to the lure of adolescent boys, which the four adults understood and applauded.

'It won't last much longer,' Paola said, voicing the eternal pessimism of the mothers of young girls. 'Some day soon she'll show up at breakfast in a tight sweater and twice as much makeup as Sophia Loren.'

Brunetti put his hands to his head and moaned, then snarled, 'I have a gun. I can shoot him.' He sensed the three heads snap in his direction and ran his hands slowly down his face to reveal his grin. 'Isn't that what the fathers of teenage girls are supposed to say?'

The Conte took a sip of his prosecco and observed drily, 'I begin to suspect I should have tried that when Paola brought you home the first time, Guido.'

'Do stop it, Orazio,' the Contessa said. 'You know you stopped thinking Guido was an interloper after a few years.' This information would have served as little comfort to Brunetti had his mother-in-law not reached across to pat him on the knee. 'It was far sooner than that, Guido.' How nice it would be to believe this, Brunetti thought.

She was interrupted by the arrival of Flavia Petrelli, who was shown into the room by the maid. She seemed less tired than she had been the other night and smiled warmly at them all as she entered. The Count was instantly on his feet and moving towards her. 'Ah, Signora Petrelli, you have no idea how delighted I am you could come.'

He took her hand and bent to kiss the air a few milli-metres above it, then linked his arm in hers to lead her towards the others, quite as proud as a hunter who'd bagged a plump pheasant to bring home for dinner.

Brunetti got to his feet at their approach but contented himself with shaking her hand and saying what a pleasure it was to see her again. Paola stood, as well, and permitted herself the liberty of exchanging kisses with Flavia. The Contessa remained seated but patted the cushion next to her and asked Signora Petrelli to sit beside her. When Flavia was seated, the Contessa told her she had admired her singing since hearing her debut at La Fenice as Zerlina. The fact that she did not mention the year of that debut reminded Brunetti that the Contessa's family had contrib-uted a large number of diplomats to both the Vatican and the Italian state.

'That was a lovely production, wasn't it?' Flavia asked, a question which led to a discussion of the dramaturgy, the sets and staging, and to the quality of the other singers in the cast. Brunetti noted that she never referred to her own performance and seemed not to have the desire, nor the necessity, to summon up praise for it. He remembered the scene-stealing woman he'd encountered years before and wondered where she had gone, or whether this quiet conversation was merely another example of the remark-able acting skill he had seen in the past.

The Conte handed Flavia a glass of prosecco and took a seat opposite her, leaving it to his wife to engage the singer in reminiscing about a performance he had not seen. When the conversation moved closer in time to the *Tosca*, he said he'd already ordered tickets for the last performance because their plans had changed and they would stay only briefly in London.

'If it happens,' Flavia said to universal confusion.

'I beg your pardon,' the Conte said.

'There's talk of a strike for the last two performances. The usual story: a contract hasn't been renewed, so they say they won't work.' Before they could give voice to their surprise, she held up calming hands and said, 'Only the stage crew, and it's unlikely anyone else will join them. So even if they do strike, we can still stand on the stage and sing.'

The maid appeared to tell them that dinner was ready. The Conte stood and offered his arm to Flavia; Brunetti took his mother-in-law's arm, and then, in a shocking breach of etiquette, pulled Paola up by one hand and, still holding it, took both women into the dining room, all of them leaving behind talk of the possible strike.

Brunetti ended up opposite the singer, who continued speaking to the Contessa, their topic having moved to Flavia's impression of the city, she having been away from it for a long time.

As the maid served *involtini* with the first green asparagus of the season, Flavia looked around at the faces at the table. 'You're all Venetian,' she said, 'so perhaps I should keep my opinion to myself.'

A silence fell. Brunetti used the pause and the way the people at the table dedicated themselves to their food to study Flavia's face. His original assessment was wrong: far from being relaxed, she bristled with tension. She had eaten little, he noticed, nor had she touched her wine. He remembered how deeply he had been struck, years ago, by the beauty of her speaking voice, not only the tone but the fluidity with which she moved from phrase to phrase, each word pronounced clearly, distinct from the others. This evening, she had occasionally stumbled over words and once had not completed a sentence but seemed to have forgotten what she was saying. The tone, however, had the same peach-ripe softness.

Unfamiliar with the stress singers faced in their work, Brunetti asked himself if they ever fully relaxed before the run of an opera was finished and they were freed from worrying about their health, their voice, the weather, their colleagues. Following this train of thought, he tried to imagine what it would be like to spend the whole day thinking about going to work, like athletes condemned to compete only at night.

When he tuned back into the conversation, Brunetti heard Flavia ask the Conte what other operas they had seen that season.

'Ah,' he answered, exchanged a glance with his wife, cleared his throat, and finally smiled. 'I have to confess I haven't been able to see anything yet,' he answered, and Brunetti heard in his voice the same nervousness he'd heard in Flavia's. 'Yours will be the first.'

Flavia's look was absolution itself. 'I'm honoured, then.' About to continue, she was interrupted by the return of the maid, who cleared the plates from the table. She was quickly back with their plates of *merluzzo con spinaci*.

When she was gone, the Conte tasted the fish, nodded, and said, 'Hardly, Signora. The theatre is honoured to have you sing there.'

Flavia raised an eyebrow in open scepticism and glanced across at Brunetti, but addressed the Conte. 'That's hardly the case, Signor Conte, though I thank you for the compliment.' In a more serious voice, she added, 'It was true forty, fifty years ago. *Those* were the singers. And any theatre was honoured to have them.'

While Brunetti's consciousness was opening itself to the new category of 'modesty in singers', the Contessa asked, 'Is that aimed at the theatre?'

'I've found it wise,' Flavia said, speaking to the Contessa but, Brunetti suspected, to them all, 'never to comment on the people who offer me work.' Then she shifted the need to give an opinion to the Conte by asking, 'You grew up with La Fenice, Conte. You've heard the change in the quality of the singers there.' When he didn't answer, she added, 'You have an *abbonamento*, so you've heard the change over the years.' Brunetti noted the way she avoided asking why he hadn't bothered to attend this season.

The Conte leaned back in his chair and took a small sip of wine. 'I suppose it's like having a cousin who's gone to the bad: stolen from the family, taken up with loose women, lied about what he's done, stayed out of jail only because the family's rich.' He smiled, sipped at his wine and, with every sign of enjoying the comparison, added, 'But no matter what he does, how much he steals, you remember how charming he was when he was younger and what good times you had with him and his friends when you were all boys together. And so, when he calls you, half-drunk, at two in the morning and tells you that he's got a great new idea for his business, or a new woman he wants to marry, but he needs some money from you to do it, you give it to him, even though you know you shouldn't. You know he'll spend it on an expensive vacation, maybe with the new woman, or one from his past; you know you'll never see anything in return; but most of all you know he'll do the same thing again in six months or a year.' The Conte set his glass on the table and shook his head in feigned despair, then looked around at all of them in turn. 'But it's family.'

'Great God,' Flavia burst out, laughing as she spoke. 'Please don't let me think of that when I see the Director.' She laughed so much that she had to cover her mouth with her napkin and look down at her plate. When she stopped, she looked across at the Conte and said, 'If I didn't know better, I'd think you worked there.'

7

As if by unspoken agreement that no one could top Flavia's remark, the topic moved away from opera. Paola asked Flavia about her children: Flavia's son was the same age as Chiara, her daughter younger than Raffi. Flavia looked pleased to say they were doing well at the international school in Milano, where she lived most of the year, and added – making what seemed an effort not to boast – that they had the advantage of being fluent in Italian, Spanish, and English. Brunetti noted that her only comment about her ex-husband was that he was Spanish.

Talk became general, and Brunetti contributed a few remarks, but his attention had been caught by the singer's nervousness. She had seemed happy enough to see him the other night, so it was not caused by meeting someone who had once known a great deal about her private life. The Conte and Contessa, when relaxed and at their ease, would soothe even a whippet, perhaps because the dog would be less likely than a human to notice the Titian portrait in the living room and the engraved crests on the cutlery. And Paola, he observed, was on her best mother-of-children behaviour.

The Contessa inquired where Flavia would be singing next, and she said she had another week there, singing Tosca, then some time off, then to Barcelona. Brunetti found it interesting that she didn't say where she would be going after Venice and didn't bother to mention what she was going to Spain to sing. He had always assumed that most people were all too ready to talk about them-selves: one did not expect self-effacement in a diva.

Paola surprised them all by saying, 'It must be a difficult life.'

Flavia's head snapped towards Paola, but then she lowered her eyes and picked up her wine glass. She took a consciously slow sip, put the glass down, and said, 'Yes, it can be. There's the constant travel, staying in a city – alone – for weeks at a time. I miss the kids, but they're at an age when they don't much want to spend their free time with their mother.'

Then, perhaps aware that this might sound like self-pity, she quickly added, 'After all these years, I've worked with so many people that there's always someone in the produc-tion I know. That makes it easier.'

'What's the worst part of it, if I might ask?' the Contessa inquired, then tried to lighten her question by adding, 'I'm so seldom alone that I have to say it sounds tempting.'

'There's no worst part,' Flavia answered, and Brunetti thought he was finally hearing her real thoughts. 'I suspect there isn't even what I could call a bad part. I'm just whining.'

She glanced around the table and saw that she had their complete attention. 'The singing is always a joy, especially if you know you've sung well and if you have good colleagues to work with.' She took a drink of water, then added, 'I suppose it's no different from any job that requires a lot of preparation and thought – like restoring paintings or making a pair of shoes: you spend a long time learning how to do it, but at the end you have a finished product that's beautiful.'

Brunetti thought the comparison worked only in part. The others had the painting or the shoes: all the singer had was the memory. Before YouTube, at least.

Flavia was not finished. 'Days can be very long if you're alone in a city you don't know. Or one you don't like. Maybe that's the bad part.'

'What ones are those?' Brunetti interrupted to ask.

'Brussels,' she said with no hesitation. 'And Milano.'

He didn't like them either, but said nothing about her choice to live in one of them.

'Do you get tired of hearing people say how exciting your life must be?' the Contessa asked, curious and ready to be sympathetic.

Flavia laughed. 'I don't know how many times I've been told that. I suppose people say it to anyone who travels a lot.'

'But no one would say it to an accountant or an insurance salesman, would they?' Paola asked.

'I doubt it,' Flavia answered. Then she lapsed into silence for a moment before saying, 'The strange thing is that the people who say it probably don't understand anything about the way we actually live our lives.'

'Are fans really curious about that?' Paola asked.

Involuntarily, Flavia moved back in her seat, as though trying to escape the words. 'What's wrong?' the Contessa asked, her alarm as audible as Flavia's was visible.

'Nothing,' Flavia said. 'Nothing.'

Brunetti felt the air stiffen: Flavia sat, unable to say any more, and the others carefully avoided looking at one another for fear of calling attention to her behaviour. Finally Flavia, in a tight voice, asked Paola, 'Did someone tell you?'

'Tell me what?' Paola asked, her confusion evident.

'About the flowers.'

Paola leaned towards the other woman, as if hoping nearness would help. 'Flavia, I don't know what you're talking about,' she said. She watched Flavia's face and waited until it was evident that she had registered the words.

Speaking slowly and clearly, Paola went on, 'I don't know anything about flowers.'

Flavia lowered her head over the empty place in front of her, reached aside and slid the knife to a horizontal position. Index fingers pushing at the ends, she swivelled it repeatedly in a half-circle, as if it were the speedometer in the car of a very erratic driver. Without looking at Paola, she said, 'Someone's been sending me flowers.' The nervousness of her tone corrupted the banality of the words.

'And that frightens you?' Paola asked.

Flavia slid the knife to vertical before looking back at her. 'Yes,' she answered. 'Dozens of them: ten, twelve bouquets. On the stage. In my dressing room.' She looked at Brunetti. 'In front of the door of my apartment.'

Brunetti asked, 'In front of the building or inside, by the apartment door?'

'Inside,' Flavia answered. 'I asked my friend who lives upstairs if he knew anything about it, but he didn't: no one asked him to open the door.'

'Are there other people living in the building?' Brunetti asked, this time sounding like a policeman.

'Yes. But they're away.'

This must be what was bothering her, Brunetti realized, not really understanding her evident fear. Flowers were not sent to menace but to give pleasure or offer praise. The delivery man could have found the main door open; a maid could have opened it for him.

The Conte saved Brunetti from suggesting either of these possibilities by asking, 'Have you had this sort of thing happen before, my dear?'

The warm concern in his voice and the final endearment proved too much for Flavia, who looked at him but found herself unable to speak; tears appeared in her eyes but did not fall. She held up her hand and patted at the air between them, and the Conte picked up his glass and held it, waiting for her courage to return. No one spoke.

Finally Flavia said, 'I've had fans, but it's always been a friendly thing. Not like this. It frightens me.'

'How long has it been happening, my dear?' the Count asked, setting his glass down untouched.

'About two months.' Then she added, 'In London and St Petersburg. And now here.'

The Conte nodded to suggest he found her reaction entirely natural and justified.

'It's too much,' Flavia continued. 'There are too many flowers, and it's all so attention-seeking.'

'To draw attention to you?' the Conte asked.

'No, to the person who's sending them. That's what's wrong with it. He sent a note saying he knew I threw them away.' Her voice was higher than usual.

'What did you do with the letter?' Brunetti asked in a normal voice.

The look she shot him was suffused with anger. 'I tore it up and threw it in the garbage at the theatre.'

Brunetti began to understand her response. People left flowers at the artists' entrance or came to the front of the stage and tossed them in homage at the feet of the singer. The audience would watch the flowers and the singer, not the person who brought them. 'The ones on the stage,' he said. 'Do you know who threw them?'

'No.'

'No idea?' Brunetti asked.

'No.' Then, in a calmer voice, she said, 'You saw it the other night, the heap of them. I didn't want them. You saw how we had to step on them when we came out for our bows.' She grimaced at the memory.

'They were for you?' Brunetti asked.

'Who else would they be for?' she snapped, sounding like the woman Brunetti had met years before. Flavia, however, had simply been clarifying something that should have been self-evident.

'Did you speak to the people there?'

'The porter at the entrance said two men he'd never seen before brought the flowers that were in my dressing room. That's all he knew.' She waved a hand, as if pointing up at the balconies, and said, 'I didn't ask about the ones that were thrown down on to the stage.'

Though the maid had brought the peaches with cream and amaretti while they were talking, none of them had much interest in them, and so, by general agreement, they went back to the main salon and to the sofas. The maid came in with coffee; the Conte asked if anyone would like to join him for a grappa, but only Brunetti was interested.

Silence settled on the room: they sat for some time, listening to the boats moving up and down the Grand Canal, looking out at the windows on the opposite side. Lights went on and off, but there was no motion to be seen behind the windows.

Brunetti was struck by how comfortable their silence

was, even in the face of events that were, at least, disquieting, at worst . . . he wasn't sure. Strange and unsettling, out of place in a world that was meant to present beauty and provide pleasure.

He thought of a friend of his father's, a man who had fought in the war with him. Angelo was probably illiterate, not so startling for a man born in the desperate Thirties, when young people went to work at the age of ten. His wife did the reading for the family, paid the bills, kept things going.

Brunetti's father had once expressed one of his bizarre opinions about the world to Angelo: Brunetti couldn't remember any longer what it was, although he did recall thinking, at the time, that the idea was strange.

Hearing it, Angelo had not opposed or contradicted his friend, and when the elder Brunetti insisted that he tell him what he thought, Angelo sat back in his chair and rubbed the side of his face a few times, then said, smiling at his friend, 'My idea is different from yours, but that's because all I have is one head, and it lets me have only one idea about things.' Angelo had made it sound as if he were apologizing for a mental handicap and could never match his friend in being able to hold some more complicated idea in that head of his, or perhaps even more than one idea. Perhaps the person sending the flowers had room in his head for only one idea about how to show his appreciation. Or perhaps he had even stranger ideas.

Looking at Flavia, Brunetti asked, 'Would you like me to try to do something about this?'

She answered him but spoke to everyone in the room. 'No, I don't think that's necessary. It helps just to be able to talk about it and hear how strange it is.'

'Nothing stronger than strange?' the Conte asked.

'If I were sitting home alone in the apartment, and no

one else was in the building, I'd probably say yes,' Flavia began. Looking around at their concerned faces, she gave a small smile and added, 'But here, with you, it seems only strange.'

'Who are the people upstairs?' Brunetti asked.

'Freddy d'Istria,' she said, and when they nodded, she amended it to, 'Federico, that is.'

'That's all right,' Paola broke in, smiling. 'We call him Freddy, too.'

'How do you know him?' Flavia asked.

'He and I were at elementary school together,' Paola said. 'We were in the same class for four years, and for three of them we sat beside each other.'

'And I met him in *liceo*,' Brunetti said; no more than that.

'A state school?' Flavia asked Paola without thinking.

'Of course,' Paola said, as if there were no other sort of school to which children would be sent. 'It's the nearest school to both our homes.'

The Contessa interrupted them. 'I wanted Paola to learn Veneziano from other children, not only from the staff here. It's her language, after all. '

'Do you speak it, Signora?' Flavia asked, stopping short of using the title and moving away from her surprise that aristocrats would go to state schools.

'No. I think it's pretentious to try to speak it if you're not Venetian,' the Contessa said. 'But Paola's home is here, and I wanted her to grow up speaking it.'

Paola sat back in the sofa and rolled her eyes, as if she had been hearing this all her life.

Brunetti watched as Flavia's eyes went back and forth between the two other women while she searched for something to say. 'I could have a word with Freddy,' he interposed. Freddy was as much his friend as Paola's, after all, perhaps even more so. There were times when Brunetti thought this was because they had met when they were boys, not children, and had been good friends while they ceased being boys and began to be men.

'Flowers in the theatre are one thing; getting into a private home to leave them is something else entirely,' he added.

He watched her consider what he'd said. Brunetti wasn't sure about the legal distinction between the two, nor that it was a crime to enter a building where you did not live and into which you had not been invited. Surely, tourists did it every day: how many times had he been told by friends about finding strangers in their courtyard or on their staircase? And what sort of crime was it to leave flowers in front of a person's door?

'It might be a good idea, my dear,' the Conte said to Flavia. 'I think Guido should talk to him, if only to show him that someone is taking this seriously.'

'But are you?' Flavia turned to Brunetti to ask.

Brunetti uncrossed his legs and took time to think, then said, 'I don't see anything that would persuade a magistrate that it's worth pursuing. There's no criminal act and no evidence of threat.'

The Conte spoke, sounding protective and indignant. 'Does that mean something else has to happen before you'll act?'

'*Papà*,' Paola broke in, sounding exasperated. 'That sounds so melodramatic: "something has to happen". All that's happened is that Flavia's been given flowers and a note. Nothing's even been *said* to her.'

'It's bizarre behaviour,' the Conte replied sharply. 'A normal person would simply sign a card and send it along. Or have a florist deliver them to the house in the usual way. There's no reason for the secrecy. It's not right.' He turned to Flavia and said, 'In my opinion, you have every reason to be concerned: you don't know whom you're dealing with, and you don't know what they'll do next.'

'You don't have to make it sound so threatening,' Paola said to her father. And, to Flavia, 'I don't agree with my father at all. Whoever's doing this just wants to be able to tell his friends how strong his passion for music is. It's all about boasting and proving how much better his taste is, how very strong his aesthetic responses.' She said it as though she thought it ridiculous.

The Conte reached for the grappa the maid had brought and poured some into two glasses. He handed one to Brunetti and took a sip from his own. 'Well, I suppose we'll find out.'

'What does that mean, dear?' his wife asked.

'This isn't over.' In one sip he finished the grappa, and then set down the empty glass.

8

Emerging from the *palazzo* a half-hour later, Paola suggested to Brunetti that they take the Accademia Bridge and walk home on the other side of the canal for a change. Both of them knew this would add fifteen minutes to their walk, but it would also mean they could go at least that far with Flavia, who was staying only a few minutes from the bridge. Since she had no reason to know where their home was, she would not see Paola's long detour as the protective gesture it was.

Brunetti, still curious about the changes that seemed to have taken place in Flavia over the years, wondered if they would talk of music and thus put her at the centre of the conversation. She, however, chose to speak of those things that parents talk about. She told them that she worried terribly about drugs, even though neither of her children had ever shown much interest in them. And she feared that one of them – she admitted that she feared more for her daughter than for her son – would fall into the wrong company and be led to do things she would not ordinarily do.

When Paola asked what she feared most, Flavia shook her head in exasperation, either with the world or with her own formless fears, and said, 'I don't know. I can't imagine the world they live in. I always have this low-grade noise in my mind, worrying about them.'

Paola leaned closer, linking her arm in Flavia's as they walked. 'People think they have babies,' Paola said. 'But we don't: we have people, and we have them all their lives, and we never stop worrying about them. Never.' Then, in a thoughtful tone Brunetti recognized, she said, 'I think someone should invent a special telephone for parents of teenage children.'

'That does what?' Flavia asked.

'That can't ring between one and six in the morning.'

Flavia laughed out loud and said, 'If you ever find it, please get me one.'

At ease as with old friends, they reached the museum and the bridge and stopped at the bottom of the steps. Flavia kissed Paola on both cheeks and stepped back to turn to Brunetti. 'I can't thank all of you enough. I had no idea how much I needed an evening like this: conversation and good food and nothing to worry about.'

A Number One vaporetto heading towards the Lido revved its engine into reverse and banged into the *imbarcadero*. So common a sound was it that neither Brunetti nor Paola really heard it, but Flavia started and turned towards the noise. When the few people from the boat had dispersed, she went on, 'I'd like to thank you for your patience.' She smiled, but it was a faint shadow of the smile Brunetti remembered from years before.

To reassure her, Brunetti said, 'I'll talk to Freddy. It's

been too long since I've seen him, and this is a good reason to call him or meet for a drink.'

'Only if you think it might be useful.'

Brunetti bent down and kissed her on both cheeks. 'It's always useful to see old friends, don't you think?'

'Yes,' she said, her eyes on his. 'Old friends.'

The night was clement, the moon only a day short of being full. They stopped at the top of the bridge and looked out towards the Lido and, behind it, the Adriatic.

'Do you think of her as an old friend?' Paola asked. There was no wind, so the moon was reflected as though on a plate of dark glass. No boats came for some minutes, and Brunetti remained silent, as if afraid that the sound of his voice would shatter the surface of the water and thus destroy the moon. The footsteps on the bridge stopped, and for a long time there was silence. A Number One appeared down at Vallaresso and crossed over to La Salute, breaking the spell and then the reflection. When Brunetti turned towards San Vidal, he saw motionless people on the steps below him, all transfixed by the now-shimmering moon and the silence and the façades on either side of the canal. He looked to his right and saw that the railing was lined with more motionless people, faces raised for the moon's benediction.

He took Paola's hand, and they descended the steps, heading home the long way.

'It feels like an old friendship, although I don't know why I think that,' he finally answered as they entered Campo Santo Stefano. 'I haven't seen her for years, and I don't think we were really friends either time I knew her.' He thought about this for some time and then said, 'Perhaps friendship comes to you with the memory of hard times together.'

'You make it sound as if you were in the trenches with her, the way your father used to talk about his friends.'

'Yes, he did, didn't he?' Brunetti answered. 'We hardly suffered as much as they did, she and I. But there was violence, and people did suffer.'

'I wonder what's she been doing all these years,' Paola said to move him away from those memories. 'Other than becoming even more famous, that is.'

They approached the bridge leading to Campo Manin, and Brunetti paused to look into the window of the book dealer. When he moved away and started up the bridge, he said at last, 'I have no idea. I've seen as much as you have; perhaps even less because I don't read the music reviews.'

'Lucky you,' Paola said. 'Overblown,' she added, and nothing more.

'The reviews, presumably,' Brunetti said as they passed in front of the lion.

This made Paola laugh. 'Flavia's name comes up now and again. The reviews are always good. More than good.' Then, as they crossed San Luca, 'You heard her the other night, didn't you? Saw her?'

'I'd like to hear her in something with music that's more . . .' Brunetti had no idea of how to twist himself out of this sentence.

'Respectable?' Paola suggested.

This time it was he who laughed.

Talking of this and that, veering away from music to discuss Raffi's apparent cooling towards Sara Paganuzzi, only to return to music, they crossed the Rialto on the left side and started along the *riva*. The restaurants were closed or closing, the waiters visibly weary at the end of a long day.

They said little as they walked along the water. Just

before they turned right under the passageway, both of them turned back and saw the moon's reflection looking as though it were about to slide under the bridge.

'We live in Paradise, don't we?' Paola asked.

The call would have slipped past Paola's parental telephone because it came at six-fifteen two mornings later. Brunetti answered with his name at the third ring.

'It's me,' a man's voice said, and Brunetti's mind chugged.

'What's happened?' he asked, identifying the voice as that of Ettore Rizzardi, one of the city's pathologists, who should not be calling him at this hour.

'It's Ettore,' the doctor said, though there was hardly need of that. 'I'm sorry to call you this early, Guido, but there's something I think you should know about.'

'Where are you?' Brunetti asked.

'At the hospital,' he answered.

To Brunetti, that meant the mortuary: where else would Rizzardi be?

'What's happened?' Brunetti asked, shying away from what he wanted to ask: Who's died?

'I came in this morning for the autopsy on that boy who shot himself,' Rizzardi said. 'I wanted to get it done before the day began.'

'Why?' Brunetti asked, though it was none of his business.

'I've got a new doctor here, just out of medical school, and I don't want her to have to see this. Not yet.'

'Is that why you're calling me?' Brunetti asked, hoping – coming as close to praying as he was capable of doing – that Rizzardi had no doubts about the suicide.

'No, it's something one of the nurses told me. You know her, Clara Bondi, Araldo's wife.'

'Yes,' Brunetti said, wondering what was going on and why none of this was making sense. 'What did she say?'

'There's a girl in the Emergency Room. She's got a broken arm, and they put six stitches in her scalp.'

'What happened?' Brunetti turned to look at the clock. Almost six-thirty. No chance of going back to sleep.

'She fell down the steps on Ponte de le Scuole.'

The elongated mass buried by covers beside him moved and made a moaning noise. He placed a calming hand on Paola's hip and said, voice consciously pleasant and friendly, 'Why are you telling me this, Ettore?'

'They brought her in by ambulance. Some people going home found her about midnight at the bottom of the bridge and called the Carabinieri. They went over and called the ambulance. She was unconscious when they brought her in.'

That was probably a good thing if she had had to have her arm set and have six stitches, Brunetti thought. 'And?'

'And Clara was the nurse on the ward where they put her.'

'And?'

'And when she woke up, she told Clara that someone had pushed her down the steps.'

Brunetti considered possibilities. 'Had she been drinking?'

'Apparently not. They checked that when she came in.'

'Blood test?' Brunetti asked.

'No, just the breath, but there was nothing.' Rizzardi let a moment pass and then added, 'Clara said the girl sounded very certain about it.'

'Why are you calling me, Ettore?'

'When Clara told the doctor, he said the girl was probably making it up, that people didn't do that here.' Before

Brunetti could protest, Rizzardi said, 'So he's refused to call the police. He doesn't want any trouble with them.'

'What does he expect the girl to do?' Brunetti asked.

'He said she can call them when she gets home.'

'When will that be?'

'I have no idea, Guido,' Rizzardi said, suddenly exasperated. 'That's not why I called you.'

'All right, Ettore,' Brunetti said, shoving back the covers. 'I'll be there as soon as I can.' He could all but hear Rizzardi calming down, so he asked, 'Have you spoken to her?'

'No, but I've known Clara since I started working here, and she's got more sense than most of my colleagues. She said she believes the girl, and that's enough for me.'

Brunetti made a noise as he got out of the bed.

'Is that the weight of the world I hear on your shoulders, Guido?' Rizzardi asked in his normal voice.

'Let me have a shower and some coffee. I'll be there in an hour.'

'She'll be here.'

9

Brunetti left for the hospital very shortly after, having decided not to make coffee at home but to stop on the way. It was not yet seven-thirty when he reached Ballarin, but to his relief he saw that there was already someone inside. He tapped on the door; when Antonella came to see who was there, he asked if he could have a coffee and a brioche. She stuck her head out and looked both ways, then pulled the door fully open to let him in. She closed and locked the door after him.

When she caught his glance, she said, 'We can't serve before opening time. It's against the law.'

Brunetti was tempted to put on his mock-severe voice and say he was the law around there, but it was too early for jokes – and he had had no coffee. Instead, he thanked her and said he would stop by another time and pay, so no law would be broken.

'There's probably some other law we don't know about,' she said as she went behind the counter, but then her voice was drowned out by the coffee grinder. She handed him a brioche, still hot, and turned to get his coffee. It took some time and two packets of sugar, but the combination worked its magical transformation, and he left the *pasticceria* a man reborn.

At the hospital, he realized he had no idea where to find the injured woman, nor even whom to ask about: he had been too dulled by sleep to ask her name. He shied away from the idea of going to see Rizzardi in the place where he worked and went to the Emergency Room, where it was likely the girl had first been taken. There, he was told that, because the other wards were already overcrowded, she had been sent to *cardiologia*. Her paperwork had been sent along with her, and four people were queuing behind him, so Brunetti decided that he had enough information to be able to find her: after all, how many girls with a broken arm and stitches in her head would be in the cardiology ward?

Indeed she was the only one, lying on a trolley in an empty corridor, apparently parked – Brunetti's choice of word – until they managed to find a room where there was space for her. He approached her. A pale-faced young woman lay on her back, apparently asleep, her left arm in a cast on her stomach, palm open on her hip. Her head was bandaged, and he saw that a swathe of hair had been shaved away to allow the tape to hold.

He went to the nurses' station and found someone. 'I've come to see the young woman over there. May I see her chart?' he asked.

'Are you a doctor?' the nurse asked, looking him up and down.

'No, I'm a policeman.'

'Has she done something?' the nurse asked, shooting a quick look in the girl's direction.

'No, quite the opposite, it would seem.'

'What do you mean?'

'She may have been pushed down the bridge,' Brunetti said, curious to see how the nurse would respond to his confidence.

'Who'd do something like that?' the woman asked in a voice now warmed by concern, as she glanced back at the young woman. Obviously, her colleague Clara had told her nothing.

'That's what I've come to find out.' Brunetti smiled when he said this.

'Ah, take it, then,' she said and passed him a file lying on the counter that separated them.

'"Francesca Santello",' Brunetti read. 'Is she Venetian?'

'She sounds it,' the woman answered. 'Well, in the little I heard her say. They gave her something when they set her arm and did the stitches, and she's been groggy or asleep since then.'

'What did she say?'

'She asked me to call her father,' the nurse answered, then added, 'but she was asleep before she could tell me his name.'

'I see,' Brunetti said and looked through the file. Her name and date of birth, residence in Santa Croce. The X-rays of her skull had clipped to them a note saying they showed no sign of fracture or internal bleeding. The examining physician wrote that the fracture of her arm was a simple one, and the cast could be removed in five weeks.

'I looked,' the nurse said forcefully, as if to deny some accusation from Brunetti.

'Excuse me,' he said, looking up from the file.

'Santello. In the phone book. But there's a dozen of them.'

Brunetti thought to ask if she had checked the addresses but limited himself to a smile.

'How long has she been here?'

The nurse looked at her watch. 'They brought her up after they put in the stitches.'

'I'd like to stay here for a while to see if she wakes up,' Brunetti said.

Perhaps because his explanations had transformed the young woman from a suspect to a victim, the nurse raised no objection, and Brunetti went back to the side of the trolley. When he looked down at her, he saw that she was staring at him.

'Who are you?' she asked.

'Commissario Guido Brunetti,' he answered. 'I came because one of the nurses said you think you were pushed down the steps.'

'I don't think it,' she said. 'I know it.' Her voice used too much breath, as if she had to pump out the words to get them free. She closed her eyes, and he saw her lips press together in frustration or pain.

He waited.

She looked at him with clear, almost translucent blue eyes. 'I know it.' Her voice was little more than a whisper, but the pronunciation was diamond-sharp.

'Would you tell me what happened?' Brunetti asked.

She moved her head minimally, but even that caused her a sudden gasp of pain. She lay still and then said, speaking very softly, as if to keep the pain from noticing, 'I was going home. After dinner with friends. When I was going up the bridge behind the Scuola, I heard footsteps behind me.' She studied his face to see if he was following.

Brunetti nodded but said nothing.

She lay still for some time, gathering more breath to enable herself to continue. 'When I started down, I felt someone behind me. Too close.

'Then he touched my back and said, "*È mia*", and he

67

shoved me and I tripped. I think I tried to grab the railing.' Brunetti leaned forward, the better to hear her. 'Why would he say "You're mine"?' she asked.

She raised her right hand to touch the bandage on her head. 'Maybe I hit it. I remember falling, but that's all. Then there were police, and they put me on a boat. That's all I remember.' She shifted her eyes around the corridor and out the windows. 'I'm in the hospital, aren't I?'

'Yes.'

'Can you tell me what's wrong with me?' she asked.

'Good heavens,' Brunetti answered with mock seriousness. 'I'm not sure that's any of my business.'

It took her a moment to understand, then she smiled and added, joining in the joke, 'Physically, that is.'

'Your left arm is broken, but your chart says it's not a bad break,' he said. 'And there are stitches in your scalp. There's no evident damage to your brain or skull: no haemorrhage and no fracture.' He had given the bare facts and felt obliged to add, 'You have a concussion, so I suppose they'll keep you here for a day or two to see that they didn't overlook anything.'

She closed her eyes again. This time they stayed closed for at least five minutes, but Brunetti remained standing beside the bed.

When she opened them again, he asked, 'Are you sure that's what you heard, "*È mia*"?'

'Yes,' she said without hesitation or uncertainty.

'Can you tell me anything about the voice?' Brunetti asked. 'The tone or the pronunciation?' It would hardly be much to go on, but if the attacker had come from behind her, that's all there would be.

She raised her right hand and waved one finger back and forth in a strong negative. 'No. Nothing.' Then, more thoughtfully, 'Not even the sex.'

'Not high or low?' he asked.

'No. Whoever spoke was forcing their voice, the way you do when you sing falsetto.'

Brunetti thought of jigsaw puzzles, the old wooden ones his father had played with in the last years of his life, and he remembered those magic moments when a single piece, perhaps containing half an eye and a dab of flesh, opened up a new colour and made sudden sense of those beige pieces lined up at the edge of the table that had been, until then, meaningless.

'Are you a singer?'

Her eyes widened and she said, 'I want to be. But not yet. I have years of work before that.' With that infusion of passion, her natural voice returned, leaving behind the whisper and the stress, freeing its beauty.

'Where are you studying?' Brunetti asked, tiptoeing towards a place he could only suspect might be nearby.

'Paris. At the Conservatory.'

'Not here?' he asked.

'No, my school's closed for the spring holiday, so I've come here to study with my father for a few weeks.'

'Does he teach here?'

'At the Conservatory, but only part time. He's also one of the freelance *ripetitori* at the theatre. I've been working with him there.'

'La Fenice?' Brunetti asked, as if the city were full of theatres.

'Yes.'

'Ah, I see,' Brunetti said. 'Does he approve of what the French are teaching you?'

She smiled and, as happened when young people smiled, grew prettier. 'My father's always enthusiastic,' she said with becoming modesty.

'Only your father?'

She started to speak, and Brunetti saw her stop herself. 'Who was it?' he asked.

'Signora Petrelli,' she whispered, as though she had been asked who she thought could heal her broken arm and had replied, 'La Madonna della Salute.'

'How is it she heard you singing?'

'She was going to her rehearsal room, and she passed the door where I was with my father, and she . . .' The girl closed her eyes. And then a soft snoring sound came from her nose, and Brunetti knew he would get no more information from her that morning.

10

Brunetti went back to the nurses' station, but the woman he had spoken to was not there. He pulled out his phone and, feeling ridiculous for his continued reluctance to go and talk to Rizzardi, called the pathologist's number.

Rizzardi answered by asking, 'You talk to her yet, Guido?'

'Yes.'

'What can you do about it?'

Brunetti had been thinking exactly this since he had spoken to the girl. 'Try to find out if we have a camera over there.'

'Camera?' Rizzardi asked.

'There are some in different places in the city,' Brunetti explained. 'Although it's not likely there'd be one there.'

After a pause that could have been polite or impolite, Rizzardi inquired, 'Too few tourists?'

'Something like that.'

All irony fled Rizzardi's voice and he asked, 'Why would anyone do something like that?'

'I have no idea.' The son of a friend of Brunetti's had been attacked on the street by a drug addict five years before, but this sort of random attack – a kind of vandalism against persons – was virtually unknown in the city. Rizzardi had no need to know that the girl's assailant had spoken to her, so all Brunetti did was thank his friend for calling him.

'I hope you find out who did it,' Rizzardi said, then added, 'I've got to go,' and hung up.

Left to his own thoughts, Brunetti mentally listed the agencies that had installed *telecameras* in the city. The ACTV, he knew, had them on the *imbarcaderi*, both to see that the ticket sellers did not cheat their clients and to identify vandals. He knew that many buildings were protected or at least kept under surveillance by them, but who would bother to put one on a bridge that was likely to be used only by Venetians?

He recalled seeing a report about the surveillance cameras his own branch of the police had installed but failed to remember where they were; the Carabinieri certainly had some; and he had seen one in the alley that led to the offices of the Guardia di Finanza near Rialto.

He walked back to take another look at the young woman, but even before he reached her bed, he could hear her quiet snoring. He left the ward and made his way out into Campo SS Giovanni e Paolo.

The scaffolding still climbed both sides of the Basilica. Although it had been in place for years, Brunetti could not remember the last time he'd seen any workmen on it. On an impulse, he went into the Basilica, only to be stopped by a word from a man sitting in a wooden booth to the right of the door. Neither the booth nor the man had been there the last time Brunetti went into the church.

'Are you a resident?' the man asked.

A flash of outrage struck Brunetti, doubled by the fact that the man spoke Italian with a foreign accent. What else would he be, a man in a suit, at nine in the morning, going into a church? He lowered his head and stared through the glass at the man who had questioned him.

'*Scusi, Signore*,' the man said deferentially, 'but I have to ask.'

This calmed Brunetti. The man was doing his job, and he was being polite about it. 'Yes, I am,' Brunetti said, then, though it was hardly necessary, 'I've come to light a candle for my mother.'

The man smiled broadly and just as quickly covered his mouth to hide his missing teeth. 'Ah, good for you,' he said.

'Would you like me to light one for yours?'

His hand fell from his mouth, and it opened in an 'O' of astonishment. 'Oh, yes, please,' he said.

Brunetti started to walk towards the main altar, his spirit uplifted by the lightness of everything before him. The sun streamed in from the east, tracing coloured patterns on the waving floor. Signs of the city's majesty – doges and their wives sleeping away the centuries – lined both sides of the nave. He refused to look at the Bellini triptych on the right, still scandalized by the violence of the last restoration it had been subjected to, poor thing.

Halfway down the right aisle, he paused to study one segment of the stained-glass windows: with advancing years, Brunetti had lost the ability to soak in too much beauty at one time and thus tried to limit the dose when he could by studying only one thing, or two. He gazed up at the quartet of muscular, spear-bearing saints.

His mother had always harboured a special devotion to the mounted dragon-killer on the left, though she alternated between believing him to be San Giorgio or San

Teodoro. Brunetti had never thought to ask her why she liked them so much, but now that she was gone, he had come to believe it was because she so hated bullies, and what greater bully than a dragon? He took a euro coin from his pocket and let it clank into the metal box. He took the two candles to which this entitled him and lit the wicks of first one, and then the other, from a burning candle. He placed them in the middle row and stepped back, watching until he was sure the flames would hold.

'One's for the mother of the guy at the door,' he whispered, just to make sure they didn't confuse things and credit both candles to his mother's account. He took a final look at the saint, an old friend after all these years, nodded and turned away. As he went along the aisle, Brunetti kept his eyes down to avoid overloading himself, but he could hardly avoid the glory of the pavement.

At the door, he bent down, caught the man's eye, and said, 'Done.'

On the way to the Questura, he thought of the things he would need to know: first the location of the *telecamere* and then the name of the organs of state in charge of them. He also had to consider how willingly the different branches of the forces of order would disclose their activities, even to each other, and whether they would be willing to do this cooperatively and not insist upon a request from a magistrate.

He went immediately to the squad room and found Vianello at his desk. Open in front of him was an enormous file of documents with the name 'Nardo' on the cover. At Brunetti's approach, the Inspector looked up at him and, pasting a tortured expression on his face and reaching out a hand he was careful to make tremble, whispered, 'Save me, save me.'

Having often been constrained to look at the same file, Brunetti raised his hands as if to ward off a malign apparition, and said, 'Not the Marchesa again?'

'The very same,' Vianello said. 'This time she's accusing her neighbour of keeping wild cats in the courtyard.'

'Lions?' Brunetti asked.

Vianello tapped the back of his fingers on the page he had been reading and said, 'No, the cats in the neighbourhood. This time, she claims he lets them in every night and feeds them.'

'Even though he lives in London?'

'She says she's seen his butler feeding them,' Vianello explained.

'Who also lives in London,' Brunetti offered.

'She's mad,' Vianello said. 'This is the seventeenth complaint we've had.'

'And have to investigate?' Brunetti asked.

Vianello closed the file and looked longingly at the wastepaper basket on the other side of the room. Resisting the impulse, he shoved the papers to the side of his desk and said, 'If she weren't the godmother of a cabinet minister, do you think we'd be wasting our time on this?'

Instead of answering the question, Brunetti said, 'I've got something more interesting.'

They found Signorina Elettra seated at her desk, turned away from her computer and reading a magazine she made no attempt to hide. They would have been no more shocked to see a painting of Eve without Adam, a statue of Saint Cosmas without Saint Damian at his side.

When he noticed that the computer screen was blank, Brunetti's shock doubled, and he could think only of turning it into a joke. 'Are you on strike, Signorina?'

She looked up, surprised, and shot a glance at Vianello. 'Did you tell him?'

'Nothing,' Vianello answered.

'Tell me what?' Brunetti asked, directing the question at both of them.

'Then you don't know?' she asked, closing the magazine and opening her eyes in feigned innocence.

'No one's told me anything,' Brunetti insisted, although that was hardly true. The young woman had told him she'd been pushed down the steps. Beside him, Vianello folded his arms, making it clear he was going to sit this one out.

'Oh, it's nothing,' she said and looked back at the magazine.

Brunetti approached her desk. *Vogue*. He'd thought so.

She caught his glance and said, 'It's the French edition.'

'Don't you read the Italian one?'

She half closed her eyes for an instant and did something with her eyelids that dismissed the worth and accuracy of the Italian edition of *Vogue* at the same time as calling into question the taste of anyone who would ask such a ridiculous question.

'What may I do for *you* this morning, gentlemen?' she asked, turning to Vianello, as if she had just noticed them coming in.

'You can start by telling me,' Brunetti began, glancing at the still-silent Vianello to include him in the accusation, 'what's going on.'

Something he didn't follow passed between her and Vianello, and then she said, 'I want Lieutenant Scarpa's head.'

Over the last few years, the black spite that existed between Signorina Elettra, secretary to Vice-Questore Giuseppe Patta, and Lieutenant Scarpa, his closest confidant and assistant, had grown more intense. She and the Lieutenant delighted in blocking any initiative put forward by the other, Scarpa with utter disregard for the cost to the rest of the people working at the Questura, and Signorina Elettra handicapped by concern for it. If she suggested compiling a list, not only of the names and convictions of repeat offenders, but of the frequency and severity of their crimes, Scarpa was sure to criticize it as an attempt to stigmatize and discriminate against reformed criminals. If Scarpa recommended someone for promotion, his letter was bound to have attached to it her list of any reprimand the officer had ever received.

'As an office decoration?' Brunetti asked, looking around as though to search for the best place to set Scarpa's head, perhaps there on the windowsill next to the silent Vianello.

'That's a charming idea, Commissario,' she said. 'I'm amazed it hadn't occurred to me. But no, I was speaking figuratively, and all I want is that he be gone from here.'

He knew her well enough to hear the clash of iron and steel behind the joking words. He adjusted his voice accordingly and asked, 'What's he done?'

'You know he hates Alvise?' she asked, surprising him by speaking the truth so candidly. Lieutenant Scarpa, upon his arrival at the Questura some years ago, had at first appeared to court Alvise but had quickly discovered that the officer's amiability was distributed equally to everyone, not to the new arrival in particular. Thus had things quickly gone wrong, and since then the Lieutenant had not missed a chance to point out Alvise's many inadequacies. For all his slowness of wit, however, Officer Alvise was generally acknowledged to be decent, loyal, and brave, qualities not shared by some of his more intelligent colleagues. But hate, like love, came even when not summoned and did what it willed.

'Yes,' Brunetti finally answered.

'He's sent an official complaint about him.'

'To him?' Brunetti asked, adding to this breach of protocol by tilting his head in the direction of the office of Vice-Questore Giuseppe Patta.

'Worse: to the Prefetto and to the Questore,' she said, naming the two highest law enforcement officials in the city.

'What's he complaining about?'

'He's accusing Alvise of using criminal force.'

Unable to believe this, Brunetti turned to Vianello, who said, 'Alvise. Criminal force', as if to allow Brunetti to hear the absurdity of the conjunction of words. The Inspector looked in Signorina Elettra's direction to pass Brunetti's attention back to her.

'The Lieutenant's accusing him of assaulting one of the protestors last week,' she told him.

'When did he say this?' Brunetti demanded. He'd been at the protest in Piazzale Roma, a hastily organized thing that involved about a hundred unemployed men who had managed to block all traffic into or out of the city. Because there had been no warning and no request for a permit from the protestors, the police were slow in arriving, and by the time they did, they found drivers and protestors screaming abuse at one another and little way to distinguish between them unless the drivers were still in their vehicles. The arrival of the police, wearing face masks and helmets that turned them into a sinister species of beetle, along with a sudden burst of rain, dampened the spirits of the protestors, who began to disperse.

One of them, however, had fallen or been knocked to the ground, where he'd hit his head on the kerb and had to be taken to the hospital in an ambulance. At the time, a witness had said the man had tripped over one of the flags that had been abandoned by the protestors.

Two days afterwards, four protestors had arrived at the Questura to make a formal statement attesting that their colleague had been knocked to the ground by the night-stick of Officer Alvise – they knew his name – for they had seen it happen. It turned out that they were all members of the same union as the victim of the purported attack. The Vice-Questore, reached by phone, had given the investigation to Lieutenant Scarpa, who had begun by asking that Officer Alvise be suspended without salary until such time as the investigation was completed.

Brunetti heard this with mounting astonishment: when had anything like this ever been done? And how in God's name was Alvise to pay his rent?

'An hour after Alvise was informed,' Signorina Elettra continued, 'we had three calls from the press, two national editions, and *Il Gazzettino*.' She glanced at Vianello and then at Brunetti, and continued, 'None of the reporters would tell me how they'd heard of this, and one asked if it was true that Alvise had a history of violence.'

Brunetti turned at the sound of a hooted laugh from Vianello, who said, 'Alvise couldn't be violent if his life depended on it.' Brunetti, who was of the same opinion, said nothing.

'When I realized how the press must have learned about Alvise's supposed history of violence, I decided to go on strike.' After waiting a moment, she added, 'But I am not failing to report for work: I am merely limiting the amount of work I'll accept.'

'I see,' Brunetti said. 'Then to what extent is it a strike?'

'As I made clear to the Vice-Questore earlier this morning, I will not do anything that aids the Lieutenant: I will not distribute his memos, I will not transfer calls to him, I no longer speak to him – however much pleasure that might afford him – but chiefly, I will neither search for nor pass on any information to him.' By the end of this list she was smiling, and her expression became absolutely beatific as she added, 'I have already told three people who phoned that I have no idea who Lieutenant Scarpa is and suggested they try calling the Corpo Forestale.'

It came to Brunetti that, years ago, she had acquired – to choose the least incorrect term – the Lieutenant's password to the computer system, but he thought it improper to ask if that fact would be of any importance, or use, at the moment. 'Might I ask what the Vice-Questore's response to this has been?' he asked, instead.

'Strangely enough, he seemed able to tolerate it, so I had to tell him that, for each day Alvise remains suspended, I will work two hours fewer for him, as well, so by the end of the week I will be doing almost nothing for him, as I am now doing nothing at all for the Lieutenant.' The woman was calm, but no less terrible for that.

'What was his response, if I might ask?'

'Modesty prevents my saying he was appalled,' she responded with some pride. 'This forced me to explain that what I was doing was really much kinder than what was done to Alvise: he was tossed out from one minute to the next.' She smiled the sharkish smile Brunetti had come to appreciate and added, 'What I am also doing is weaning the Vice-Questore from what has become, over the years, an embarrassing dependence on my abilities.'

'Did you tell him that, too?' Brunetti asked, unable to disguise his astonishment.

'Of course not, Dottore. I think it's best for us all if he doesn't realize this.'

11

Brunetti agreed fully with Signorina Elettra's judgement. 'You're on strike only against them?' he asked, wanting to clear this up before he asked for her help.

'Of course. If you have something you'd like me to do, I'd be only too happy to abandon this,' she said, flipping closed the magazine. 'I don't know why I bother to read it.'

'That's exactly what my wife says about *Muscoli e Fitness*,' Brunetti said, deadpan.

But Signorina Elettra was not to be trapped. 'I'm sure she's interested because those things were so vital to Henry James,' she said.

'Have you read him?' Brunetti asked, not sure if he was astonished or worried.

'Only in translation. I'm afraid my mind has been so dulled by reading police reports that it's hard for me to concentrate on such complex prose and psychological penetration.'

'Indeed,' Brunetti said in a soft voice. And then, sensing Vianello's impatience with their quips, said, 'What I'd like you to do is find out if anyone has *telecamere* in place by Ponte de le Scuole.'

'Is that the one behind San Rocco?' she asked.

'Yes.'

It took her only a moment to visualize the place, and when she did, she said, 'I wouldn't think so. It's so far from anything.' Turning to Vianello, she asked, 'What do you think, Lorenzo?'

'We should try the Carabinieri,' he said, looking very pleased with himself. 'I remembered one of them, years ago, telling me they were putting up a lot of cameras, and he said they . . .' he paused here, catching their attention, '. . . wanted to put them in places where people didn't go much.'

'Is that a Carabinieri joke?' Signorina Elettra asked.

'Sounds it, doesn't it?' Vianello confirmed. 'But, no, it's actually what he said.' Neither one of them was willing to comment. Then, after a few seconds, he added, 'And did.'

Vianello was about to continue when, all of a sudden, their heads, like sunflowers towards the sun, turned in unison towards the sound of the opening door of the office of the Vice-Questore, and with the same involuntary phototropism, their faces reddened at the sight of his.

'You,' Patta said at the sight of Brunetti, ignoring Vianello, who was in uniform that day and, as such, unworthy of his attention. 'I want to talk to you.' At first Patta seemed not to notice Signorina Elettra, but then he gave her a brusque nod and turned back into his office.

Brunetti, his face as stern as the Vice-Questore's had been, glanced at his colleagues and followed his superior inside.

Patta stood in the middle of the room, a sure sign to Brunetti that their dealings were likely to be, regardless of subject, brief.

'What do you know about this strike business?' Patta demanded, waving an angry hand towards the door.

'Signorina Elettra was just telling me about it, Vice-Questore.'

'You didn't know anything?'

'No, Dottore.'

'Where have you been?' Patta asked with his usual gossamer delicacy of manner, then, without bothering to wait for Brunetti's answer, walked to the window and studied the buildings on the other side of the canal. When he had them memorized, he asked, not turning around, 'What are you working on?' It sounded to Brunetti like the kind of pro forma question Patta would ask while he was thinking about something else – the strike, probably.

'A woman was pushed down the stairs of a bridge last night. She's in the hospital.'

Patta turned. 'I thought that sort of thing didn't happen here.' Then, in case Brunetti had not been sensitive to his tone or to his heavy emphasis on the last word, he added, 'In peaceful Venice.'

Although Brunetti had to swallow his immediate reaction, his answer could not have been more bland. 'That certainly used to be true, Dottore, but we've had so many people coming in these last years, it's no longer the case.' Having edited his remark to remove 'from the South' after 'people' and replace it with a long pause, Brunetti considered his response both true and moderate.

As if he had read Brunetti's mind, Patta's voice became soft and almost menacing. 'Does it bother you that so many of us are here, Commissario?'

Brunetti gave a small, but visible, start to demonstrate

surprise and said, 'I meant the tourists, Vice-Questore, hardly the people who come here to work . . .' he toyed with saying it, thought he would, thought he wouldn't, and then decided to hell with it and finished his sentence, '. . . for the good of the city, such as you.' He smiled and applauded his own restraint in not having included Lieutenant Scarpa among those who worked for the good of the city.

He wondered which way Patta would jump and whether he had finally gone too far in provoking his superior. Patta could not fire him directly, but both of them had worked in the system long enough to understand that the Vice-Questore had friends who were sufficiently powerful to make life unpleasant for Brunetti, just as his own connections could cause significant trouble for Patta. Brunetti could be transferred somewhere awful, and there were enough awful places to make his head spin. Or Patta could take the easier path and see that Brunetti's friends and supporters at the Questura were transferred: there were surely enough awful places to go round.

Musing upon these things, Brunetti stood with his hands held behind his back, his eyes glued to the large photo of the President of the Republic hanging behind Patta's desk. He began to make an alphabetical list of the terrible places he might be sent and had got to Catania when Patta said, 'Tell me about this thing on the bridge. What happened?'

'Late last night, a young woman was pushed down the steps by someone who spoke to her before he did it.'

'Spoke to her how?' Patta asked. He walked to his desk and took his place behind it, waving Brunetti to the chair in front.

Brunetti sat down. 'She told me he said, "You're mine" just before he pushed her.'

'Do you believe that?' Patta asked, unable to prevent the instinctive suspiciousness from slipping into his voice.

Ignoring the scepticism and concerned only with the question, Brunetti said, 'Yes, I do.'

'What else did she tell you?' Patta asked. Then, not at all to Brunetti's surprise, he added, 'Is she important?'

In ordinary circumstances, Brunetti would turn a remark like this on its head and hand it back to his superior as a philosophical inquiry about how importance could best be determined, but today he wanted no trouble, and so he said, 'She's a guest at La Fenice, and it seems that Signora Petrelli thinks highly of her.' Both statements were true, he knew, and joined together like this they were utterly misleading.

'Petrelli?' Patta asked, then added, 'That's right; she's back. What's she got to do with this girl?' Brunetti didn't like the question, nor its insinuation.

'From what I was told, she heard this young woman singing at the theatre and stopped to compliment her,' he answered, as if he had not heard or understood the undertone in Patta's question.

'So she is singing there, this other woman?'

'Of course,' Brunetti said, as if the entire city were lined up and asking for her autograph. 'We were there for a performance a few nights ago, and Signora Petrelli's enthusiasm seems justified.' Brunetti left it at that: at least one of these was unquestionably true.

'In that case . . .' Patta began, and Brunetti waited as his superior pulled out some mental calculator that only he knew how to operate and worked out the relationship between the importance of the victim and the amount of police time that he should order to be spent on her. As Brunetti watched, Patta returned the calculator to a pocket in his mind, then said, 'Can you look into it?'

Brunetti took his notebook from his pocket and paged through it. 'I have a meeting at two' – this was a lie – 'but after that I'm free.'

'All right, then. See what you can find out,' Patta said. 'We can't have this sort of thing happening.' The head of the Tourist Office could not have phrased it more clearly.

Brunetti got briskly to his feet, nodded at the Vice-Questore, and left the office. He found Signorina Elettra alone in front of her computer, doing for him what he refused to learn to do.

'Lorenzo?' he asked.

'He had to meet someone.'

'Anything?' he asked.

'Before he left, he told me he called the Carabinieri and they do have a camera on the other side of the bridge where the girl was found: it shows the right side leading to San Rocco.' She pushed her chair back and pointed at the screen, saying, 'They just sent me this.'

Making no attempt to disguise his astonishment, Brunetti said, 'The Carabinieri actually sent this?'

'He's done them some favours in the past.'

Brunetti had no idea what they might have been, nor did he want to know. 'I'll never tell another Carabinieri joke,' he lied.

Giving him a sceptical glance, Signorina Elettra rolled her chair to one side to create space for him.

He moved behind her and leaned down, the better to view the screen. The image at first reminded him of an X-ray: grey, grainy, and utterly without definition. He made out – but only because he knew he was looking at a bridge – the parapet, at the top of the screen, and the back wall of the Scuola di San Rocco, though it could have been the wall of any building. Motion appeared: a small, round, wavy dark grey shape at the bottom right of the screen. Very quickly, it grew shoulders, a torso, legs, feet, moved away, and then disappeared in reverse order as the person walked down the other side of the bridge. 'That's all?' he asked, unable to disguise his disappointment.

Signorina Elettra shrugged and slid her chair forward. She clicked a few keys; other grey shapes hurried across the bridge as if they were skating over the steps. He watched two of them, three, crossing the bridge in both directions, then he lost count. There was a long blankness on the screen: only the parapet and the wall at the back. Signorina Elettra touched a key, but nothing changed.

Suddenly a shape crashed into the screen, startling a gasp from both of them. Brunetti watched as something thin projected down from the shape and poked at the stairs, then gave way, after which the whole shape collapsed on top of it, bringing with it another of those small round shapes, though this one bounced against a step, and then it all stopped moving.

Time passed. Signorina Elettra said, 'I'll speed it up again.' Nothing changed on the screen: nothing moved for a time.

Suddenly two round shapes appeared at bottom right; by now Brunetti recognized them as heads and watched as the bodies caught up with the heads, and then the men hurried up the steps to the unconscious woman. One knelt beside her while the other moved his arm and held something to his ear. The kneeling one took off his jacket and spread it over the shape on the ground, then both of them got to their feet and stood motionless.

Signorina Elettra fast-forwarded the video, and the two men moved to the side of the bridge with the jerky animation of speeded-up film. Twice one of them hurried to kneel beside the shape, which did not move. Then both heads whipped to the left at the same time, after which two more men, dressed in black, hurried on to the scene.

She leaned forward and touched a key, and things returned to normal speed. The men in black knelt beside the shape, which appeared to move. One of the carabinieri put his hand on the woman's shoulder and bent over her, speaking into her ear. The shape stopped moving.

Again Signorina Elettra fast-forwarded the tape: one of the uniformed officers leaped to his feet in defiance of the law of gravity; then the other did the same. All at once the screen filled with figures as two men in white uniforms arrived with a stretcher. They appeared to speak to the carabiniere who was not speaking with the other two men, then they ran to the top of the bridge and set down the stretcher. Signorina Elettra slowed things down and the white-uniformed men carried the woman to the top of the bridge, one of the carabiniere following close behind. The men lowered her to the stretcher then lifted it and disappeared with her at the bottom left of the screen.

She touched another key, and the figures on the screen froze as in a children's game.

'May I see the scene where she falls again, please?' Brunetti asked.

Signorina Elettra did as he requested, and again they watched the young woman fail to block her fall. They saw her arm give way and her head crash against the edge of the step.

'Again, please,' Brunetti requested, and they started from the beginning. This time he ignored – or tried to ignore – the falling woman and looked behind her for any sign of motion. There was something.

'Can you slow it down?' he asked.

She started it again, and this time the young woman looked as though she were falling under water, floating down to make elegant contact with the surface that would break her arm and cut open her head.

Brunetti ignored this and studied the top of the bridge behind her. And he saw it again: a dark vertical bar that came into sight from behind, then swirled away, to be followed immediately by something thin and striped and horizontal. It flashed out from the top of the place where the vertical bar had been, and was then sucked back to the left.

Signorina Elettra sent the scene back to the beginning, and they watched the same apparitions: first the dark vertical and then the striped horizontal, both appearing from the same place and returning there.

She hit the keys and it started again, and then again.

When the slow-motion scene stopped the fourth time, leaving only a few centimetres of the disappearing horizontal image, she froze the last image and turned to Brunetti to ask, 'What do you think it is?'

'A coat and a scarf,' he said with no hesitation. 'He walked across the top of the bridge, took a look at what he'd done, then turned around and walked back down the other side.' He leaned forward and touched the screen with his finger. 'That's his scarf swirling out to the side.'

'Bastard,' Signorina Elettra whispered, the first time in all these years that he had heard her use strong language. 'He could have killed her.'

'Maybe he thought he had,' Brunetti said in a grim tone.

12

Signorina Elettra remained silent, staring at the last wave of horizontal lines. She rested her chin on her palm and continued to study it. 'There's not much else it could be, is there?' she finally agreed. She leaned closer, hit a key, and the picture on the screen suddenly grew larger. 'Look,' she said, 'you can even see the fringe.'

Brunetti bent closer and saw that she was right. He stepped back, put his hands into his pockets, and stared at the image on the screen, working out what might have happened. 'She fell from the top of the stairs,' he said. 'So either he was following her, or he was waiting near the bridge, which means he knew which way she would be going. Then, after he pushed her, he couldn't resist the temptation to see what had happened.' He thought it through again and said, 'She didn't move until those men found her.'

'So he did think he'd killed her,' Signorina Elettra finished for him. Then, voice tight with rage and disgust, she said, 'God, it's awful.' Brunetti saw that she had closed her eyes and decided not to speak to her until she was calmer.

He went over to the window and studied the vines in the garden of the *palazzo* where, for the last decade, he had seen no sign of life other than the yearly renewal of this ever-expanding plant. In a month, the wisteria would be in full bloom, but for now the vine would lurk menacingly on the wall, apparently unwilling to divulge its secret until that day when – zap! – the panicles were there, where they had not been the day before, and the perfume filled every room of the Questura.

From behind him, he heard Signorina Elettra say in her normal voice, 'It's usually the husband or boyfriend or an ex or someone she's trying to make become an ex.'

Brunetti had reached the same conclusion and had decided he had no choice but to go back to the hospital to speak to the girl again.

'Her name's Francesca Santello,' he said.

'How old is she?' Signorina Elettra asked.

'Young,' was all Brunetti could say, failing to remember what had been written on the hospital chart. 'Looks about eighteen. Not much more than that.' Then, 'She's studying in Paris.'

'Would you like me to see if I can find out anything about her?' she asked.

Brunetti nodded. 'She seemed a nice girl,' he said.

'Nice girls don't always have nice boyfriends,' Signorina Elettra answered.

Brunetti gave a combination of nod and shrug to indicate agreement and resignation to the way of the world.

'The way he stood on the bridge and looked at her is strange,' she said in a sober voice. 'A crank wouldn't do that: he'd just push her for the fun of it and run away.

But this guy wanted to see what he'd done.' She looked thoughtful. 'I'll have a look,' she said.

Brunetti checked his watch and decided to go home for lunch and then to the hospital during the time when the wards were, at least theoretically, closed to visitors.

'Where is she?' Signorina Elettra asked.

'*Cardiologia.*'

Signorina Elettra failed to hide her surprise. 'What?'

'They had nowhere else to put her.'

When she finally responded, it was to ask, 'You think she's safe there?'

'As safe as anyone is there.'

He had thought of asking Vianello to go along with him after lunch, but the girl had still been so groggy she might not remember having spoken to him: better she wake up to see a woman standing near her bed. He phoned Claudia Griffoni and asked if she could meet him at the front door of the hospital at three, to serve as 'a calming feminine presence' when he questioned a young woman who had been assaulted.

That done, he walked home, dawdling through the nearly empty streets while he still could. In Campo Santa Marina, he noticed that the small tables in front of Didovich were all full, most of the customers sitting, eyes closed, faces towards the sun. Seeing them, Brunetti remembered overhearing an American tourist say, 'Sunscreen's for sissies.' He also remembered that his repeating it to Rizzardi had provoked one of the pathologist's rare smiles.

As he suspected, he found his family lined up in a row on the terrace much like the clients at Didovich: Paola, wearing gloves and with a woollen scarf wrapped around her neck, sat reading. Chiara wore a T-shirt the sight of which made goose bumps break out on Brunetti's arms. She sat, chair tipped back, feet on the railing, eyes closed, with every evidence of having slipped into a deep coma. Raffi wore headphones and sat, eyes closed, shaking his head from side to side as though in the grip of Parkinson's or St Vitus's dance.

None of them registered his arrival. He stood and studied them. His wife had been transported by her worship of words, his daughter by the sun, and his son by something Brunetti refused to call music. In their flight to altered states, they'd left all thought of him behind. And, it seemed, all thoughts of lunch.

He retreated to the kitchen and saw the red light that said the oven was on, so there would be something to eat once the living dead arose and joined him. Having nothing better to do, Brunetti set the table, being careful to make as much noise as possible. He let the plates clunk on the wooden surface, clanged two of the forks against the plates, slid the knives to the other side of them, one making a very satisfactory scraping sound. Napkins, disappointingly silent things, glasses that went cling. There was a loaf of bread in a paper bag on the counter, and he made a great fuss of unwrapping it, thought for a moment of blowing air into the bag and popping it but decided that would be unfair. He pulled out the wicker bread basket and sliced half of the loaf into pieces of the thickness he liked and no one else did, deciding to content himself with one of life's smaller victories.

He took out a bottle of mineral water, then opened the fridge and found an unfinished bottle of Pinot Grigio. Once they were on the table, Brunetti saw no reason to continue waiting: besides, it was well after lunchtime and he was hungry.

He went back to the the terrace and saw them, petrified

as the plaster casts of the victims of Pompeii. 'Shall we have lunch now?' he asked in a normal voice. None of them responded, something he could forgive only Raffi, who was now drumming out a spasmic rhythm on his thighs.

'Shall we have lunch now?' Brunetti repeated, louder this time. Paola looked away from her book and towards him but, he was sure, didn't see him. Her eyes remained focused on some inner place or world where people spoke in well-considered, full sentences and did not make a fuss about what time they ate their lunch.

Chiara opened her eyes, raised a hand to shade them from the sun and saw him. 'Oh, you're here,' she said, smiling. 'How nice.' Irritation packed its bags, opened the door and, pulling impatience along by its sleeve, began the long walk downstairs.

Paola set her book face down on the wall of the terrace and got to her feet. 'What time is it?' she asked. 'I didn't hear you.'

'I just got here,' Brunetti explained.

She moved towards him, still seeming slightly dazzled, either by the sun or by her book. As she reached him, she placed her hand on his arm and aimed a kiss at his left ear. 'There's frittata with zucchini and stuffed turkey breast,' she said.

'Am I taking you away from anything important?' he asked with a glance at the book she had abandoned.

'Truth, beauty, elegant prose, lacerating psychological penetration, thrilling dialogue,' she listed.

'Just can't stay away from Agatha Christie, can you?' Brunetti said and turned back towards the kitchen.

Paola retrieved her book, set it down in front of Raffi and prised off his earphones, then moved her lips as though she were speaking.

It took Raffi a moment to realize she was joking, and then he had the grace to laugh. 'I'm starved,' he said to his mother's retreating back, quite as if he had not said this at least once every day since he first learned to speak.

He and Chiara followed their mother into the kitchen and took their places. Paola bent over the oven and said over her shoulder, 'Thanks for setting the table, Chiara.'

Chiara looked at her in surprise, then at Raffi, who shook his head and, keeping his right hand close to his chest and covering it with his left, pointed a finger at Brunetti, who held a finger to his lips, a gesture which freed Chiara to say, 'Well, you always do all the cooking, *Mamma*. It seemed the least I could do.'

This time Raffi jabbed his forefinger repeatedly into his open mouth but said nothing to reveal his sister's perfidy.

The meal passed quietly, with the idle chat of people who were at ease with one another. Paola asked Raffi if Sara would be coming home from Paris for Easter, and when he said she would, Paola asked him if he missed her.

Raffi looked up from his dessert, a pumpkin and raisin cake, set his fork on his plate, and clasped one hand to his heart. 'I think of nothing else. I long for her as a ship-wrecked sailor longs for the sight of a sail on the horizon, as a man lost in the desert longs for the sight of a trickling stream, as . . .'

'A starving man longs for a crust of bread. As a . . .' Chiara began, only to be interrupted herself by Paola.

'Isn't it interesting,' she said in the voice she used for speculation, 'that longing is so often expressed in physical terms: hunger, thirst, physical safety?'

'What should we long for instead?' Brunetti asked. 'Universal peace?'

'That's not what I'm saying,' Paola insisted. 'I find it

interesting that longing is usually expressed in physical terms rather than in spiritual or intellectual ones.'

'It's more immediate,' Chiara said. 'You suffer from physical need: water, food, sleep. You *feel* it.'

'You suffer more from the lack of freedom or peace of mind, I'd say,' Brunetti offered.

Raffi continued with his cake, as if he found it far more interesting than this sort of speculation.

'But physical pain *hurts*,' Chiara insisted. 'Nobody dies of a broken heart.'

Paola placed a hand on her own anguished heart. She reached across the table and grabbed at Brunetti's hand. 'Guido, we've raised a savage.'

Time, Brunetti decided, to go and meet Griffoni.

13

Claudia was there at three. Tall, blonde, blue-eyed, her appearance gave the lie to every Venetian preconception about Neapolitans, while her quick intelligence and perception confirmed another. The kindness of the day invited them to stand on the steps of the hospital while Brunetti explained about the attack and the film footage from the bridge.

'All you see of him is the coat and the scarf?' Griffoni asked.

'Yes.' Brunetti took a step away from her and stopped, then swung around to face her again, letting his arm mimic the scarf swirling out to the side. A woman coming across the *campo* gave them a strange look before entering the hospital.

'He just stood there and looked?'

Brunetti nodded. 'Then turned around and went back down the other side of the bridge.'

Griffoni glanced aside at the bridge leading down into

the *campo*, as if trying to imagine the same events taking place there. 'Shall we go and talk to her?' she finally asked.

Brunetti led the way across a courtyard filled with the scent of earth yearning to open itself to springtime. Letting his feet follow the serpentine of memory as they made their way through the hospital, he told Griffoni the little he knew of the girl: she was studying singing in Paris but was here on school holiday and practising at the theatre with her father, one of the *ripetitori*.

'Is she a good singer?' Claudia asked.

'Her father must think so.' Brunetti considered the possible, but not very likely, link between Francesca Santello and Flavia Petrelli. They both sang: they had both been provoked, though he realized this was a feeble word for what had happened to Francesca. Finally he decided to say it, as much to test how it sounded as for any other reason. 'She was complimented for her singing by Flavia Petrelli. Someone might have overheard it.'

Claudia came to a sudden stop. 'Would you say that again, please?'

'Signora Petrelli has a fan who seems to have followed her here,' Brunetti said, speaking slowly to allow himself time to shape the story. 'He sends her flowers, enormous quantities of them. It started in London; happened in St Petersburg, and then he sent more to her dressing room after the opening night here. When she got home, she found more of them inside the building where she's staying, outside the door of her apartment. No one had let anyone in.'

Claudia rubbed at her cheek, then ran her fingers up into her hair and tugged at a few strands. 'And the girl? I don't understand what connection you're trying to make.'

Neither did he; not in a linear way that anyone else would find plausible. He started walking again, with

Claudia beside him. They passed the bar and barely noticed the people in slippers and bathrobes standing inside and drinking their coffee.

'I'd say sending someone flowers . . .' she continued, turned and saw the look on his face, and added, 'all right, a lot of flowers, is different from trying to kill them.' She tried for irony but achieved only scepticism.

'They're both excessive actions,' he insisted.

'Does that mean one leads to the other?' she asked in the voice he had been hearing prosecutors use for years.

He stopped. 'Claudia, stop playing bad cop, all right? If you think about this as the behaviour of a person with an unbalanced mind, you might see what I mean.'

She stared back at him, obviously unpersuaded. 'If you're trying to relate two unrelated things, nothing's better than saying a crazy person did them, is there? You don't need a reason because there's the crazy person to blame.'

'That's exactly what I'm saying,' Brunetti insisted. 'It's crazy to send hundreds of flowers to someone over a period of months and in three countries and not tell them who you are.'

'Hundreds?' she asked, clearly surprised.

'Yes.'

'Ah.' Her pause was long-drawn-out. 'Did you see them?'

'The ones on the stage, yes. And she told me there were at least ten bouquets in her dressing room on opening night, and more in front of the door of her apartment when she got back there.'

'You spoke to her?'

'Paola's parents invited her to dinner a few nights after the opera, and she told us about it.'

'Was she telling the truth?'

Reluctant to ask Claudia why she would doubt Flavia's word, Brunetti answered mildly, 'I think so. She seems a reliable witness.' Freddy, when Brunetti phoned him, had verified the story of the roses inside their building but had added that he thought Flavia was overreacting to them. 'After all, Guido,' he'd added, 'this is Venice, not the Bronx.'

Brunetti's voice must have revealed his frustration at Claudia's reluctance to believe him, for she said, just as they started up the stairs to *cardiologia*, 'I don't need confirmation, Guido: I believe you. And her. It's just hard for me to believe that someone would be this . . .'

'Crazy?' Brunetti suggested.

She stopped at the door to the ward and turned to him. 'Yes. Crazy.'

He reached in front of Griffoni and pushed open the door, then followed her into the ward. When they walked up to the nurses' station, he saw the same nurse who had been on duty that morning standing behind the desk.

Looking up, she recognized him and said, 'We've found her a room.' The nurse seemed genuinely pleased to be able to tell him this. The girl had been rebranded as a victim, Brunetti recalled, so now she was everyone's darling.

'Good,' he answered and smiled. He thought it best to explain who the attractive blonde was, so he indicated Griffoni and said, 'I've brought a colleague with me. It might be better to have a woman with me when we speak.' The nurse nodded in agreement.

'How is she?' Brunetti asked.

'Better. The doctor changed the painkiller, so she's much less groggy than she was this morning.'

'May we see her?' Griffoni asked with the deference beautiful women – if they are intelligent – use when dealing with women who are less attractive than they are.

'Of course,' the nurse said. 'Come with me.'

She led them down the corridor and stopped at the second door, opened it and went in without knocking. Griffoni put a firm hand on Brunetti's arm and stopped him from following the nurse into the room. 'Let her invite us in,' she said.

After a moment, the nurse came back and said, addressing them both, 'She'd like you to come in.'

Brunetti stepped back to allow Griffoni to precede him. It was a double room with a view over the tops of tall trees just coming into leaf. The other bed was empty, though the covers were turned back, the pillows propped up and dented by the head of the person who had been resting against them.

Griffoni stopped two metres from the bed and stood still to allow Brunetti to approach the girl. She looked better: her hair was brushed, and there was some colour in her face. From her expression, it was evident that she remembered Brunetti and was glad to see him again.

Her smile broadened, and he again saw the beauty there. 'I'm glad to see you looking better,' he said and extended his hand. She took it with her good hand, saying, 'Thank God I'm not a pianist.' She lifted the cast a few centimetres to show her other hand, swollen and blue. Again, that sweet voice and precise diction.

Brunetti turned to Griffoni, who joined him next to the bed. 'This is my colleague, Claudia Griffoni.' Thinking truth would sit well with the girl in the bed, he added, 'I thought I should bring a woman along.'

'So I would be less frightened?'

'Something like that.'

The girl looked at Griffoni and caught her eye. She pulled her lips together and raised her eyebrows in surprise at the quaintness of Brunetti's remark. 'Thank you.' Then, looking at Griffoni, she added, 'She doesn't look very threatening.'

Griffoni laughed, and Brunetti felt strangely excluded from this feminine affinity. To re-establish his position, he said, 'I'd like you to tell me again about last night, at least as much as you remember.'

Griffoni moved a step closer, set her bag on the floor by the wall, and took a pad and pen from it.

The girl smiled, as if not yet ready to take the risk of moving for fear of the whack her head had taken. 'I've been thinking about it since I saw you this morning, trying to remember, but it's hard because of what happened. I know that he pushed me. I don't want to invent things that might have happened before that or let them change my memory.'

She raised her hand and let it fall helplessly back on the bed. 'I'm sure of it: I really did hear something when I was walking, maybe from the time I left the pizzeria, or I sensed something, but I'm not sure what it was.' She paused, and Brunetti again saw just how clear her eyes were, strangely at odds with her dark hair. Were she an older, or a vainer, woman, he'd suspect she dyed it. As it was, he thought she'd merely had the luck of the genetic grab that had put that chestnut hair above those clear blue eyes and that very pale skin.

'Did you look back to see what it was?' Griffoni asked.

The girl's face relaxed at the ease with which Griffoni posed the question, as if she already believed the girl had indeed been aware of something and needed only a clearer idea of what it might have been.

'No. It's Venice. That doesn't happen.'

Brunetti nodded. And waited.

'When I got on to the bridge, I heard steps behind me, but before I could turn I heard him say, "*È mia*", in a really creepy voice, and then I felt this shove. All I could think about then was not falling, of somehow getting to the bottom of the steps on my feet. But I didn't. Then there was that man kneeling over me and asking me if I was all right.'

'And here we are,' Griffoni said, lifting her pen from the page and waving it at the room. Then, more seriously, she asked, 'What do you mean by "creepy voice"?'

Francesca closed her eyes, and Brunetti knew she was putting herself back on the bridge. 'It had too much breath,' she said and opened her eyes. 'Like it had been hard for him to follow me or come up the steps. I don't know. There was a gasping sort of sound. Like you'd use to frighten children.'

'Could he have been trying to disguise his voice?' Brunetti asked.

The blue eyes looked out of the window and studied the trees for a long time. Singers, he had once been told, often had extraordinary memories. Had to have them. He imagined her remembering the voice on the bridge, and then she said, 'Yes, that could be it. It wasn't a real voice. I mean, it wasn't a person's real voice.'

'You're sure you heard correctly?' Brunetti asked. 'He said you were his.'

'Yes.' Her response was instant and unhesitating.

Brunetti glanced aside at Griffoni, wondering what she would make of his next question, but decided to ask it anyway. 'Are you sure he meant you?'

'Of course he did,' she answered heatedly. 'I told you, he said, "*È mia*." He was talking to *me*.'

He heard Griffoni's sudden intake of breath, but it was the girl who asked, 'What?'

Brunetti watched as Claudia worked out the grammar. At the same time, he saw her studying Francesca's face, her youth displayed there and in the small body under the covers.

'He didn't say, *"Sei mia"*?' Griffoni asked, making no effort to disguise her disbelief. 'To someone he's pushing down the steps?' The girl had told Brunetti twice that her attacker had addressed her formally, and both times he, like Claudia, had been surprised by this. Her youth was beyond question, and her attacker might well have been older. To address her with the formal was absurd. In that case, he was referring to some other woman: *'She's* mine.'

14

'I think he was telling me I was his,' Francesca said, still not understanding that she might not have been the attacker's main target. 'That's what's so awful, that he just decides who belongs to him.' Hearing her anger, Brunetti began to think she would come out of this unscathed: it was a much healthier response than fear and caution.

'You said you didn't see anyone following you,' Brunetti reminded her.

It took her some time to answer. 'On the bridge, I *felt* it.'

As she spoke, Brunetti saw her begin to fade, like a child who has played too hard all day and now needs to sleep. He turned to Griffoni and said, 'I think that's enough information for us to go on with, don't you, Claudia?'

She closed her notebook and picked up her handbag. She put it over her shoulder and approached the bed. 'Thank you for talking to us, Signorina Santello.' Claudia reached down and placed her hand on the girl's arm. She gave it a small squeeze and stepped back, leaving space for Brunetti.

'Does your father know what's happened?' he remembered to ask.

'He's gone to Florence for a few days,' she said in a voice that was sinking towards sleep. 'He works there, for the Festival, playing for auditions.'

'Did you tell him what happened?' Brunetti asked.

'Only that I fell and broke my arm,' she said, drifted a bit and then came back to add, 'I didn't want to frighten him.' Her lips turned up, either at the thought of her father or of having spared him worry, and then she was asleep.

They watched her for a while and then left. At the desk, Brunetti asked the nurse if anyone had been to visit her and was told that an aunt had come that morning and would return the next day and take her home the day after. 'The aunt told me her parents are divorced and the mother lives in France,' the nurse said, then shrugged. 'Modern times, Commissario.'

Brunetti thanked her for her help; he and Griffoni left the hospital and started back to the Questura.

As they were crossing the *campo*, Claudia said. '"*È mia.*" Of course he was talking about another woman. He wouldn't call her "*Lei*". She's little more than a kid, and he's trying to kill her, for the love of God. He'd hardly address her formally.'

'And the other woman?' Brunetti asked.

'Don't be coy with me, Guido,' she said with real irritation. 'I believe in the possibility of what you said.'

'Only the possibility?' he asked, doing his best not to sound coy.

Griffoni smiled and punched at his arm. 'All right, more than the possibility.' They turned left at the bottom of Ponte dell'Ospedaleto and walked along the canal, Brunetti completely unconscious of choosing the direction and Griffoni tagging along like a pilot fish beside a shark, content to let it lead the way.

They came down the next bridge and stopped. She asked, 'What do you want to do?'

'Send Vianello to talk to people in the neighbourhood to see if they've seen anyone spending a lot of time near the place where she's staying,' Brunetti answered, then added, 'I'd like to have someone keep an eye on the girl, but staffing's so short with Alvise gone, I don't know if there's any way to do it.'

'Why not ask him?' she asked.

'Who? Alvise?'

Griffoni nodded and said, 'I haven't known him very long, but he's loyal and able to follow simple orders. And he's bound to be eager to get back to work. So if he's told this is a special assignment, to see that nothing happens to her at the hospital, he'll jump at the chance to do it.'

'He's been suspended, which, as I understand it, means he cannot work and is not being paid,' Brunetti said. 'I can't ask him to take the risk of working, and I certainly can't ask him to do it for nothing.'

Griffoni looked thoughtful, then said, 'I don't think that will be a problem, Guido.'

'Of course it is. How do we pay him – by going around and collecting from the rest of the staff?' Even as he said it, he realized how bizarre this conversation was. Would they ask Scarpa to contribute to Alvise's salary and thus make sure that Patta found out what they were doing?

Griffoni looked at him and started to speak but then stopped and studied the water in the canal. Finding no answer there, she returned her attention to Brunetti and said, 'It's possible that Signorina Elettra failed to file the request that his pay be stopped before she stopped working herself.'

'She did not stop working,' Brunetti said emphatically, trying to introduce some sense into this conversation. 'She's on strike.' Was this how Alice felt, he wondered, lost in a forest of words she didn't know how to escape?

Griffoni did not dispute this, and so he sought to enforce his argument.

'Besides, he's paid from Rome, not from here,' Brunetti explained. 'We all are.' Surely, she must know at least this.

'The order to stop his salary would originate here, wouldn't it?' Griffoni inquired. 'From Lieutenant Scarpa, countersigned by the Vice-Questore.' Taking his silence for assent, she added, 'There are, however, ways to circumvent that.'

Brunetti put his right hand to his face and rubbed at the short hairs that had grown up under his bottom lip since he'd shaved that morning. He scratched them lightly, telling himself he could actually hear them springing up as soon as his nails passed over them. '"Circumvent",' he repeated.

Griffoni's face remained strangely immobile as she said, 'If that order were not passed on to Rome, and if he were assigned to a new employment category, then there would be no interruption in his salary.'

'"If he were"?' Brunetti repeated the subjunctive, a mood which tended to creep into many conversations with both Commissario Griffoni and Signorina Elettra. And then, '"New employment category"?'

Griffoni raised an eyebrow and both hands, as if to suggest the limitless meaning of that phrase.

Brunetti studied Griffoni's face. Had it changed since her friendship with Signorina Elettra began? Was there not a certain veiled quality about her eyes that had not been there before?

He could not prevent the question escaping him. 'She did all of this?'

'Yes.'

'What's he been told?' Brunetti asked.

'Only that there will be a change of assignment while this matter is settled.' She looked away, looked back. 'He's been helping in the archives.'

'Helping how?'

'To the degree that he is capable of helping,' she answered, nothing more.

Brunetti looked at the buildings on the other side of the canal. The shutters on the largest of them were sun-bleached, some of them hanging askew. A drainpipe had come loose, and water had made a trail down the façade.

'Tell him to go over to the hospital and check on her a few times a day, would you?' he asked her. 'Plainclothes work. He'll like that.' How easily these two women could suck a person into complicity.

'And when she goes home?' Griffoni asked. 'What then?'

'If she stays in the city, he can still go and check on her,' he said. It wasn't much. Alvise wasn't much. But it was something.

He continued down the embankment towards the Questura.

She followed him. 'I'd like to hear her sing,' she surprised him by saying.

'Why?'

'Her voice is beautiful. Seems strange, though, coming from that wisp of a girl.'

As they entered the Questura, Claudia asked, 'Is there anything you'd like me to do after I talk to Alvise?'

The fact that she was not Venetian had at first made Brunetti reluctant to ask her to go to the theatre, for people there might be reluctant to talk to a foreigner. Well, he tempered the word: a non-Venetian. But he had begun to suspect that her charm and beauty might be enough to overcome that handicap. 'See if anyone at the theatre has noticed anything or anyone that ought not to be there.'

Without commenting on how broad that request was, she nodded and left him at the top of the stairs to go to her own office. Brunetti went into Signorina Elettra's and found her sitting upright at her desk, the magazine replaced by a book. 'Using the strike to catch up on your reading?' he asked.

She didn't bother to look at him, either because he was now included in her strike or because she was enthralled by the book.

Brunetti came closer and, reading upside down, made out the name on the binding.

'Sciascia?' he asked. 'Don't you learn enough about crime and the police by working here?'

His question proved sufficient to distract her. 'I'm trying to limit my direct contact.'

'With crime?'

She glanced in the direction of the door to the Vice-Questore's office. 'With the police,' she said, then, responding to Brunetti's false agitation of hands, she clarified, adding, 'But only those of certain ranks.'

'I hope I'm not included.'

She took the red ribbon hanging from the binding and slipped it between the pages before closing the book. 'Hardly. In what way can I be useful to you, Commissario?'

He saw no reason to tell her he knew about Alvise's salary or his new employment category: so long as he didn't know, he would not have to do anything.

'The girl we saw,' he began, waving at the computer, 'told me she received compliments about her singing from no one less than Flavia Petrelli.' He gave her the chance to ask about this, but all she did was set her book to the side of the computer and continue to look at him attentively.

'She – Signora Petrelli – has a fan whose behaviour is, well, is excessive,' he continued. Still she said nothing.

'So far, all he's done is send flowers, hundreds of them, both to her dressing room and to her home.'

After a long pause, Signorina Elettra asked, '"So far"?'

Brunetti shrugged to express his own unease. 'I have no concrete reason to believe this has anything to do with what happened on the bridge. It's all supposition.'

She considered that, face impassive. 'Do you have any idea who this fan is?'

'None,' he said but then realized he really hadn't given his identity much thought. 'It's got to be someone with enough money to travel to where she's singing and buy that many flowers. And who is clever and rich enough to get the flowers delivered pretty much wherever he wants.' He tried to imagine what else this man would have to know and be able to do. 'He'd have to know the city well enough to be able to follow the girl without being seen or losing track of her.'

'And without her seeing him. You think that means he's Venetian?'

'Possibly.'

'Shall I try to find out about the flowers?' she asked with the enthusiasm of a hunter set loose in the fields.

'Yellow roses. There were so many of them, it must have been a special order. The florist would probably have to have them sent in from the mainland.'

She leaned forward to switch on her computer. 'Have you missed it?' Brunetti risked asking, nodding towards the screen.

'No more than my friends miss their children when they

go off to university,' she said, waiting for the screen to light up.

Brunetti was struck by how little, after all these years, he knew about her. She had friends who had children of university age, yet she was surely not old enough to have a child ready to begin studying. He didn't even know how old she was. If he had chosen, he could easily have had a look at her file, learned her date of birth and her educational history. But he had never done it, just as he would never read a friend's letters – at least would not have done so in the era when people still wrote letters. Paola, whose mother was a passionate reader, had inherited the sense of ethics and honour of the gentlemen heroes of nineteenth-century novels. While he, strangely enough, had been given pretty much the same ethical grounding by a woman who had never gone beyond the fourth year of middle school and a perpetually unemployed dreamer whose health had been ruined and mind affected by years as a prisoner of war.

'Excuse me,' he said, having not attended to her last remarks.

'I said that I'm allowing myself to use it selectively.' She indicated the computer screen. 'I use it as I always have, only there are now two people for whom I don't use it.' He was impressed at how very reasonable she made it sound.

'Since I'm among those for whom you still work,' Brunetti said, speaking with false earnestness to demonstrate how sincere was his hope that he was, 'I'd like you to find out whatever you can about the girl on the bridge. Francesca Santello: parents divorced; mother lives in France; she lives with her father when she's here; somewhere in Santa Croce. She's studying singing at the Conservatory in Paris.' He spoke slowly when he saw that she was taking notes.

'I've asked Claudia to see if she can find out about anything strange that might have happened at the theatre. Even though she's not Venetian.'

Signorina Elettra nodded, as she would if he had mentioned the limitations created by a physical handicap.

'Do you know anyone who works there?' he asked, adding, 'The only person I know retired about five years ago and moved to Mantova.'

It took her only a second to answer. 'Someone I was at school with works in the bar on the corner, just opposite the theatre. I can ask him if he's heard them talking about anything strange. Most of the stage crew and staff go in there for coffee, so he might have heard something.' She made a note of that and looked at Brunetti. 'Anything else?'

'I'd like you to see what you can find out about fans,' he said.

She held up her pencil to get his attention. 'It might be more accurate to refer to stalkers.'

'Of?'

'Signora Petrelli.'

'And the girl?' he asked, though he thought he knew.

'She was someone who got in the way.'

'"In the way",' Brunetti repeated, pleased to hear her confirm his own opinion.

'Shall I take a look at Signora Petrelli's ex-husband?' she asked.

'Yes. And see if you can find out – do gossip magazines have an online edition?'

'I have no idea,' she answered blandly. 'I always read them at the hairdresser's.'

'If they do, could you go back through the last few years and see who Signora Petrelli's been involved with?'

'Are you thinking the same thing I am?'

'Probably,' Brunetti said. 'Just check the magazines,' he added, thinking that it would save a great deal of Signorina Elettra's time if he simply asked Flavia directly. If nothing else, it would allow Signorina Elettra more time to get on with her strike.

15

In his office, he turned on his own computer and, telling himself he was a man and not a mouse and could certainly do basic research, looked at the crime statistics about stalkers: yet another term, like 'serial killer', that English had brought into the language. Well, he told himself, they've also given us 'privacy', so take the bad with the good.

He began to read the Questura's internal documents and statistics, then turned to the wider world of the records kept by the Ministry of the Interior. He read with growing interest and increasing distress, and after an hour he said aloud, 'So much for the Latin lover.'

Two women a week, or close to it, were judged by the police to have been murdered, and usually the killer was an ex of some sort. There were countless other cases of accidental deaths and various vicious attacks, and when had it become fashionable to throw acid in women's faces?

He remembered, years ago, attending a seminar in Rimini, where a pathologist in a suit and tie who could easily have been mistaken for a small-town pharmacist had spoken of the many murders that passed undetected each year: falls were very common, as were overdoses of pills taken by women who had also been drinking. Women sometimes hit their heads and drowned in the bathtub, the doctor had told them: he had once performed an autopsy on one whose husband had come home from work to find her floating there, having, he told the police, left her asleep in bed that morning. A very wealthy man, he was also a very careless one, for he had forgotten the surveillance cameras in the house that had filmed his wife going into the bathroom, only to be followed by him eight minutes later, naked and carrying a large sheet of bubble wrap, traces of which the pathologist had found under her fingernails. 'Young, healthy people don't fall in the bathtub. Please remember that, ladies and gentlemen,' he had said before moving on to his next case.

And young girls don't trip and fall down bridges, Brunetti added, though he was the only one listening.

He called up the statistics for the last few years, and saw that aggression against women kept inverse pace with the crumbling economy: one went up as the other went down. Quite a large number of men, when faced with fiscal ruin, had opted for suicide, but more of them turned their rage or despair – or whatever the emotion that drove them was – against the women nearest to them, killing or maiming them with a frequency that frightened Brunetti.

These, he reflected, were women they knew and said they loved or had once loved, in many cases women with whom they had raised children. They were not some distant, unattainable diva on the stage, singing for thousands and not for you.

He closed the program and stared at the verdant hillside of the screen saver that had been in the computer when it had come to share his office, and his life. Green hills, one rolling to the left and, behind it, one to the right, almost as if the photographer had told them how to pose. He leaned forward and opened Google and tapped her name into the window provided, hit the Return key, and, within seconds, had Flavia Petrelli smiling upon him, as if to thank him for his attempt to help her. There she was, costumed, beautiful, radiant. He looked at the clothing and tried to figure out the roles that would require it. He got the Contessa in *Nozze* right and, having just seen the same production, Tosca. The cowboy hat and pistol identified her as Minnie, even though Brunetti had never seen *La Fanciulla*. In the next photo, she wore a bosom-exposing gown with a crinoline and with her hair – or her wig – piled high on her head. He didn't bother to read the caption.

He moved on to Wikipedia and was reminded that she had been born in Alto Adige more than forty years ago and had begun her musical training there. He jumped over the summary of her career and started reading the short paragraph entitled 'Personal Life'. There was the husband, listed correctly as Spanish, and two children whose names were not given. Her marriage, he read, had ended in divorce. There was the usual reference to 'early talent', 'astonishing debut', and 'technical mastery', as well as a list of the roles she had sung, but there was nothing beyond this.

Returning to Google, he opened another article, which consisted chiefly of photos, but he soon tired of the wigs and ball gowns. He had the number of her *telefonino* in his and he called it.

'*Sì*,' she answered on the fourth ring.

'Flavia,' he began, 'it's Guido. I'd like to talk to you; this evening, if possible.'

There was a very long pause, and finally she said, 'How long will it take and what do you want to talk about?'

'It's about a girl you spoke to, and I have no idea how long it will take,' he answered.

'A girl?'she asked. 'What girl?'

'Francesca Santello,' he said, but the name was met with silence. 'You spoke to her at the theatre a few days ago.'

'The contralto?' Flavia asked.

'I think so. Yes.'

'What about her?'

'Could I come and see you?'

'Guido, I'm in the theatre. I have to sing tonight. If whatever you have to tell me is going to upset me, I don't want to hear it, not this soon before a performance. Besides, there's nothing I can tell you about her. We met at the theatre, I complimented her, and that was that.' He heard a noise from her end of the phone: it sounded like a door closing. Then he heard a woman's voice – not Flavia's. Then silence.

'Could I come to see you after the performance?' he asked.

'Has something happened to the girl?' she asked.

'Yes. But she's all right.'

'Then why are you calling me?'

'Because I want you to tell me as much as you remember of your meeting with her.'

'I could do that right now,' she said, her voice less friendly than it had been.

'No, I'd rather do it in person.'

'So I can betray my guilt with my facial expression?' she asked, perhaps as a joke, perhaps not.

'No, not at all. I just don't want us to be rushed: I want you to have time to remember what happened and what you said.'

118

There was another long pause, during which he could hear the other woman's voice again and then some noises that might have been objects being moved around or set down.

'All right,' she said brusquely, the sort of voice one used with importuning salesmen. 'You know what time we finish. I'll wait for you.'

'Thank you,' Brunetti answered, but she had broken the connection before he spoke the second word.

He should have checked to see if there was a performance before he called, but the story troubled him: inexplicable violence always did. If his interpretation of events was correct, then there was every possibility that the violence directed at Francesca might expand to include Flavia.

He explained at dinner that he had to go out to speak to Flavia Petrelli that evening, after the performance. Neither of the children seemed interested, though Paola listened to his speculations attentively. At the end of his account, she said, 'People become fixated on other people.' She tilted her head and looked into the far distance, the way she did when some new idea came to her. 'I think that might be why Petrarch has always made me so uncomfortable.'

'What?' Brunetti asked in open astonishment.

'His thing with Laura,' she said, and Brunetti pondered these words – in the mouth of the most serious reader he had ever known, and said of the man who had taught his country how to write poetry. *His thing with Laura?*

'I've always wondered if he simply wound himself up about her, although I suspect he got into a state because that kept the poetry coming.'

'Beautiful poetry,' Brunetti said, aiming for precision here.

'Of course, beautiful poetry, but one does get so tired of all the unrequited love.' That said, she stacked the dishes prior to putting them in the sink, the children long since having slunk off to their rooms to engage in idle pursuits while leaving the work to their mother. 'And what about Laura? She might have thought he was a pest, a creep, or, if you will, a stalker, which is why I thought of him in this context.' She turned on the hot water and set the plates in the sink, then looked at Brunetti and said, 'You think, if he were living now, he'd have Laura chained in the cellar, and she'd be the mother of his two illegitimate children?'

Unable to find an adequate response to her question, the best Brunetti could do was say, 'You never told me you thought this way about Petrarch.'

'I'm simply tired of the fuss. People quote him, but how many people actually read him any more?' she demanded. 'And how many times can a poet get away with something like:

> *"Aura che quelle chiome bionde et crespe*
> *cercondi et movi, et se' mossa da loro,*
> *soavamente, e spargi quel dolce oro,*
> *et poi 'l raccogli, e 'n bei nodi il rincrespe"*. . .'

That said, Paola brought her lips together and said apologetically, 'I used to know the whole thing, but now that's all I can remember.' She pulled the silverware from the soapy water, rinsed it under hot, and set it in the drying rack above the sink, saying, 'Next thing, they'll be calling you to say I'm lost on the street and can't find my way home.'

Brunetti looked at his watch, kissed her without saying anything and left for the theatre.

* * *

His flight from further discussion of Italian poetry brought him to the theatre fifteen minutes before the end of the performance. He showed his warrant card at the stage door and said he'd find his way backstage. The guard displayed little interest and told him the elevator was on his left.

When he got out on stage level, he saw a man about his own age, dressed as he was, in suit and tie, and asked him the way to the stage. The man, a sheaf of papers in his hand, pointed straight ahead and told him he'd hear it, then walked off and left him there without having bothered to ask him who he was.

Brunetti followed his directions and walked down a dimly lit corridor to a soundproof door that failed to stifle the throb of the orchestra. He opened the door just as poor old Mario got it in the chest from some of Rome's finest: the sound swept over him, and the voices. Music, confusion, general noise. After pausing to allow his eyes to adjust to the brighter light, Brunetti took a few steps forward and stopped behind three stagehands who stood with their arms folded, watching the opera, and two others who were busy with their *telefonini*. And there on the stage was Flavia, hair crowned with a jewelled diadem, red gown trailing behind her, standing again on the ramparts of Castel Sant'Angelo, announcing her death. And then over she went, the music crashed out again, the curtain closed slowly, and one of the stage-hands turned his attention to the screen of his colleague's phone.

The audience, as they had the night he was there, went wild, erupting into the frenzy that Tosca's suicide and those final chords were meant to provoke and, in the hands of someone who could sing and act, usually did. Brunetti shifted a few metres so that he could see the entire area behind the curtain, where the singers loitered in a group, talking among themselves and laughing. Minutes passed.

A man holding a clipboard waved it to herd together the three principal singers and shooed them to centre stage, then turned and waved everyone else to the sides. The curtains pulled back, and the three singers, all miraculously returned to life, appeared, to receive their tumultuous applause. After some time, Flavia slipped to the side and brought out the conductor – whom she had referred to, at the Faliers', as 'a mediocrity that thumps' – then stood back and joined in the applause. Everyone linked hands again, and the curtains closed on them.

Brunetti stood on the side and watched for minutes as various performers walked from behind the curtains to receive their due. He saw the way Flavia put on a smile, flashing with delight each time she appeared to the public, then saw it dissolve the instant she returned behind the curtain.

As the applause thundered on, the man in charge clapped his hands briskly and pulled back the edge of one of the curtains to create an opening for the principals. He clapped again, more loudly, and the four people looked towards him. Tosca was drinking a glass of water and passed it to her dresser; the conductor was nowhere to be seen; Scarpia shined his shoes by rubbing them against the back of his trousers, Cavaradossi stuffed his *telefonino* into the pocket of his bloodstained doublet. Brunetti had once been told that it was done by squirting red ink from the inside of whatever they were wearing, so that the blood erupted just at the moment they were shot or stabbed. He wondered idly, as the audience continued its mad noise, if it washed out and, if so, whether the theatre had washing machines. Singers sweated a lot when they sang: the lights, the tension, the sheer physical strain of singing. They probably had dry cleaning machines, as well. Showbiz.

The man with the clipboard nodded, and Scarpia walked out to centre stage. Loud applause. He returned at the moment the applause peaked, and out went Mario. Louder applause, longer applause. He came back behind the curtain, pulled out his *telefonino* and continued his conversation. Tosca walked slowly from behind the curtain and stood entirely still. Pandemonium.

From the angle where he stood, Brunetti saw her right arm rise, as if to salute all that enthusiasm, all that love. Then it sank as she lowered herself in a slow curtsey that ratcheted up the applause. He watched her wave as she stepped unerringly backwards to the opening in the curtain and slipped through it, giving place to the conductor, who had returned to the stage and was enveloped in applause. Quickly back, he walked past the singers without bothering to speak to them.

After some time, when there was no lessening of enthusiasm from the audience, all four of them joined hands, filed on to the stage and took their united bow. They repeated this twice, and then left the diminishing applause and retreated behind the curtain. The man directing the bows made a quick horizontal gesture with his hands, as Brunetti had seen ground staff do when a plane was safely docked at the terminal. Gradually, the applause trickled down and stopped.

Behind Brunetti, the stage crew were busy disassembling Castel Sant'Angelo. They lowered the massive blocks of the stone ramparts that ringed the tower on to dollies and wheeled them offstage. Windows came apart as easily as the pieces of a jigsaw puzzle, were placed on different dollies, and sent to join the pieces of the ramparts.

When this ceased to interest Brunetti, he looked around

and saw that he was the only person, other than the head of the stage crew and the workers, to remain onstage. He approached and asked the man giving the orders if he could tell him where Signora Petrelli's dressing room was.

The man gave him a sharp look and asked, 'Who are you?'

'I'm a friend,' Brunetti answered.

'How'd you get back here?' he asked.

Brunetti removed his wallet and pulled out his warrant card. The other man took it and studied it carefully, looked at him to check the photo, then handed it back.

'Could you take me there?' Brunetti asked.

'Follow me,' he said and turned back the way Brunetti thought he had come, then down a long corridor: turn right, turn left, into the elevator and up, he thought, two floors. They turned left into a corridor, and on the third door on the left he saw Flavia's name. The man left him there. Brunetti knocked, and a woman's muffled voice shouted out something that did not sound inviting. A few minutes later, the door opened and a woman came out of the room, carrying the red gown on a hanger. She stopped when she saw him and asked, 'Are you Guido?'

Brunetti nodded, and she held the door open, then pulled it closed after him.

Flavia, barefoot and wearing a white cotton dressing gown, sat in front of the mirror, running both hands through her short hair; her wig stood on a stand to her left. She removed her hands from her hair and shook her head wildly: drops flew from it on all sides. Grabbing a towel, she rubbed her head for what seemed a long time. Tiring of this, she threw the towel on the counter and turned to Brunetti. 'He got in here again,' she said with an unsteady voice.

'Tell me,' Brunetti said, taking a seat to her left so as not to tower over her while they were speaking.

'When I came back after the performance, this was here,' she said in an uneasy voice, pointing to a wrinkled bundle of dark blue wrapping paper. A piece of thin gold ribbon lay on the floor.

'What is it?' Brunetti asked.

'Look,' she said and reached for the paper.

'Don't touch it,' he said more loudly than he should have. Her hand froze, and she shot him an angry look in which he saw the automatic response of a wilful person who is stopped from doing what they want to do.

'Fingerprints,' he said calmly, then added, hoping she watched crime shows on television, 'DNA.'

Chagrin replaced the anger on her face and she said, 'Sorry, I should have thought.'

'What is it?' he asked again.

'You have to see it.' She picked up a long-handled comb from her dressing table. Reversing it, she used the pointed end to push at the paper, moving it to one side. There was a flash under the makeup lights; she caught something with the sharp end of the comb and pulled it free of the paper.

'*Oddio*,' Brunetti said. 'Is that real?' Lying next to the wrinkled paper was a necklace. Every so often, the gold links thinned and wove around stones the size of Fisherman's Friend throat lozenges, though these were deep green, not dusty dark brown. 'Are they real?'

'I have no idea,' she said. 'All I know is that someone left this package here, and I opened it when I got back from the curtain calls.'

'Why did you open it?' Brunetti asked, resisting the impulse to add, 'with everything that's going on'.

'Marina, my dresser, told me a few days ago that she'd found something she thought I might like at the street fair in San Maurizio and would bring it tonight.'

Glancing at the necklace, Brunetti said, 'That's hardly the sort of thing one sees on sale at the street fair in Campo San Maurizio, is it?' Then he asked, 'Did you ask her about it?'

'No, I didn't have to. When she came in to collect my costume, she said she had to take care of the grandchildren yesterday and she forgot all about it.'

'Did she see it?' he asked, eyes on the hypnotizing green.

'No. I put a towel over it. I thought you were the person I should show it to.'

'Thank you,' Brunetti said. His eyes roamed back to the green, and he counted the lozenges: there were at least a dozen. 'How does it make you feel?' he asked, pointing with his chin towards the necklace.

She closed her eyes and clenched her teeth, then opened them just enough to whisper, 'It terrifies me.'

16

'Can't you lock the door?' he asked gently, to show he understood her reaction.

She shrugged the idea away. 'I suppose I could, but people always need to come in: if I forget a fan or a shawl, Marina has to get it, and the makeup artist leaves her things here.'

These sounded flimsy arguments to Brunetti, but he said nothing. Looking into the mirror, she caught his eye and said, 'The real reason is I wouldn't know where to put the key when I'm onstage. My costumes for this production don't have pockets, and I'm certainly not going to stuff it down my bodice.'

'I've always wondered about that,' Brunetti said, then immediately wished he had not.

'About what?' she asked, running her hands through her hair, this time evidently satisfied that it was dry.

'I've read or been told those stories about old-time sopranos,' Brunetti said, 'who wouldn't sing until they were paid in cash, and then put the silk bag of ducats or dollars or God knows what down their bodice.'

'The days of being paid in cash are long gone, I'm afraid,' she said with real regret. 'Today it's all agents and bank transfers and financial records.' She studied her face in the mirror. 'How lovely it would be to be paid in cash,' she said, sounding wistful at the passing of a finer era.

She turned away from the mirror to face him squarely. 'Tell me about the girl.'

'Someone pushed her down a bridge last night, saying, "*È mia*."'

'Oh, the poor thing. What happened to her?'

'She broke her arm and hit her head badly enough to need stitches.'

Her face tightened. 'Why are you telling me this?'

'Because of her age and because of the language.'

She shook her head. 'I don't understand.'

'Her attacker didn't say "*Sei mia*", which you'd ordinarily use with a young person and, I think, with someone you're pushing down a bridge.' He had hoped she'd smile when he said that, but she did not, so he went on. 'He said, "*È mia*."' Again he waited, and Flavia said nothing. 'Either he was speaking formally, or he was speaking about some other person: "She's mine."'

He saw the moment when she understood. 'And I'm that other woman?' she asked, sounding as if she couldn't – or wouldn't – believe it.

Brunetti chose not to answer this and, instead, asked, 'Can you remember what you said to the girl and who was there when you said it?'

She looked at her hands, clasped together in her lap, as she tried to reconstruct the scene. 'I was with my *ripetitore*, Riccardo Tuffo. I've always worked with him here. I heard someone singing in one of the other rehearsal rooms and wanted to know who it was: she was that good. So Riccardo knocked on the door, and when he opened it, another pianist came out, and then I recognized the girl. She'd been waiting inside the stage door after the performance the night before. The same night you came. She wanted to thank me for the performance.'

Flavia looked up from the consideration of her hands and said, 'She has a remarkable voice: it's a real contralto, deep and true.'

'What did you say to her?'

'The usual things: that she was very good and would have an important career.'

'Was anyone else there who might have heard what you said?'

She thought about this for a moment. 'No, only the four of us: me, the girl, Riccardo, and the other *ripetitore*, who is her father. That's all.'

'No one else could have heard you?' Brunetti insisted.

Most people, when asked to verify their memory of a conversation or incident, answered immediately, as if to demonstrate that to question their memory was to insult it, and them. But Flavia looked at her hands again, then swivelled on her chair to look at the necklace. 'After Riccardo and I left and were going down to our rehearsal room, some people walked towards us from the other end of the corridor. I was still praising the girl, and they might have heard me.'

'Did you recognize any of them?'

'No. It's been years since I've sung here, and there are a lot of new faces.' She picked up the comb and pushed the necklace back into the paper, removing it from their sight. 'I wasn't really paying attention,' she concluded.

Then she asked him, with a casual wave towards the necklace, as though it were a few pages of a score someone had left in her room, 'What do you want to do with that?'

'The usual,' Brunetti answered. 'Take it to the Questura. Fingerprints.'

'You really do that?' she asked.

'Yes.' Then he asked, 'Whom do I say it belongs to?'

'Why bother?'

'Because when they're finished with the tests, it goes back to the owner.'

'Really?' she asked, incapable of disguising her wonder. 'It's worth a fortune.'

'I can see that,' Brunetti said. 'Or I think I can.' He glanced at the necklace, but all he could see now was the blue wrapping paper.

'Why would he give me something like that?' she asked, bewildered.

'To impress you,' Brunetti explained. 'To give you proof beyond question of his regard and attraction.'

'But that's crazy,' she said, this time sounding angry rather than confused. '"Attraction"?' It was as if she had only now heard the word. 'What's that supposed to mean?'

'Just what I say, Flavia, that this person is attracted to you in some way. And the gift is an attempt to make you interested in the giver who treats you with this sort of . . . largesse.' Then, before she could react, he said, 'I know it's crazy. But we're hardly dealing with a normal person here.'

She tried a light voice and asked, 'Is that the sort of thing policemen are supposed to say?'

Brunetti laughed and said, with robot-like precision, 'Never. We remain open-minded and respectful of all persons at every minute of our working day.' He let his voice relax and finished by saying, 'It's only with our family and friends that we can say what we think.'

She looked at him and, smiling, placed a hand on his arm. 'Thank you for that, Guido.'

Brunetti thought this might be the best time to say it. 'There's one thing we haven't considered in all of this,' he said.

'I think it's enough that you've considered that he's crazy and that he knows where I live,' she said angrily. 'I don't think I can take any more surprises.'

'It shouldn't really be a surprise,' Brunetti said, knowing this was not true.

'What are you talking about?' she demanded and removed her hand from his arm.

'We've been assuming that this person is a man. Everyone uses "he" and "him" when talking about what's happened, but there's no way we can be sure of that.'

'Of course it's a man,' she said in a tight voice. 'Women don't go around pushing other women down bridges.'

'Flavia,' he began, concerned that he might be about to lose her and trying to find the way to say it without offending her. But why waste time with suggestion and more questions; why not just say it and have done with it?

'The last time you were here . . . in fact, the last two times you were here, you were living with a woman.'

She reeled back as though he had tried to hit her, but she said nothing.

'A very nice one, I might add,' Brunetti said and smiled, but she gave no answering smile. 'People in your business don't pay much attention to things like that, but other people do. Obsessives more so.'

'And so this is the revenge of the lesbians for my having given that up?' she asked, her anger not at all disguised. 'Or a woman who wants me to transfer my love to *her*?'

'I have no idea,' Brunetti said calmly. 'But your past life is no secret, so – like it or not – we have to consider the possibility that the person who is stalking you' – he'd finally said the word – 'is a woman.' She said nothing, so he went on. 'The fact that women are less violent than men might make it a good thing, but this person has already acted violently, and if it's because you spoke to that girl, it was for very little reason.'

Her response surprised him. 'Is there someone in the hospital with the girl?'

'There's someone, a police officer, who will look in on her now and again.'

'What does that mean?'

'It's as much as I can do,' he said, choosing not to explain. 'She'll go home soon, and then she'll have the protection of her family,' he continued, without being at all sure of this.

Flavia was silent, shifting repeatedly in her seat, then asked, 'So if it's a woman, are you saying she'll attack any woman I talk to?'

'I'm not *saying* anything, Flavia. I'm merely asking you to consider a possibility.'

Again she was silent, but Brunetti waited her out. 'A friend of mine,' she began, 'a mezzo-soprano, told me she once had a woman fan who threatened her with a knife.' Brunetti waited.

'The woman had sent her a couple of notes, always very complimentary and intelligent, after performances. But not often, once a year, maybe twice. Over the course of eight or nine years. And then the woman wrote to suggest they have a drink after a performance in London. My friend said she sounded so articulate and clever that she agreed.'

Flavia's voice drifted away, and Brunetti wondered if he were going to hear the end of the story. But Flavia jump-started herself and continued. 'So they met in a bar after a performance, and as soon as she sat down, my friend said, she knew the woman was crazy.' She caught Brunetti's puzzled glance and said, 'You know, the way you just *know* someone's mad.'

'What happened?' Brunetti asked.

'The woman went on about how my friend was the only woman in the world for her, that they were meant to be together, and when my friend started to get up to leave, the woman pulled out a knife and said she'd kill her if she didn't come with her.'

'What did she do?'

'She told me she smiled and found the presence of mind to say that they should get a taxi and go back to her hotel.'

'And then?'

'When they got outside, my friend hailed a taxi, and when it pulled up, she gave the other woman a shove, got in and slammed the door and told the driver to drive. Anywhere.'

'Did she go to the police?'

'No.'

'What happened?'

'Nothing. She never heard from her again. But it took her months to get over it.' Then, after a long time, 'I'm not sure you ever get over something like that, not really.'

'Yes,' Brunetti agreed, then he asked, 'Have your fans ever behaved like this before?'

Flavia shook her head, almost violently. 'Mine? No. Absolutely not.' She looked away from him and stared into the mirror, but Brunetti, who could see her reflection, realized she was looking at something invisible to either of them.

He noticed the moment she became aware of his gaze. Quickly she turned to face him and said, 'Most of them are women.'

'Who?'

'The fans who make me nervous, who make us all nervous.'

'By doing what?'

She shook her head, as if finding the correct words was too difficult. She reached out to the things on the table and moved a few of them around, picked up the hairbrush and stroked the bristles with the tips of her fingers. It was so quiet in the room that Brunetti thought he could hear them snapping back into place.

'These women are needy,' Flavia finally said, sounding uncertain about that word. 'They try to hide it, but they can't.'

'What do they need?'

'I don't know. Something. From us,' she said and then was silent. 'Maybe they want love.' Another pause, even longer. 'But I don't want to think that.' She set the brush back on the table then nodded a few times, as if to convince herself of what she had said.

Just as Brunetti was about to speak, Flavia said fiercely, 'Fans are fans; they aren't friends.'

'Never?'

'Never,' she said with enraged certainty. 'And now this.'

'Yes.'

'What can I do?' she asked.

'You're not here much longer, are you?' he asked.

'Less than a week, and then I have some time free to be with the children.'

Talking seemed to have calmed her a bit, so Brunetti asked, hoping that more information might help, 'You said it started in London.'

'Yes. And in St Petersburg, there were masses of flowers, but that's normal there: lots of people bring them.'

'Were they yellow roses?' he asked, remembering what

he had seen after her performance and what she had described at dinner.

'In St Petersburg, only some. In London, yes.'

'Anything else?'

'Things have disappeared from my dressing rooms. Never money, only things.'

'What things?'

'A coat, a pair of gloves, and in Paris my address book.'

Brunetti considered this and asked, 'Have any of your friends mentioned receiving strange phone calls?'

'Strange how?'

'Someone asking where you were? Maybe saying they were a friend of yours and you hadn't answered your phone for a long time?'

She started to speak, and he saw something flash into her memory. 'Yes. A friend in Paris said she'd had a call from someone who said they couldn't get in touch and asking if she knew where I was.'

'What happened?'

'There was something about the voice she didn't like, so she said she hadn't heard from me for a month either.'

'Was it a man or a woman who called?' Brunetti asked.

Flavia pulled her lips together and said, as if about to tell him something that would prove him right, 'A woman.'

Brunetti resisted the impulse to say, 'I told you so.'

17

Flavia leaned forward, rested her elbows on the dressing table, and lowered her head into her hands. Brunetti heard her mutter something but couldn't make out the words. He waited. From beside her, he saw her shake her head a few times, and then she sat up and looked at him. 'I can't believe this is happening.' She closed her eyes and bit her lower lip, then looked at him and said, voice not as steady as it had been, 'That's just cheap melodrama, isn't it? Of course I believe this is happening: that's what's so horrible.'

Brunetti, much as he would have liked to offer her comfort, refused to lie to her. The brief conversation between Flavia and Francesca, containing nothing more than a compliment about the girl's talent, was perhaps the link to the attack on the bridge. '*È mia.*' Did a polite compliment lead to this assertion of absolute possession, and was any person in whom Flavia showed interest to be put in danger?

Brunetti had been fortunate in his career in that, regardless of how many bad and very bad people he had been forced to encounter in his years of police work, he had rarely had to deal with the mad. The behaviour of the bad made sense: they wanted money or power or revenge or someone else's wife, and they wanted them for reasons that another person could understand. Further, there was usually a connection between them and their victims: rivals, partners, enemies, relatives, husband and wife. Find a person who stood to gain – and not only in the financial sense – from the death or injury of the victim and put some pressure on that connection or start to wind in the connecting line, and very often the returning tug would lead to the person responsible. There had always been a line: the secret was to find it.

Here, however, the reason might have been nothing more than a casual conversation, a bit of praise, a bit of encouragement, the sort of thing any generous-spirited person would give to a young woman at the beginning of her career. This appeared to have provoked rage against the girl sufficient to cause violence.

'What do I do?' Flavia asked at last, and Brunetti withdrew from his speculations to return to her. 'I can't live like this,' she said, 'trapped between this little room and my apartment. I don't want to be afraid of everyone I see coming close to me on the street.'

'And if I said you're not likely to be in danger?' Brunetti asked.

'My friends are, anyone I speak to is. Isn't that the same thing?'

Only to the purest of Christian spirits, Brunetti thought, but did not say. Over the years, he had seen diverse reactions to physical danger. So long as it is speculative, we respond as heroes, lions; in the face of real physical danger, we become mice.

'Flavia,' he began, 'I don't think this person wants to harm you; he or she wants to love you. And be respected, or loved, by you.'

'That's disgusting,' she spat. 'It's better to be harmed. Cleaner.'

'Stop it, Flavia, would you?' he said so sharply he surprised even himself.

Her mouth and eyes flew open and stayed that way for seconds. 'What?' she began, and he feared she'd tell him to leave.

'It's not better to be harmed. Think of that girl, with a broken arm and stitches in her head, and God knows what fear. Most things are better than that. So stop it, would you? Please.'

He'd gone too far. He knew it but he didn't care. Either she could stop the melodrama, leave it on the stage and behave like an adult, or . . . That was the part he couldn't be sure about: what would happen if she stuck to big statements and grand gestures? He remembered her as being far more sensible than this, far closer to the earth in terms of practical realities.

She picked up the comb and used the sharp tip to move aside the blue wrapping paper, again exposing the necklace. She stared at it, then shifted to the side of her chair to allow Brunetti a clear view of the jewels.

'Only a person who's crazy would give that to someone they don't know and have never met,' she said. 'Do you think he,' she began, paused and added, '– or she – really believes something like that would make me interested in them or make it not have happened, what he did to that poor girl?'

'We're not sharing the same reality with this person,

Flavia,' Brunetti said. 'The rules you use to talk to me or to your dresser or your colleagues don't apply here.'

'Which ones do?'

Brunetti raised his hands in the universal gesture of ignorance. 'I have no idea. They're the ones this person makes.'

She leaned forward to look at the watch on the dressing table and said, 'It's almost midnight. God, I hope we're not locked in here.'

'Don't they have a watchman?' Brunetti asked.

'Yes, after the fire, they do, and he really has to walk around the building, or at least that's what they've told me.'

'Shall we go, then?' Brunetti asked. 'I'll walk you home.'

She looked at him, confused. 'I thought it was more convenient for you to walk to Rialto.'

Casually, as though he believed it, Brunetti said, 'It's only a few minutes' difference if I take the Accademia.' Then, before she could question him, he said, 'Come on. Let's go. You've spent enough time in this place today.'

She held up her watch again. 'It's already tomorrow.'

He smiled and repeated, 'Come on. Get dressed and we'll go.'

She went into the bathroom, and he heard the familiar feminine noises: water splashing in the sink, a dropped shoe, a few clicks and clacks, and then the door opened and she was there: brown skirt and sweater, low-heeled shoes, and light makeup. Brunetti gave thanks that he lived in a country where a woman who had just spoken of being in fear of her life would put on eyeliner and lipstick for a ten-minute walk across a deserted city after midnight.

It took them some time to figure out what to do with the necklace, but she finally succeeded in wrapping the package in a white towel and shoving it into a plastic bag. That in its turn went into a dark green canvas shoulder bag he recognized as being from Daunt's bookshop in London. Flavia passed it to him and he strung it over his shoulder.

She led the way back down the corridor to the elevator. As they were waiting for it to come, her phone buzzed in the pocket of her jacket: neither of them managed to disguise their shock. She grabbed the phone and looked at it. The name she saw there softened her expression. She glanced at Brunetti and said, 'Freddy', then answered by saying, 'Ciao, Freddy' in an entirely natural voice: happy, calm, curious.

The doors to the elevator slid open and they stepped inside. 'I know. I know. I'm sorry I didn't call, but the place was filled with fans, and I had to sign programmes and discs for ever.' Long silence. 'I know I said I would, but there were so many of them, and it made me so happy to see them there that I forgot about it entirely. I'm sorry, Freddy; really I am.' Freddy spoke for some time, and she said, 'I'm just leaving now.'

The elevator stopped. The doors opened. She stepped into the corridor and turned, waiting for Brunetti to get out; she put her hand on his arm to stop him from continuing towards the exit. 'There's no need for you to worry, Freddy. I couldn't be in safer company. Guido Brunetti – he said he was at school with you – came back after, and I've been talking to him.' More silence. 'Yes, I told him everything the other night, so he came along after the performance. He's leaving with me.' She looked at Brunetti, who nodded.

'No, Freddy, don't bother. He said he'd walk me home.' She lowered her face and turned a bit aside. 'No, really, Freddy, you don't have to.' Suddenly, she started to laugh, nothing faked or forced about it.

'Oh, you are a goose. You always were one. All right, at the top of the bridge. But if you're wearing your pyjamas, I'll know you were lying.'

She clicked off the phone and returned it to her pocket. Where did she keep that, he wondered, during a performance? 'He was worried,' she said in explanation. 'But you heard it all. He said he was still up and would meet us on the bridge so you didn't have to take me all the way home. He was always a worrier, Freddy,' she added and continued towards the exit.

They found the watchman sitting inside the *portiere*'s enclosure, drinking from the metal top of his thermos, a half-eaten sandwich in front of him. 'Good evening, Signora,' he said. 'There were lots of people here tonight, waiting for you.' With his cup he toasted the empty space just to the side of his booth. 'But they all went home.'

Turning to Brunetti, she said, her own surprise audible, 'I've never done that before, just forgotten about them.' The guard gave Brunetti a closer look and, when Brunetti met his gaze, took a sip from his cup.

Flavia shrugged. 'Can't be undone,' she muttered, said goodnight to the watchman, and pushed open the door to the *calle*. Outside, she turned to the right and headed towards Campo San Fantin. He was about to tell her they should have turned left but then thought of the *calle* he would have led them to, narrow and dark. She turned at the hotel, and Brunetti was happy enough to let her lead the way. There had been no one standing in the *calle* outside the theatre, though that probably didn't mean much: she would have to cross the Ponte dell'Accademia to get home. Freddy would meet them there, but that was also the place anyone else who was waiting for her would be.

Since the city illumination had been changed about a decade ago, Brunetti had grumbled about how bright the night had become: some of his friends complained that they could read in bed with the light that came in the windows. But here, nearing the underpass that would lead them to the narrow *calle* into Campo Sant'Angelo, Brunetti was relieved at the brightness.

They emerged into the *campo* and she asked, 'Do you often do this?'

'What? Walk women home?'

'No. Stay out after midnight without having to call home.'

'Ah,' he said. 'Paola is just as happy to sit alone and read.'

'Than to have you there?' she asked, her surprise audible.

'No, she'd rather have me there, and she'll probably stay up until I get home. But if she's reading, it doesn't make much difference who's around her: she ignores them.'

'Why?'

It was a question he'd heard a number of times. To serious readers like him and Paola, reading was an activity, not a pastime, and so the presence of another person added nothing to it. The children distracted Brunetti; he envied Paola her ability to disappear into the text, leaving them all behind. But he knew most people saw this as strange, almost inhuman, and so he said, 'She was raised that way, reading alone, so it's her habit.'

'Did she grow up there?' Flavia asked. 'In the *palazzo*?'

'Yes, she lived there until her last year of university – that's when I met her – but then she went away to finish her studies.'

'She didn't stay here?' she asked.

'No.' He wondered what his own children would decide to do, and soon.

'Where did she go?'

'Oxford.'

'In England?' Flavia asked, stopping to face him.

'Not in Mississippi,' Brunetti answered, as he often had.

'Excuse me?' she asked, obviously confused.

'There's a university in Oxford in Mississippi,' Brunetti explained.

'Oh, I see,' Flavia said and began walking again. 'You met her and then she went away. For how long?'

'Only a year and a half.'

'"Only"?'

'The course was meant to last three, but she finished it in half the time.'

'How?'

Brunetti smiled as he said, 'I suppose she read very fast.'

Flavia stopped beside the *edicola*, closed now, just at the entrance to Campo Santo Stefano. There were few people and all were in motion, he noticed; no one seemed to be standing still, waiting to see who came in from the direction of the theatre. In a very untheatrical gesture, she tipped up her chin towards the statue in the centre and everything surrounding it. 'This is all normal for you?' she asked, using the plural.

'I suppose it is. We saw it as kids, on the way to school, going to see friends, walking home from the movies. Nothing more true than this.'

'You think it's why you are the way you are?'

'Who? Venetians?'

'Yes.'

'How are we?' he asked, expecting her to talk about their fabled aloofness, their arrogance, their greed.

'Sad,' she said.

'Sad?' He could not keep the surprise, and the resistance, from his voice.

'Yes. You had all of this, and now all you have is the memory of it.'

'What do you mean?'

She started walking again. 'I've been here almost a month, and all I hear in the bars, where people chat and say what they're really thinking because they're talking to other Venetians, is how terrible it all is: the crowds, the corruption, the cruise ships, the general cheapening of everything.' They were just at Palazzo Franchetti, and she pointed to the windows: stone woven into gossamer, the light filtering through from the other side of the canal. The gates closed off the garden and the building.

'I imagine an enormous family once lived there,' she said, continuing around it until they reached the small *campo* at the foot of the bridge. She looked across the canal at the *palazzi* that lined the other side and said, 'And families lived there, as well.'

When it was clear that she had nothing else to say, Brunetti started towards the bridge and began to climb the steps, hoping to be able to walk away from the irritation that her words had created in him.

From behind him, he heard her footsteps. And then she was beside him, walking on his right, near the railing. He shifted the cloth bag to his other shoulder, hearing the paper crinkle inside.

'Don't you have anything to say?' she asked.

'Nothing I say will change anything. Hamburg isn't Hamburg any more, and Parisians whine about the changes to their city, but everyone and his dog thinks it's his right to moan about the changes here. I'm just keeping out of it.'

'Flavia,' a man's voice called from above them, and Brunetti, distracted, stepped in front of her and blocked her ascent, causing her to crash into his back. Both of them danced about to keep their footing on the steps, while Brunetti looked up to see whose voice it was.

And saw Freddy, Marchese d'Istria, dressed in a pair of light blue jeans, white shirt, and dark blue jacket, looking years younger than his real age, just starting to walk down the steps in their direction. As always, Freddy broadcast good health and calm. Brunetti noticed that the buttons of the jacket were pulled tight, but no one could think of accusing Freddy of being fat: he was merely '*robusto*', another sure sign of his continued good health.

Brunetti stepped to the left, and Flavia took her hand away from the railing and walked up to the landing between ramps. Freddy bent and kissed her on both cheeks, then turned to Brunetti and, pretending he had not seen his instinctive protective move, embraced him warmly. 'How wonderful to see you, Guido: it's seldom I get to see two of my favourite people at the same time.' He indicated the Church of the Salute with one arm, placed the other protectively across Flavia's shoulders. 'And in such a wonderful place.' Then, as an afterthought, he added in a serious voice, 'I'd like the circumstances to be different, though.'

With eel-like grace, Flavia freed herself and turned to Brunetti. 'Thanks for taking me this far, Guido. Now Freddy gets to do the other half. Soon they'll be moving me around the city on rollers, someone new taking over at every bridge, I suppose.' It was meant to be light-hearted, but Brunetti chose to hear a different tone, and a far more sober one.

Freddy asked how the performance had gone, and Flavia made some critical remarks about the conductor, both of them striving to make this sound like a normal conversation. Brunetti was careful to turn his head towards them every so often as they walked, three abreast, down the steps, but his attention was concentrated on the other people crossing the bridge, both those going down with them and those coming up towards them. At this time of night there were few, and most were couples or groups. A man with a Jack Russell came towards them, the unleashed dog dashing to the top of the bridge, only to turn around instantly and scamper back to his approaching master. A tall woman with a scarf wrapped high around her neck talked on her *telefonino* as she passed them, going down more quickly than they, but she paid them no attention at all. Brunetti noticed the toes-out angle of her feet and the care she took in placing them, favouring one, a wise precaution on these humid steps.

When they reached the last landing of the bridge, Brunetti stopped. He decided it would be best to let them go, they to the left and he to the right, without asking Freddy if they could talk the next day. Flavia was sufficiently upset; he did not want to give her the chance to believe that they were going to meet to talk about her. He gave Flavia twin kisses, shook Freddy's hand and said goodnight, then started down the final ramp of steps and towards home. Just as he got to the small *campo* in front of the museum, he turned and saw that they had disappeared. He walked back to the corner; ahead of him, they were just turning left into the *calle* that would take them over the bridge and down into San Vio. Feeling entirely foolish, Brunetti walked quickly to where they had turned, then stopped and watched them until they reached the bridge. He set off after them, embarrassed that they were the only three people on the street and with no idea of what he was doing.

At the bridge into San Vio, some animal instinct told him to look to the right, and he saw a figure, really half a figure, standing at the point where a *calle* opened on to the *riva*. He saw a coat, perhaps a raincoat, perhaps a scarf. Brunetti's step faltered and he came down heavily on his left foot. The bag started to slip from his shoulder, and he turned to put a hand on it. When he looked again, the figure was no longer there, the only trace of it the sound of diminishing footsteps. He ran to the entrance to the *calle*, but by the time he got there, the entire length of it was empty, and though he could still hear the footsteps, there was no way he could tell the direction from which they came. He ran to the first crossing: no one to the right and no one to the left. And off in the distance, those ever-fainter footsteps. He stopped and held his breath, but he could still not tell where they were going, whether towards the Salute or towards the Accademia. The sound died away. Brunetti turned around and started towards home.

18

Paola had abandoned all hope of Brunetti's coming home, and so Brunetti, having seen that no one was up and waiting for him, went into the kitchen in search of something to eat and drink but quickly decided he wanted nothing but to be in his bed, alongside his wife. But first he had to find a place for the green cloth bag. He gave this some thought before good sense intervened and reminded him that the place would hold the bag for no more than eight hours, so he left it on the top of their dresser and went into the bathroom.

His arrival beside his wife was greeted with a grunt, which he chose to read as an affectionate one, and he was soon lost in images of disappearing scarves and footsteps, and yellow roses in rising, suffocating piles.

The following morning, he gave Paola a brief account of his meeting with Flavia the previous night, but she was more interested in the emerald necklace and asked to see it. She had chastised his pedestrian comparison of the stones to Fisherman's Friend lozenges and insisted that they must be the size of 'plovers' eggs', explaining that she had read the phrase many times but had no idea of how big they were.

'We can't touch it until they've taken the prints, all right?' he asked, not ready, after only one coffee, to enter into a discussion of how large a plover's egg might be. Indeed, he was in some doubt as to what a plover might look like and thus could make no accurate calculation as to the size of its eggs.

He left the apartment carrying the bag and was careful to keep it over his shoulder when he stopped for coffee and a brioche. At the Questura, he went immediately to the lab to speak to Bocchese. The chief technician's perpetual air of self-sufficiency often provoked Brunetti to acts of needless bravado: this time he walked to Bocchese's desk, the bag in his hand, and, saying nothing, tilted it and let the package slide on to the desk. As luck would have it, the paper wrapping caught in one of the straps of the bag so the necklace materialized on the desk bedded on the royal blue wrapping paper.

'For me?' Bocchese asked, looking up at Brunetti and pasting a smile of idiot delight on his face. 'How did you know today's my birthday, Guido? Well, never mind that: thanks for remembering, and I think I'll wear it with my red dress.' He spread the fingers of his right hand and wiggled them over the necklace, as if about to pick it up, but Brunetti refused to play his game and stepped back to let him touch what he willed.

Bocchese accepted partial victory and pulled his hand back. He opened the front drawer of his desk and poked around in it until he found a jeweller's loupe. He put it to his eye and bent over the necklace, careful to avoid coming into contact with it or the paper on which it rested.

He studied the stones for a moment, then moved to the other side of his desk, forcing Brunetti aside, to look at them from another angle. He moved over each one, humming a little song that Brunetti had heard from him only in moments of great contentment.

Bocchese set the loupe on his desk and went back to his chair. '*Maria Vergine.* You certainly do have good taste in stones, Guido. In a setting like this, they're probably genuine, and if they are, they're worth . . . a great deal.'

'Probably?' Brunetti asked.

Bocchese pushed out his lips as though about to kiss a baby as he considered Brunetti's question. 'It's almost impossible to tell with the ones that are coming out of South America today.' He shook his head in disapproval of forgery he could not detect.

'But if the setting is as old as I think it is,' the technician went on, 'at least thirty years, and hasn't been messed with, then they're priceless.'

'I've always wondered what that word means, especially when it's used in reference to things that people are buying and selling,' Brunetti said, adding, 'for a price.'

'That's true, isn't it?' Bocchese exclaimed with pleasure. 'I wonder why we continue to say it?'

'How much is the price they're beyond?' Brunetti asked.

Bocchese sat back and folded his arms, studying the stones. 'What I usually do is show them to a friend of mine who's a jeweller – he really knows stones – and ask him what he thinks they're worth.'

'Who's that?' Brunetti asked.

'Vallotto.'

Making no attempt to disguise his shock, Brunetti said, 'But he's a thief.'

'No, Guido,' Bocchese began, 'he's far worse than a thief. He's a cheat and a swindler, but he's very convincing, so after you deal with him, you can't say that he's robbed you because you've signed a form saying you agree to his prices, and that means there's no way you can stop him.'

'He buys as well as sells, doesn't he?' Brunetti asked, thinking of the man's slick shop not far from Rialto.

'Yes, and my guess is that he's not satisfied unless he can sell what he's bought for five times what he paid.'

'But you trust him?'

Bocchese looked at a small Renaissance bronze plaque he kept on his desk as a paperweight or good luck token. He prodded it with his forefinger, moving it a few centimetres to the left. 'I did him a favour once, so though we're not friends, he'll still help me; well, he'll still give me an accurate estimation.'

'Even though he knows you work for the police?'

'Who could pay him to do it, you mean?' Bocchese asked.

'No, not that. Who might come to arrest him some day.'

Bocchese pushed the plaque back to where it had been. 'He thinks it was a big favour.'

'What did you do?' Brunetti asked, sensing that the technician, usually a man wrapped in privacy, wanted him to ask.

Bocchese looked at the plaque again, as if the two human figures on it had also expressed interest in the story. 'We were at school together. This is forty years ago; more. His family was miserable; the father drank and had been arrested a few times. The mother made do with what she could earn. But the kids went to school clean and studied hard.' Brunetti had heard this story countless times: it was the youth of his friends and companions.

'Anyway,' Bocchese said, as if in response to a signal from the men on the plaque that he hurry things up, 'one day I was in a grocery store getting some things for my mother and I saw his mother, standing in one of the aisles, looking around her as if the fires of Hell were coming to get her. She saw me, but she didn't answer when I said hello. Then all of a sudden the owner was there, screaming at her, "I saw you, I saw you take that rice", and it was then I saw her hand was under her coat.

'She looked like she was going to faint, poor thing, and then he was walking towards her, screaming, "Thief, thief, thief. Someone call the police."

'And I thought of Leonardo and the other kids, and what it would be like for them if their mother was arrested, too.'

'So what did you do?' Brunetti asked.

'While the man was walking towards her, I went past her, to where he was, and reached up and grabbed a box of pasta, and I made sure I knocked some others off, so he'd look to see what was going on. When he saw me, he made a grab at me, but I ran around him and out of the store, and he forgot all about her and followed me. I moved just slowly enough that he would try to catch me, and when I'd led him two streets from the store, I really started to run and lost him.'

Bocchese looked back at the memory without smiling. 'When he got back to the store, she was gone. I don't know if he recognized her; he didn't know me, that's for sure.'

'How'd Vallotto find out?' Brunetti asked.

'I suppose his mother told him,' Bocchese said without much interest. 'He never talked about it until years later, when I met him on the street, and he told me he'd heard I was getting married, and to come to him for the rings.

'He must have seen my expression because he said, "I remember what you did for my mother. I'll never cheat you, and I'll help you if I can."' He looked at Brunetti and added, 'And he has.'

'How?'

'Remember, about six years ago,' Bocchese asked, 'we found a diamond bracelet and some rings in the home of a suspect, and he said they were his mother's?'

Brunetti nodded, although he had only the vaguest memory of the case.

Bocchese went on. 'I took them to Leonardo and told him it was police business but would he help.'

'And?'

'And he told me the name of the family they'd been stolen from.' Bocchese paused, but Brunetti could think of nothing to say.

'What do you want me to do with this?' Bocchese finally asked, waving towards the necklace.

'Check it and the papers for prints, and, if you'll send me some photos, I'll have Signorina Elettra see what she can find out.'

'Then what do I do with it?' Bocchese asked.

'You have a safe, don't you?' Brunetti asked.

'I do,' Bocchese said and slipped the paper and necklace back into the cloth bag.

His next stop was to see Signorina Elettra and ask whether she was still on strike and, if so, how Vice-Questore Patta and Lieutenant Scarpa were faring. He also wanted to know if she had learned anything about who had sent the yellow roses that had gone to the theatre and to Flavia's apartment, and to ask her about the necklace. When he saw her at her desk, Brunetti decided not to bother to ask her about the flowers, so clear did her expression make it that she had had no success.

'Nothing,' she volunteered. 'My friend in the bar by the theatre is on vacation. I tried the few florists that are left in town, but not one of them had had a sale that big. I tried Mestre, and Padova, but then I gave up.' Had he ever heard her use that phrase before?

Before he could comment, she said, 'I found a number of articles, in Italian and English, about fans and stalkers, but I'm afraid they don't say anything common sense doesn't tell us. The operatic ones are almost all women.' She looked at him and smiled, saying, 'Also, women for rock music, but men for jazz.'

He was reminded of a friend who had once owned a CD shop, in the era when people still bought CDs in shops, who had told him that the weirdest customers were people who liked organ music. 'Most of them shop at night,' his friend had said. 'I think it's the only time some of them ever leave their houses.'

'As to Signora Petrelli,' she went on, 'I spent the morning chasing her through the gutter press: at the beginning, they loved her affair with that American woman, but they grew tired of it and it dropped off the front pages, then the back pages. The last time they mentioned her – they never take any interest in her singing – was because her husband took her to court to try to get his payments to her reduced.'

'And?' Brunetti asked.

'She must have had the best lawyer in Spain draw up the settlement for the divorce. Public sympathy was with her at the time and the judge who held the hearing to review the case told him, in essence, to stop wasting the court's time and pay his wife, or he'd go to jail.'

'Did that last word have its usual sobering effect?' Brunetti asked.

'Exactly.'

'You think he's involved in this?'

She gave the question the consideration it deserved and answered, 'I doubt it', then quickly clarified, 'not because

154

he wouldn't do it but because he's intelligent enough to know he'd be the first suspect if anything happened to her. Besides which, he's in Argentina.'

'After the divorce, has the press paid much attention to her?' Brunetti asked.

'Only the press that's interested in music. She's won awards and been on the covers of magazines. But her private life seems not to interest them any more.'

'Is that because of her age?'

'Probably,' Signorina Elettra conceded. 'And the lives of pop stars are much more exciting.'

He nodded, having heard and overheard the conversation of his own children and seen the magazines they'd left lying about the house. 'We were no different, my generation,' he said.

'Nor mine,' she said and shrugged.

He was tempted to add, 'Nor Nero's', but thought he'd spare her that.

'The American?' he finally asked.

'Nothing about her for years other than the articles and books she's written about Chinese art.'

'No mention of where she is?'

'Every reference I found placed her in China, though some of them said she had just arrived for a conference. No mention of where she arrived from.'

He frowned. Dead end. From the way Flavia had spoken, it had sounded like that's what it was. 'Pity,' he said out loud. Signorina Elettra looked up in surprise.

19

'What about Alvise?' he asked.

Surprise vanished. 'He's been suspended.'

Brunetti interrupted her to ask, 'Since when can that happen?'

'I beg your pardon?'

'I've never heard that an officer can be suspended so easily, without an investigation or a hearing, yet we've all gone along, acting as if Scarpa has the authority to do this. But has he?'

She sat, open mouthed, looking at him as though he had suddenly started speaking to her in Hungarian. 'It's a procedure used to stop officers' pay without actually bringing charges against them,' she said as if a commissario, of all people, should be aware of the rulings of the Ministry of the Interior.

'Who told you about it?' Brunetti asked.

Again, she stared at him, a cardinal confronted with sin. 'I think it's common . . .' she started to say, but then he saw illumination arrive. 'Lieutenant Scarpa told me,' she said, no longer a cardinal but now an Inquisitor who had just stumbled upon the distinct possibility of human heresy.

'I see,' Brunetti said coolly. Then, keeping his voice carefully level, he asked, 'Had you thought of having a look in the regulations of the Ministry?'

She turned to her computer, saying under her breath, 'I don't want to believe this.'

Brunetti resisted the temptation to stand behind her while she searched, certain that there was no way he could be of the least help to her, equally certain that he would not understand what she was doing. He went to the windowsill and, folding his arms, leaned back against it. Her nails clicked on the keys. He studied the laces in his shoes, noticing that they were a bit worn and should be replaced. Lieutenant Scarpa should be replaced, as well, though not because he was worn. Time clicked by.

'It's not possible,' she said, eyes still on the screen. 'No regulation exists. Even if you're accused of a crime, you're still paid and still considered a member of the force.' She looked up, iron-jawed, from the screen. 'He can't do it. They can't stop his pay.'

Brunetti remembered that he was not supposed to know that she had kept Alvise on the payroll. He returned his attention to his laces and considered consequences. Signorina Elettra had, for years, thrived in open violation of many laws, especially those regarding privacy. She had raided banks, broken into the files of ministries, had even gone trawling through the files of the Vatican. At times, she had gone too far and provoked flurries of alarm among the people who knew what she was doing, often the same people for whom she was doing it. But she had always managed to scamper free without leaving tracks.

Discretion seemed a luxury at this moment. The ship was sinking: he tossed discretion overboard. 'Under whose name did you write to reinstate Alvise's salary?'

Her face did not move. She put the first three fingers of her left hand to her lips and rubbed them. 'This isn't good,' she said.

'What did you do?'

'I put in a request for authorization of payment for overtime to Alvise. I didn't want to create suspicion by countermanding the order to stop his pay, so I merely moved his name to a different category and had him paid for extra shifts. Five of them in a week.' She paused, then added, 'I really believed Scarpa had the power to suspend him. I don't know what was in my head that made me believe him.'

'Who authorized those payments for the extra shifts?' Brunetti asked, uninterested, as he often was with the children, in explanation or excuse.

'That's why it's not good,' she said. 'You authorized them.'

'Ah,' Brunetti said, dragging out the sound to give his mind time to follow the consequences. He looked at her, but her eyes veered away from his. 'The people in Rome have records of a man who worked eighty hours this week?' he asked.

'Yes,' she said, avoiding his eyes.

'And if these numbers were called to their attention, what would they think was going on?'

Without hesitation, she answered, 'They'd think that whoever was authorizing the hours for him would be dividing the extra money with him.'

Brunetti, were he working in Rome, would probably come to the same conclusion. Were he working anywhere, for that fact.

'So Scarpa catches two pigeons with one bean. They get Alvise for making the false claim, and they get me for approving it, and who cares if I got the money from him or not? Why else would I do it?'

She would have figured this out, would probably now be inventing newspaper headlines: 'Corruption Not Only in the South'. 'Paid Double after Injuring a Worker'.

Signorina Elettra started counting something on her fingers.

'What?' Brunetti asked.

'Counting how many days until we're paid,' she said.

'Seven,' Brunetti said, saving her the trouble. 'Why?'

She looked at him but seemed not to see him. 'I'm trying to think of how to fix this,' she said at last.

'I could have a mental breakdown, and then I'd never be blamed for anything,' Brunetti suggested.

It was as if he had not spoken. She stared into the middle distance, then turned to her computer and tapped in a short string of words, saw what that produced and tapped in some others. Her eyes contracted as she read the second screen, and the third, then almost closed with concentration at the next.

Telling himself that his days at the Questura might well be numbered, Brunetti decided to spend these last ones as pleasantly as he could, and there were few things that gave him as much delight as watching Signorina Elettra enter the trance state that was the first stage of her passage to illegality. Look at her, he told himself: today she is disguised as a Captain of Industry, with a black wool waistcoat buttoned tight over a white cotton shirt, charcoal grey pinstripe trousers and a sober tie: if the gods had turned Patta into a woman, she would dress like this.

Time passed, and Brunetti continued to watch Signorina Elettra work. Or plot, or corrupt, obstruct, defy, pervert the course of justice – well, of the law, at any rate. Brunetti had no idea what she was doing, but he settled in to watch her success or failure as people did in the lobbies of the larger banks, entranced by the screens on which were posted prices of the major stocks at play at the Borsa in Milano. One had but to study their faces, rapt in contemplation of the god in the terminal, to read their fate: prices went up or down, and their hopes were dragged along with them.

Brunetti floated free of all sense of time. His only contact with the world was Signorina Elettra's expression. He saw her defeated, then defiant, completely stunned, fearful, hopeful, worried, then terrified, and suddenly absolutely certain that she had found the way, the truth, and the light.

She took her eyes from the screen and opened them wide in surprise at seeing him there. 'Have you been here long?' she asked.

He glanced at his watch. 'Half an hour,' he said, then nodded towards her computer. 'Found something?'

'Ah, yes. There's a back door to the overtime applications.'

'Back door?'

'It's a way to get in and change the requests.'

'What can you change?'

'Everything,' she answered. 'Purpose, duration, uniformed work or not.'

'Can you change the name of the superior officer authorizing it?'

'I've just done that,' she said and ran a self-satisfied palm down the front of her tie, just as he had seen Patta do.

'Need I ask?'

'Lieutenant Scarpa has requested that Officer Alvise

liaise – I've always wanted to use that word – with the staff of the hospital so as to keep an eye on the victim of an attack. Because he especially wants Officer Alvise to take this assignment, he has authorized unlimited overtime.'

'You have no shame, do you?' Brunetti asked with a wide smile.

'And less mercy,' she answered, smiling in her turn.

Thinking it more discreet that they be silent in their celebration, Brunetti took his phone from his pocket and, trying to appear casual, held it up. 'Bocchese's sent me some photos of a necklace. I'd like you to see what you can find out about it.'

'Is it stolen?'

'I don't know,' Brunetti said, tapping his finger on the face of the phone until he had the photos there. 'I'll send them to you.' He tapped an icon, tried to remember what Chiara had taught him to do, and went through the processes just as she had shown them to him. With a soft whoosh, the first photo slid out of his phone – or so he visualized it – and crossed the two-metre distance to Signorina Elettra's computer. The others followed. He looked up, self-satisfied and trying to hide it, but Signorina Elettra was looking at the first photo, already displayed on her screen.

'*Maria Santissima*,' she whispered. 'I've never seen anything like it.'

Brunetti read the message Bocchese had attached, saying that the setting was at least forty years old, and thus the stones were likely to be genuine.

'Where'd he get it?' she asked.

'Signora Petrelli gave it to me. Someone left it in her dressing room.'

She moved closer to the screen. 'Left it?'

'That's what she told me.'

'You want to know where it comes from?'

'Yes. If possible.'

'If it was stolen, it might well be: Interpol has a file of major pieces that are stolen.' She raised a hand towards the stones but stopped herself from touching the screen, perhaps out of the same fear he had of leaving fingerprints on something so beautiful.

'Is there any way you can check with jewellers?' Brunetti asked.

She nodded, still looking at it. 'Anyone who sold this would remember it, I'm sure.' She removed her attention from the photo and said, 'I have a list in here of jewellers where something as valuable as this might be sold. I'll send the photo and ask if they bought or sold it within the last . . . ?' She looked at Brunetti inquisitively.

'I don't think it's necessary to specify,' he answered. Brunetti, who had no special affinity with stones, would certainly not forget it; a jeweller, with a better idea of its worth and a finer sensibility for its beauty, would be even less likely to do so.

'In this country or internationally?'

'Everywhere, I think,' Brunetti answered.

She nodded, then asked, 'Anything else?'

'You could tell me what will happen to the Lieutenant,' he said mildly and smiled.

'Ah,' she said in response. 'He's bound to be well protected in Rome, so nothing is likely to happen to him.'

'Protected by whom?' Brunetti asked in the same mild tone, remembering that she'd said she wanted the Lieutenant's head.

'I refuse to speculate, Commissario,' she said, then, turning towards a noise from behind him, added, 'Perhaps you can ask the Vice-Questore about it, Dottore.'

With the gracious condescension to inferiors that so characterized his every interchange, Vice-Questore Patta gave his attention to his subordinates. He turned to Signorina Elettra and, his face softer, asked, 'If you're talking to him, does that mean you're talking to me?'

'Of course I'm talking to you, Dottore,' she said amiably. 'How could I not?' Her voice could have been used to sell something: honey, washing powder.

'What are you talking about?' Patta asked, using the tone he reserved for her and not the one he used with Brunetti. Honey, washing powder.

Signorina Elettra waved in Brunetti's direction: he took the cue and said, in his most sober voice, 'I was telling Signorina Elettra how pleased I am that Officer Alvise is keeping an eye on the girl in the hospital.'

Like a lighthouse rotating towards a new ship, Patta turned his sleek head to face Brunetti and asked, 'Girl?' And then, 'Alvise?'

'It was very wise of the Lieutenant to think of it.'

'You aren't usually so complimentary about the Lieutenant, are you, Commissario?' Though the Vice-Questore tried to disguise his self-satisfaction, traces of it showed in his voice.

Brunetti, finding self-satisfaction better than suspicion, risked a small, chastised grimace, added a slight shake of the head, and answered, 'I have to admit that's true, Dottore. But there are some times when credit has to be given, whoever makes the decision.' He considered the wisdom of pulling his lips together and giving a small affirmative nod, but he thought this might be excessive and fought back the impulse.

Patta looked back at Signorina Elettra, but she was occupied with re-knotting her tie; Brunetti was amazed that this masculine activity could be so imbued with grace and delicacy. It was a dark grey tie with almost invisible red stripes, for heaven's sake, and the person knotting it wore a black wool vest and pinstripe trousers: why did the motion of the cloth as she slipped it through the knot remind him of the way Paola used to remove her stockings, before stockings disappeared?

'Are you here to see me?' Patta's question pulled Brunetti back to the office.

'No, Dottore. I came to ask Signorina Elettra to try to trace a piece of jewellery for me.'

'Stolen?' Patta demanded.

'Not that I know of, sir.'

'Valuable?'

'To the owner, I suppose,' Brunetti answered. Then, before the clouds forming in Patta's eyes at his answer could become inclement, he added, 'I suppose most people place a greater value on what they own or like than other people do,' he said, thinking of the value the Vice-Questore placed on the Lieutenant.

Signorina Elettra broke in to say, 'I doubt it's of great worth, Commissario, but I'll see what I can find.' She managed to sound both bored and faintly annoyed to be bothered with such trivia.

That she should speak to Brunetti in this manner seemed to please the Vice-Questore, so Brunetti allowed himself a surprised glance in her direction before saying, 'If you have nothing else, Dottore, I'll go back to my office.'

Patta nodded and turned towards his door. Behind his back, Signorina Elettra pulled her tie straight, glanced at Brunetti, and winked.

20

Once behind his desk, Brunetti had no idea what to do. He had little desire to congratulate himself about his nugatory victory over Patta, for he had, in the last years, ceased to enjoy baiting his superior, though he proved unable to stop himself from doing it. Colleagues of his in other cities and provinces continually told him of the sort of men and women they worked for, hinting – though never daring to say it outright – that some of them had given their allegiance to an institution other than the State, something that could not be said of the Vice-Questore.

Patta had given his, Brunetti had discovered over the years, to his family. Without reservation, without reflection or restraint: Brunetti liked him for it. Patta was vain and lazy, selfish and at times foolish, but these were not active failings. There was a great deal of bluster in the man, but there was no deep malice: that was left to Lieutenant Scarpa.

Patta's motives, too, were easily read and just as easily

understood: he sought the advancement of his career and the approval of his superiors. Most people did, Brunetti admitted; had he not had the cushion of his wife's family's wealth and power, he would hardly be as cavalier about his job, and his superior, as he was.

But why Patta's loyalty to Scarpa, which was hardly likely to impress his superiors or advance his career? Brunetti had never seen them together outside the Questura, nor had anyone else ever mentioned having seen them in each other's company. They were both from Palermo. Family ties? Old debts of patronage to be paid?

Brunetti pushed himself back in his chair, folded his arms, and stared across the *campo*. From there, the single round window near the top of the façade of the church of San Lorenzo stared back at him like that of a flat-faced Cyclops. Scarpa, to the best of his memory, had simply appeared one day, years ago: Brunetti had no memory of the Vice-Questore's mentioning his arrival before it occurred. Nor did Brunetti have the impression that the men had known one another beforehand, though it was difficult to reconstruct those first months, when Lieutenant Scarpa was merely a tall, thin presence, more noticeable for the perfection of his uniform than for anything he did or said.

He recalled his recognition of the first symptom, observed when he chanced upon the two men in the corridor outside Signorina Elettra's office, talking with deep nasality in a language that reminded him of Arabic, Greek, and – vaguely – Italian. He heard – or thought he heard – 'tr' transformed into 'ch' and verbs dislodged to the end of sentences. He understood nothing.

That had been at the beginning of the second investigation of the Casinò, so it would have been about eight years ago. And it was from then that Patta had become Scarpa's paladin. And why was that?

No matter how sternly Brunetti stared at the Cyclops, it refused to answer him. Odysseus had hidden his men, and then himself, under the rams to outwit the Cyclops: Brunetti could think of no stratagem that would do the same for him.

There was a quick triple knock on his door and Griffoni let herself in, now among the people who took the liberty of not waiting for an answer. Perhaps in anticipation of a hot summer, she had had her hair cut very short, thus providing the Questura with another boyish woman, this one with a crown of golden curls and a black dress that fell just below her knees. At least she wasn't wearing a tie.

Brunetti indicated the more comfortable of the two chairs facing him. 'Looks good,' he limited himself to saying, then asked, 'Anything at the theatre?'

'While I was talking to the *portiere*, three men came in and punched their time cards and left.'

'And?' Brunetti asked.

'It reminded me of home,' she said in a voice warmed by nostalgia.

Naples? 'How so?' he asked.

'I had an uncle who was a cab driver but who had a friend in the office at Teatro San Carlo,' she said, as though that explained everything.

'And?'

'And he was on the payroll as a stagehand, but all he had to do was drive by twice a day and check in and check out.' She saw Brunetti's surprise and said, 'I know, I know. But there had been an audit, and they'd introduced the time cards to be sure that everyone on the payroll did at least check in and out.'

Brunetti, puzzled, said, 'He didn't work there?'

'Good heavens, no. He had five kids, so he drove his

taxi twelve hours a day, seven days a week.' She smiled, and Brunetti realized she was enjoying this.

'And checked in and checked out and was on the payroll?' When she nodded, he asked, 'And no one ever noticed?'

'Well,' she said hesitantly, 'it wasn't as if he were the only person doing it. And he never had a licence for the taxi, so the only job he had – officially, that is – was at the theatre.'

'How many years did he . . . work at the theatre?'

She hesitated, looked down at her fingers and counted the years. 'Twenty-seven.' Then, after a moment, 'And he drove the cab for thirty-six.'

'Ah,' Brunetti sighed and said the only thing that came to mind. 'He must have come to know the city very well.'

'In every sense,' Griffoni said. She sat up straighter, as if to banish the temptation of idle chat. 'The *portiere* told me that all sorts of people come in on the night of a performance, not just the cast and musicians: relatives of the singers, friends, understudies . He said there are times the lobby is so crowded that anyone could come in and he wouldn't notice.'

Brunetti remembered the crowd that had been there the night he and Paola had waited for Flavia.

Claudia went on. 'He told me the worst time is about an hour before a performance, when everyone comes in, especially with an opera like *Tosca* where there's a chorus and a second chorus of children, so there's madness when they start arriving.' Before he could speak, she said, 'It's the same afterwards, when people come into that room outside his office and wait for the singers.'

'What about the flowers?' Brunetti asked.

'The porter didn't remember much: two men brought them. Her dresser and the woman who does the wigs didn't notice anything until after the performance, when they saw the flowers in her dressing room. I spoke to some of the stage crew: no one saw anything unusual.'

'But someone managed to get into her dressing room with the flowers.'

'And the vases,' she added: 'at least if what the dresser told me is true.'

'And someone managed to take more of them into one of the side boxes and toss them down at her,' he said, recalling what he had seen. 'How could that happen?'

'Maybe an usher took them in. Who knows?' Then she added, 'If crazy people have friends, maybe a friend helped bring them.'

Seeing little chance of success here, Brunetti decided to change the subject. 'What about Alvise?'

'He introduced himself to the girl at the hospital and told her he was there to keep an eye on her and see that no one disturbed her.' Griffoni hardly needed to tell Brunetti that secrecy was alien to Alvise.

'How much time does he spend there?' Brunetti asked.

'He told me he'll go during visiting hours: ten until one and then from four until seven.'

'And the rest of the time?'

Griffoni could only shrug. Alvise was, after all, Alvise. 'It hasn't occurred to him that something might happen outside visiting hours.'

'No,' Brunetti agreed. 'It wouldn't, would it?'

'Do you think she's *safe*?' Griffoni couldn't stop herself asking.

'That's anyone's guess, but I'm sure she feels safe, which probably helps her. And there's no one else we can ask at the moment except Alvise.'

They lapsed into the comfortable silence that exists between colleagues who find that, over the years, they have become friends. The sound of a boat approaching from the right drifted into the room.

'It might be a woman,' Brunetti finally said, and explained about the theft of Flavia's address book and the phone call from an unknown woman to her friend in Paris.

Griffoni shot him a surprised glance, then turned to consult the Cyclops. She crossed her legs and let her shoe, which had an inordinately high heel, dangle from her toe. She swung it up and down, apparently unconscious of what she was doing. First Signorina Elettra's tie, and now this shoe. Brunetti found himself wondering what Petrarch would have done had Laura worn those shoes or that dark tie. Written a sonnet to them? Turned away in horror from such unseemly dress?

He was trying to compose the third line of a sonnet to the shoe when Griffoni said, 'I suppose it could be.'

Brunetti abandoned his search for a rhyme for 'scarpa', happy to do so because he feared 'arpa' would not aid in the expression of deep sentiments, however much the harp would sit comfortably in a sonnet.

'Flavia Petrelli said that it's female fans who make her nervous because they want something from her.'

'Do you think that's because of her sexual history?' Griffoni asked, as if inquiring about hair colour.

'I don't know,' Brunetti answered. 'I have no idea how women think.'

She raised her eyebrows. 'That probably depends on the woman,' she said, adding, 'If this fan is a woman, she's hardly representative of the species.'

'Probably not,' Brunetti temporized.

'I meant only that we aren't prone to violence, and this one seems to be.' She looked out the window, as if pursuing the thought. 'But she's not very good at it, is she?'

'What do you mean?'

170

'Assuming she pushed the girl,' she began, 'she didn't do a very thorough job. She took a look and walked away.'

'Meaning?' Brunetti asked.

She looked back at him when she answered. 'I'd guess it means she didn't want to kill her, only hurt her or threaten her. Or maybe she had second thoughts. God knows what's in her mind.'

Brunetti was interested by the way both of them had fallen so easily into changing the pronoun they used to describe the assailant. There was no proof, only the voice of the person who made the phone call to Flavia's friend in Paris, and that could just as easily have been a real friend, calling to ask where Flavia was.

He wondered if he and Claudia were giving in to the thinking that characterized former centuries: bizarre behaviour was all womb-driven, hysteria, failure to find a man.

'I think I'll go to lunch,' he said and got to his feet.

She looked at her watch and stood too. They went down the stairs together, Brunetti amazed that she managed to walk so easily on heels so high they would have catapulted him down the stairs unless he chose to walk sideways and one stair at a time. What talented creatures they were, women.

21

Brunetti remained distracted all during lunch, still resisting the idea of a violent woman. He had known some in the past, had even arrested some, but he had never encountered one in, as it were, his real life.

The family chattered around him quite happily, distracted from his silence first by lentils with hot salami and candied currants and then by veal roll filled with sweet sausage. Even though Brunetti especially loved the lentils, he did little more than tell Paola they were wonderful before lapsing back into consideration of what, for him, remained an oxymoron: a violent woman.

He ate his crème caramel and for once did not ask for more. Paola said she'd bring coffee into the living room or – if he thought it was warm enough – they could drink it on the terrace.

It wasn't warm enough, so Brunetti went to the sofa and thought about literature. When Paola joined him a few minutes later, two cups of coffee on a wooden tray, he asked her, 'Can you think of violent women in literature?'

'Violent?' she asked. 'Murderously violent, or just violent?'

'Preferably the first,' he answered and took his coffee.

Paola spooned sugar into hers and went to stand by the window, looking out at the bell tower. She stirred the spoon round a few times and then continued stirring until the noise began to grate on Brunetti's nerves. He was just about to ask her to stop when she turned to him and said, 'The first that comes to mind is Tess of the D'Urbervilles, but God knows she's got cause.' She picked up her cup and raised it to her lips, then replaced it on the saucer, untasted. 'There's Mrs Rochester, but she's mad, and I suppose Balzac is full of them, but it's been so long since I read him that I don't remember. I'm sure the Russians, and probably the Germans, have them, but none comes to mind.'

She finally took a sip and asked, 'What about Dante? You're better on him than I am.'

Brunetti looked at his cup and hoped she had not seen his flash of surprise, quickly replaced by delight, at her compliment. He, a better reader? He sat back and crossed his legs. 'No,' he said easily, 'I can't think of a single one. Francesca got slammed away for adultery, and Thaïs is there for flattery. Medusa and the Harpies probably don't count.'

How interesting – he'd either forgotten it or never considered it – how easily women got off in Dante. Well, he was another one of those guys in love with a woman he barely knew, though Brunetti thought better of pointing this out to Paola and risk having her take a whack at another pillar of Italian culture. 'If anything, he defends them: why else punish the Panderers and Seducers?'

She came back to set her cup on the tray. 'Can't you think of any more?' he asked.

'There are lots of unpleasant ones who do very nasty things to people: Dickens is full of them.' She raised a hand in the air, reminding him of an Annunciation they had seen in the Uffizi. 'Ah,' she said, as the Virgin had probably whispered. 'There's the French maid in *Bleak House*.' She stood, awaiting Illumination, while he watched her scroll through the collected works of Charles Dickens, stopping at *Bleak House* to page through to the scene. He saw the memory grace her, whereupon she turned to him and said, 'Hortense.'

Brunetti spent the time it took him to walk back to the Questura trying to understand how it was done. It was not a party trick, nor did Paola show off, ever, her ability to recall what she had read. Well, he had known men who could give a play-by-play account of every soccer game they had ever seen, so perhaps it was a skill more common than he knew. He certainly remembered the clever things he heard people say, and he remembered faces.

He was two minutes from the Questura, the canal already in sight, when his phone rang. He recognized Vianello's number. 'What is it, Lorenzo?'

'Where are you?' the Inspector demanded.

'Almost at the front door. Why?'

'I'll meet you there. Get on the boat.' Before Brunetti could question him, Vianello was gone. Brunetti turned the corner and heard the boat before he saw it, in front of the Questura, with Foa at the wheel.

Vianello, wearing his uniform, catapulted from the door and jumped on to the boat without bothering to look in Brunetti's direction. Spurred by this, Brunetti ran the last twenty metres and leaped aboard without thinking.

'Go,' Vianello said, clapping Foa on the back. The boat, already unmoored, slid from the dock. Foa turned on the siren; they picked up speed and headed towards the *bacino*. Vianello grabbed Brunetti by the arm and pulled him down the steps and into the cabin, closing the swinging doors behind them in a vain attempt to block out the sound of the siren.

'What is it?'

'A man was stabbed in the parking garage at Piazzale Roma,' Vianello said, sitting opposite him, leaning forward, hands clasped on the edge of the velvet-covered seats.

As they turned into the open water, Brunetti asked, 'Why aren't we going to the hospital?'

'When they called, there was no ambulance there to go and get him, so they took him to the hospital in Mestre.'

'How can that be?' Brunetti asked.

'Sanitrans had an ambulance there already, delivering a patient back from Padova, so they drove into the garage to get him.'

'Who is it?'

'I think he's a friend of yours.'

Cold fingers grasping at his heart, Brunetti asked, 'What friend?'

'Federico d'Istria.'

'Freddy?' he asked, recalling the last time he'd seen him. On the bridge. With Flavia. Brunetti stayed very still. Freddy had been stabbed, Freddy, who'd met Paola when they were six and had decided to call her Poppie, a name she'd hated then and which could still drive her wild. 'How bad is he?' he asked in a voice he fought to keep level.

'I don't know.'

'When did it happen?'

'We got the call about fifteen minutes ago, but he was already on his way to the hospital.'

'Who called?'

'The people at the garage,' Vianello answered. 'They said a man had been stabbed and left near his car. He managed to crawl out into the aisle, and someone saw him and called them, and they called the hospital and then us.'

Brunetti had to fight to make what he heard have a meaning. 'So he's still on his way there?' he asked.

Vianello glanced at his watch. 'No, it was longer ago than that. A half-hour: he should be there by now.'

Brunetti started to reach for his phone, but then spread his palm flat on his thigh. 'Will there be a car?' he asked, thinking of Piazzale Roma and the ride out to the hospital.

'It's already waiting,' Vianello assured him.

'They didn't tell you anything?' Brunetti was unable to stop himself from asking.

Vianello shook his head. 'Nothing. I called the hospital and asked them to call the men in the ambulance, but they refused. Said we'd find out when we got there.'

'Did they call his wife?'

'I don't know.'

Brunetti took out his phone and scrolled through the numbers until he found Silvana's, but on the seventh ring an impersonal female voice gave him the option of leaving a message. He couldn't bring himself to leave a message or send an SMS.

'How'd you know he's a friend of mine?' he asked Vianello.

'You mentioned him last year when you went to the reunion of your class at *liceo*: you said he was there.'

'Why would you remember something like that?' Brunetti asked, honestly puzzled.

'Nadia's mother was his parents' cook – this was ages ago – and I remember she said he was a nice little boy.'

Brunetti's fingers entwined themselves and he leaned forward, stabbing them between his legs. Head lowered, he said, 'I didn't know him when he was a little boy. But he's a very nice man.'

The only sound for the next few minutes was the siren, and then the motor slowed and they were at Piazzale Roma. Forgetting to thank Foa, Brunetti jumped from the boat and ran up the steps to the roadway. The blue car with its flashing light was there; he and Vianello got in, and Brunetti told the driver to use the siren.

It took twelve minutes. Brunetti knew because he timed it, urging them around a slow-moving bus and a bicycle that had no business to be on the road. The driver remained silent, concentrating on the traffic. They took a new turn-off, and within seconds Brunetti was completely lost. He looked out of the window, but everything he saw was ugly, so he shifted his eyes to the back of the driver's head. At a certain point, the car stopped, and the driver turned to look at him. 'We're here, Commissario.'

Brunetti thanked him and went into the hospital, which was only a few years old but already looking a bit worn. Vianello led the way deeper into the central part of the building. The second time someone in a white uniform asked who they were, Vianello pulled out his warrant card and held it in front of them, waving it back and forth as though it were a talisman that would ward off evil. Brunetti hoped it was.

The Inspector pushed open the doors to the Emergency Ward and, still holding out his identification, stopped the first person he saw, a tall woman with a stethoscope around her neck. 'Where's the man who was just brought in?'

'Which one?' she asked. She was very tall, taller than either of them, and sounded harassed and impatient.

'The one who was stabbed,' Vianello answered.

'He's in surgery.'

'How bad is he?' Brunetti asked. She turned to look at him, wondering which of them was in charge, and Brunetti pulled out his own warrant card. 'Commissario Brunetti. Venice.'

She gave him a level look, and it came to him to wonder if people who have great experience of human pain develop a defensive coolness they can project from their eyes. She pointed to a row of orange plastic chairs, most of them already occupied, and said, 'You can wait over there.' Seeing their reluctance, she added, 'Or you can go and find some other place if you prefer.'

'Here is fine,' Brunetti said and tried to smile. Then, as a concession, he added, 'We'd be grateful for any information you can give us.'

She turned and left the room. Brunetti and Vianello went and sat in the only two adjoining chairs that were free. To their right, a young man with blood on his face held one swollen hand upright in the other; on their left sat a young woman with her eyes closed, mouth twisted with pain.

After some time, Brunetti realized that the young man next to him stank with the peculiar sour sharpness of fear and alcohol, an odour Brunetti had smelled more times than he wanted to. From the other side came the occasional low moans of the woman.

They sat there for fifteen minutes, not moving and not speaking, Brunetti growing gradually accustomed to both the smell and the sound. The door opened and the woman with the stethoscope gestured to them.

They got to their feet and followed her.

She led them down a corridor and opened the door to what turned out to be a small, disordered office. She went to the desk, removed the stethoscope, and tossed it on the surface, where it landed on a pile of papers and beside a book left there face down. She did not take a seat, nor did she suggest they sit while she spoke to them.

'The man who was brought in is still in surgery and will probably be there for some time,' she began. 'He's been stabbed four times. In the back.' As she spoke, Vianello pulled out his notebook and began to write. Brunetti thought of the good eating Freddy had indulged in for years and the resulting thickening of his torso and waist, so well disguised by the jackets he had had made. Oh, please let that fat have helped him now, Brunetti thought, and promised he would never kid Freddy about it again.

'That's the only information I have. If you want reason for optimism, I can tell you that the chief surgeon told one of his assistants he could leave, that he and the other surgeon would deal with it.'

Brunetti's impulse was to ask why the surgeons would then take so long, but he said, instead, 'Thank you for talking to us, Dottoressa.' She smiled, but it barely changed the expression on her face.

Brunetti was suddenly aware that he had brought the scent of the young man into this room with him. He extended his hand to hers, not at all certain that she would take it. But she did, and shook Vianello's as well, and then was quickly gone.

As soon as the door closed behind her, Brunetti pulled out his phone and dialled Silvana's number again, but still there was no answer. He called Signorina Elettra's office number.

When she answered, he said, 'I'm at the hospital in Mestre. My friend Freddy d'Istria was stabbed at the parking garage at Piazzale Roma, and they brought him here. Call the garage and tell them to close that floor off, then see if they have closed-circuit cameras and if his car – he was stabbed near his car – is in view of any of them. Get the tapes.' He gave this some thought and added, 'Get a magistrate to ask for all of them for the entire day. Then call Bocchese and tell him to send a crew over.'

He paused to think of what else might be necessary, glanced aside at Vianello, who shook his head.

'It's the man who owns the apartment where Flavia Petrelli's staying,' Brunetti told her.

'*Oddio*,' he heard her whisper. 'Should there be a guard?'

Brunetti thought about this, considering the distance from Venice. 'I don't think we need it here, not in Mestre.' Freddy had been followed, and that certainly showed an amount of planning, but to stab a man four times and not succeed in killing him did not. Like the attack on the bridge, impulse and momentary rage had taken over. In both cases, the victim had been left lying helpless, but the attacker lacked the killer drive to have done with it and finish them off while the chance was there.

When Brunetti returned from his reverie, the line was dead. He saw Vianello looking at him, notebook open in his hand. 'What now, Guido?'

'You stay here,' Brunetti told him. 'Talk to him as soon as the doctors let you. Ask him what he remembers.'

Vianello nodded. 'And you?' he asked.

'I'm going to talk to Signora Petrelli and find out who did this,' he said and turned towards the exit and back to the city.

22

As he walked towards the door, Brunetti considered crass carnality as a motive. Flavia had gone out of her way to speak to the girl and had shown interest in her. Further, she was living at Freddy's *palazzo*, and his affair with her had been much-documented. Brunetti himself had seen Freddy put his arm around her shoulders last night.

This fan, indeed any fan of Flavia's – be it a man or a woman – would know about Freddy, and anyone who managed to enter the theatre might have heard about her praise of the young contralto.

The little Brunetti knew of stalkers told him that people usually stalked their ex, whatever the involvement had been: business partnership, marriage, love affair, boss, employee, though love involvements seemed to be the most common motivator. Life moved along and things changed, and some people were cast aside or replaced by others. Most people took this as normal and went on with their lives. Others refused change, refused the idea of a future different from what they had known or apart from the person they loved.

A number of them decided that someone had to pay for what had happened. Sometimes it was the ex who had to pay, and sometimes it was the new partner or love interest. Here, Brunetti realized, he was in the world of lunacy, and so he could only speculate. How reason with a person who thinks that he can win back his former lover by killing the person they now love? Is it possible to threaten a person into love? If Paola fell in love with the meter reader from the gas company, what would it serve Brunetti to kill the man?

Brunetti reproached himself for deviating into irony, a habit he shared with his wife; indeed, with his children. He hoped it wasn't a bad legacy.

He left the hospital by the front door and looked around for the police car. It was twenty metres from him, parked on a yellow line, the driver outside, smoking, leaning back against the door. Brunetti moved towards him, but a sudden wave of tiredness flowed over him, and he doubted whether he could reach the car without having to sit down and rest. He stood still for a moment, and the feeling slowly passed, though it left him wondering if he had eaten too much or too little, drunk too much coffee or too little.

When he felt steady, he pulled out his phone and dialled the number Flavia had given him. She answered on the third ring, saying, her voice unsteady, 'Silvana told me. She's on her way to the hospital. She said you were already there.'

'There's no news yet: he's still in surgery. Where was Silvana?' he asked as he stepped into the car.

'Down here with me. She left her *telefonino* at home.

When she went back up, there was a message telling her to call the Mestre hospital, and that's when they told her. She called me from a taxi on her way there. Nothing since.' He thought she was finished, but then she said in a ragged voice, 'Oh my God. Poor Freddy.' And, insistently, 'Why won't they tell you anything? You're a policeman, for God's sake.'

'I have to talk to you,' Brunetti said, ignoring her question. 'I can be there in half an hour.' That, he knew, was optimistic, but if he could arrange to have a boat waiting at Piazzale Roma, it might be possible.

'But I don't know . . .' she started to say before Brunetti cut her off.

'I'm on my way. Don't go out.'

He heard her say something but couldn't make out what it was.

'Flavia,' he said. 'I'll be there.'

'All right,' she agreed and broke the connection.

He called the Questura immediately and asked that a boat meet him at Piazzale Roma in ten minutes. The driver, from in front of him, pumped a fist in the air and increased their speed.

As he hoped, the boat was there. Brunetti told the pilot where he wanted to go and went down into the cabin and called Signorina Elettra again. She answered by saying, 'I found a magistrate, who wrote an order for the videotapes, and Bocchese's sent two men to the garage to check the site.'

Brunetti was tempted to go and search for Bocchese's technicians in the parking garage, but he knew he would soon be told whatever they had learned, while it was imperative he speak with Flavia while she still felt the impulse of fear. If he gave her time, and if Freddy was not critically injured, she might prove unwilling to unburden herself to Brunetti.

The pilot used the siren sparingly, snapping it on and off only when he wanted to overtake another boat. They passed under the Scalzi Bridge and then the Rialto, Brunetti barely attending to the buildings they passed. When they approached the Accademia, Brunetti went up on deck and told the pilot to leave him at San Vio.

As the boat pulled to a stop beside the *campo*, Brunetti glanced at his watch and saw that it was exactly thirty-two minutes since he had spoken to Flavia: how wonderful, to be a policeman and to break the law with impunity. He thought he could develop a taste for it. He stepped up on to the *riva*, thanked the pilot, and headed down towards La Salute.

He turned left into the narrow *calle* leading to Freddy's place and stopped at the door. He saw two bells, one unmarked and one with 'F. I.'. He rang the first.

'*Sì?*' a woman's voice inquired.

'It's Guido,' he answered.

The door snapped open and he started towards the stairs. When he arrived at the second floor, he saw her at the door to the apartment, half hidden behind it, a position that would allow her to slam the door at the first sight of whoever came up the stairs or out of the elevator. She wore a black skirt and a beige sweater; incongruously, she also wore a pair of dark blue felt gondola slippers, the sort of thing tourists would buy, take home, and abandon.

When she saw him, her body relaxed and she released her hand from the door, but it took a moment for her face to soften and her lips to move into a smile. Brunetti paused at the top of the steps to give her enough time to adjust entirely to his presence and assure her body there was no danger.

Flavia backed away from the door and said, 'Come in.'

He did, asking permission as he crossed the threshold, making his behaviour so formal and formulaic as to calm her even more. He stopped just inside and closed the door very slowly. Then, turning to her, he asked, 'This can't open from the outside without a key, can it?'

'No,' she said, sounding relieved.

Brunetti waited for her to make the first move. 'We can talk in here,' she said, turning to the right and passing into a room. He and Paola had been to Freddy's a number of times, and Brunetti had imagined this apartment would be a copy of the one above it.

He was proven wrong by the sight of a small, narrow room with a single window looking across to the side wall and similar window of the house on the other side of the *calle*. No majesty, no Grand Canal, only this dreary, constricted room that must have been created by adding the wall to his left, thus making two small rooms out of one normal one and, in the process, almost entirely depriving this one of natural light. It also seemed to have no purpose: there were two armchairs, a round table, and a small chest against one wall. No paintings, no decoration: it reminded him of the interrogation rooms at the Questura.

'What are you looking at?' Flavia asked him.

'This room,' Brunetti answered. 'It's so . . . different from Freddy's place.'

Flavia smiled and her beauty came back. 'He's so un-Venetian, Freddy. Always has been. Most of them – you – would be using this place as a bed and breakfast.'

Grudgingly, Brunetti conceded her point with a nod.

She moved to the left and sat on the arm of one of the worn velvet chairs. Brunetti sat in the other. 'Can we forget about Venetians for a moment and talk about what's going on?' he asked.

Her face changed, as if she were offended by his brusqueness, but she answered him. 'Silvana called and said the doctors haven't told her anything yet, except that she can see him tomorrow morning,' she said in a tone she tried, and failed, to make sound optimistic. She pressed her lips together and looked at the carpet.

Brunetti let some time pass. 'As I said, it's time we talked about what's going on. And what's going on is that someone tried to kill Freddy: that's what we're talking about.'

Her response was immediate, and sharp. 'I can't think of anyone who'd want to hurt him, let alone kill him.' Again she consulted the pattern on the carpet and added, 'I've kept in touch with him ever since . . . since we broke off with one another.' She looked at Brunetti as if to ask if he knew what she was talking about. He nodded.

'And he's never spoken of serious problems with other people.' She spread her arms in a show of exasperation. 'You know him, for God's sake: can you imagine Freddy – *Freddy* – having an enemy?'

'Exactly,' Brunetti said.

She opened her eyes in a response that was meant to display confusion, but it didn't work; at least it didn't work with Brunetti.

Saying nothing, she pushed off the arm of the chair and moved around to sit in it, facing him and recrossing her arms on her chest. Finally she said, 'All right, what do I have to tell you?' putting on the trappings and the suits of truth.

'How long have you been living here?'

'Four weeks. I had permission to come late to the rehearsal, so I got here a week after the others.'

'How is it that you're staying here?' Brunetti asked, waving around the small room.

'I didn't tell Freddy I was coming,' she said, as if to refute the accusation of freeloading. 'He saw my name in the programme when the season was announced last autumn.'

'And?'

She gave an exasperated breath, the way a child does when it wants to show that an adult is being needlessly difficult. 'He called me and told me I had to stay here, in this apartment.' She saw the way Brunetti greeted this and added, 'It's really not so bad. This is the worst room in it: I don't know why I brought you in here.'

Brunetti assumed she had chosen it because it was closest to the door, and it would thus be easier to get rid of him quickly. But he said, 'The theatre didn't find you a place?'

'Them?' she asked, genuinely surprised. 'All they do is send a list of agents.'

'Did you call any of them?'

She started to speak, but then looked at him and stopped. 'No. I didn't have time. Besides, it was easier to stay here.'

'I see,' he said mildly. 'Did you spend much time with them?'

'Who them?'

'Freddy and Silvana. Or with Freddy.'

'I went out to dinner with both of them a number of times,' she said. Brunetti waited. 'Sometimes with Freddy alone,' she added. Before Brunetti could ask about this, Flavia said, 'Silvana isn't interested in opera, not at all; besides, it's an awkward . . .' The sentence dragged to a stop as Flavia failed to find the proper word.

Brunetti shrugged but didn't bother to answer. 'So you could have been seen with him?'

'I suppose so,' she answered, this time like a child with the sulks.

Brunetti got slowly to his feet and walked over to the window. Though his closeness enlarged his angle of view, all it showed him was more of the brick wall of the house on the other side of the *calle*. How could Freddy have kept this small, poky room and not knocked down the wall again to give it more light, more life, more freedom? At that thought, Brunetti paused to wonder what the doctors had discovered and how much light, life, and freedom Freddy was going to have.

He turned back to her and, with no introduction, said, 'I need to know about your lovers during recent years, Flavia. I don't care who they were, or are, but I need to know their names and how things ended, whether there were bad feelings.' If he had leaned across a dinner table and spat in her soup she could have looked no more shocked. And disgusted.

'And do you want to know what I did with them, too?'

'Save the drama for the stage, Flavia,' he said, suddenly tired of her. 'Whoever did this to Freddy is the same person who's been leaving you flowers and who pushed that girl down the bridge. You're the only connecting link between them.' Brunetti gave her a chance to object or voice her anger, but she sat silent, staring at him, her face still stiff with surprise and red with a rush of anger.

'I'm assuming this person is jealous, either of something you once had together and lost, or that you have now with some other person. Or both. Nothing else makes any sense.'

'I don't agree with you,' she said, voice loud, anger on the rise.

'Do you have a better explanation?' Brunetti demanded.

'No, of course I don't,' she said. 'But there's no proof the two attacks are connected.'

Brunetti walked back towards her and stood less than

a metre from her chair. 'Don't be stupid, Flavia,' he said, leaning towards her. 'You're not that, whatever else you might be.' Then, 'How much proof do you need? That someone gets killed?'

As if resisting his words, she got to her feet and moved away from him.

'How many more people have to be attacked before you'll admit this?' he asked, making no attempt to muffle his own growing anger. 'You've been here a month, and this person has been watching you. I'm sure you've spoken to a lot of people: how many of them have to be hurt before you'll admit what's happening?' He took a step in her direction.

No sooner was he opposite her than she went to stand by the window but turned to face him. They stood like that, each of them waiting for some concession from the other. They waited a long time, but Brunetti refused to break the silence.

'How many years?' she asked, turning to look out the window.

'Two. Three,' Brunetti said.

'There aren't many,' she said, as if confessing to weakness. Brunetti took out his notebook, opened it at random, and pulled a pen from the pocket of his jacket. With her back to him, she didn't see what he was doing.

'Franco Mingardo. He's a doctor in Milano. I took my daughter to him when she had a throat infection.' She paused but Brunetti said nothing. 'Three years ago. It lasted a year. He met someone else.' Brunetti wrote the name and briefly noted the bare bones of a love affair. He waited.

'Anthony Watkins,' she said. 'He's an English stage director. Married, two children. It lasted as long as *Così* at Covent Garden.' Then, with wry resignation, 'I'd thought it would last longer, but apparently he sees it as part of his job, and it ends when the production does.' Just in case Brunetti didn't get it, or perhaps to remind herself what a fool she had been: 'He thinks it's his right to have an affair with the prima donna.' He heard the change in her voice and glanced in her direction to see she had turned and was facing him. 'I suppose if I'd been singing Despina, he wouldn't have bothered with me.'

Brunetti made no response, and she continued. 'There's one more,' she said, 'and that's all. Gérard Piau. He's a lawyer. I met him at a dinner in Paris, where he lives.'

Brunetti nodded. 'No one else?' he asked.

'No,' she said.

To save Signorina Elettra time, he asked, 'Do you know where these three men are? Now?'

'Franco's married and has a baby boy. Anthony is in New York, directing *Puritani* at the Met,' she said, then added, 'and having an affair with the Elvira, who is a friend of mine.' She let a moment pass. 'Gérard will come to Barcelona.'

He was reluctant to ask again, but thought he had to. 'No one else? I mean something that wasn't serious?'

'I don't do that,' she said simply, and he believed her.

'Do you think any of these men capable of what's happened?'

Without hesitation, she shook her head. 'No.'

Like antagonists who sense a lull in the battle, both of them returned to their chairs. Briefly, they observed a truce, but then Brunetti decided it was time to resume.

'Aside from what you've told me about the things disappearing from your dressing rooms, the phone call to your friend, and the flowers, has anything else happened that might be related to this?'

She shook the question away.

'Has anyone come to thank you after a performance and seemed particularly insistent?' She shot him a quick glance, then shook her head again. 'Or behaved in a way that seemed strange to you?' he added.

She propped her elbows on her thighs, rested her chin in her hands and began to push the skin back from both sides of her mouth. She did this a number of times, then put her palms together as if in prayer and rested her lips against her raised forefingers. She nodded once but said nothing. Then she nodded again a few times and said, 'Yes. One time.'

'Tell me.'

She lifted her head and said, 'It was in London, the night the flowers came down the first time.' She looked at him, then lowered her head and pressed her fingers against her mouth. But it was too late: she'd begun to tell him.

'It was a woman. I think French, but I'm not sure.'

'What language did you speak to her in?' Brunetti asked.

It took her a moment to remember. 'Italian, but I heard an accent. It might have been Spanish, but it might have been French. She acted French.'

'What does that mean?' Brunetti asked.

'The Spanish are warmer, friendlier. They call you "*tu*" from the very beginning and will touch your arm without thinking about it. But she didn't. She stood back from me, used "*Lei*" and seemed very uncomfortable. The Spanish seem more relaxed, happy.'

'What did she say?' Brunetti asked.

'The usual. She enjoyed the performance, had seen me sing before, said my singing gave her pleasure.'

'But?' he inquired, hoping to lead her to remember or to reveal what she had thought at the time.

She nodded, and her nose bumped against the top of

her fingers, though she seemed not to notice. 'She was crazy.'

'What?' Brunetti asked. 'And you think of this only now?'

'I saw her just that once, two months ago. And then I forgot about it.' Then, almost reluctantly, she added, 'Or made myself forget about it.'

'What did she do that made you think she was crazy?'

'Nothing. Nothing at all. She was very formal and polite, but underneath it there was this awful longing.' She saw his failure to understand and went on. 'You get to recognize it. They want something: friendship or love or acknowledgement or . . . something. I don't know.'

She raised a hand towards him. 'It's terrible. All this wanting, and you don't want to give them anything, don't even know *what* they want. They probably don't, either. I hate it.' Her voice had grown jagged. She placed her hands flat on her thighs, pressing down on them as if to push her ideas away.

'What did she look like?' Brunetti asked.

Flavia kept pressing on her hands. 'I don't know,' she finally said.

'How could she cause this strong a reaction in you, yet you don't remember what she looked like?' Brunetti demanded.

Flavia shook her head repeatedly. 'You don't know what it's like, Guido, to have all those people crowding round, all of them wanting something, to tell you something about themselves. They think they want to tell you how much they liked your performance, but what they really want is to make you remember them. Or like them.'

She looked across at him, face tense. 'She might have been wearing a hat. She was thin and didn't wear any makeup.' She closed her eyes, and he imagined she was back there, after the opera, tired, pleased or displeased with her performance and thinking about that, but having to seem relaxed and happy in front of her fans. Of course her memory would be vague.

'Do you remember anything she said?' Brunetti persisted.

'No, only this terrible anguish she made me feel. She was so out of place there.'

'Why? How?'

'I don't know. Maybe because she seemed so alone in the middle of all of those people. Or maybe because I sensed how strange she was and didn't want her around me and didn't know how to disguise it.' She pushed herself back in the chair and placed her hands flat on the arms. 'It's awful, to have to do this after a performance. All you can think about is having a glass of wine and something to eat and maybe talking to friends or colleagues, but you've got to stop and smile at people, and sign discs and photos, when all you want to do is see people you know and talk about ordinary things until the buzz starts to disappear and you know you'll be able to get to sleep.'

As she spoke, the fingers of her left hand ran back and forth against the pile of the velvet covering of the chair. She looked at him with the open, direct gaze he remembered from years before. 'You know, if it weren't for the singing, none of us would do this,' she said fiercely. 'The travel, living in hotels, eating in restaurants, always having to be careful not to be seen doing anything that might damage your career, always thinking of the consequences of what you say because of the risk of bad publicity, trying to sleep enough, not eating or drinking too much, always being polite, especially to fans.'

Brunetti thought most of these limitations applied to any public person, but he didn't think it wise to voice his opinion, not with Flavia in this mood.

'And then there's the physical strain of it. Hours of practising every day, every day, every day, and then the stress of performance, and more study, and every year at least two or three new roles to prepare.'

'And the glamour?' Brunetti asked.

She laughed, and he thought she was going to lose control of herself, but then he realized it was a natural, easy laugh, as at the end of a good joke. 'The glamour? Of course, the glamour.' She reached across and tapped his knee. 'Thanks for reminding me about it.'

'All right; forget the glamour,' he said, and returned to more important things. 'Have you seen this woman here?'

Flavia shook her head. 'I wouldn't recognize her if I did, I'm afraid.' Before Brunetti could ask, she explained, 'My response to her was so strong that I didn't want to look at her. The idea of any sort of physical contact with her – even shaking her hand – was repellent.'

Brunetti knew what she meant. It had happened to him a few times; the feeling was no respecter of sex: he'd felt it both with men and women. It was the way animals sometimes reacted to one another, he supposed. So why not we?

'Did she say anything that made you feel that way? Ask questions about your life? Say anything that frightened you?' What he wanted to ask her was whether the woman had done anything *real*, but he knew that the feeling Flavia was trying to describe was not real in a sense that could be conveyed in words, though it was no less *real* for that.

'No, nothing at all. Just what I've heard from fans for years. It had nothing to do with what she said: it was about the way she *was*. *Is*.'

A dull noise came from outside the room, freezing them both. Brunetti rose to his feet and slipped around her chair, placing himself between Flavia and the door. He flexed his knees and looked around for anything he could use as a weapon. But then he recognized the wasp-buzz coming from the hallway.

Flavia hurried past him and out into the hall, and he heard her answer with her name. He went back to his chair and lowered himself into it, thinking what a fool he was.

Brunetti had some time to consider this theme before she returned to the room, without her *telefonino*. 'It was Silvana. The doctors said the blade couldn't get through the fat and muscle. One hit his belt and slipped off into his buttock. Two went between his ribs, and one went towards his right lung, but the blade was too short.'

He looked away from her stunned face, as he would look away from a friend if he came upon them naked. He thought of his vow never to chide Freddy about his weight. Now he vowed to take him, or send him, the biggest box of chocolates he could find in the city.

He heard a choking noise and turned back to see Flavia, one hand propped against the back of her chair, her face buried in the other. Her shoulders heaved with each sob. She cried the way a child does: relentlessly, as at the end of the world. After some time, she wiped her face with the sleeve of her sweater.

'I can't do the last performances,' she said in an unsteady voice. 'I can't do this. It's bad enough being up there in normal circumstances, but this is too much.' Though she had wiped her face, tears continued to run from her eyes. When they reached her lips, she wiped her face again.

'I've never seen an opera from backstage,' Brunetti said before he thought about it.

Confused, she looked across at him. 'Most people haven't,' she said, then choked back another sob.

'I could come to the performances.' Again, he spoke

without considering the consequences of what he proposed, and no sooner had he made the proposal than he wondered if Vianello would want to come along.

'And do what?' she asked, utterly at a loss. 'You've already seen it.'

He thought he might have to hit her over the head with a stick to make her understand. 'To see that nothing happens,' he said, only then realizing how very presumptuous that was. 'I'll ask someone else to come with me.'

'And you'll be backstage?'

'Yes.'

She wiped at her face again, and he saw that she had stopped crying. 'With another policeman?'

'Yes.'

'In *Tosca*,' she said, 'all of the policemen are bad.'

'We'll be there to show that some aren't,' Brunetti said, which made Flavia smile but also turned his thoughts back to Lieutenant Scarpa.

23

Brunetti left soon after, assuring Flavia that he and Vianello would be there for the last two performances. Glancing at his watch, he was astonished to see that it was almost nine. He called Paola and said he was on his way and would be there in fifteen minutes. She muttered something he didn't understand and hung up.

He called Vianello, who must have been at home or at least in a place where there was a television, for in the background Brunetti could hear the patently artificial voices of the Italian-speakers who did the voice-over for foreign films. Vianello told him to wait, and the sound diminished as he moved away from it. Brunetti explained what he had volunteered them for, and Vianello said that the idea of going to the opera appealed far more than the thought of another two nights of reruns of *Downton Abbey*, which he could not abide but with which Nadia was enchanted. 'You think you could organize a permanent assignment until this series is over?'

Brunetti laughed and said he'd see him the following morning. When he reached the Accademia Bridge, he heard the sound of a boat approaching from the right and quickened his steps to catch it. Luckily, it was a Number One, which would take him closer to home than the Two. He went into the cabin to look for a seat, and the sudden warmth of the enclosed space triggered the same rush of exhaustion he had felt in front of the hospital. He turned away from the sight of the passengers and faced front, but that did not relieve the heat or lessen the assault of tiredness. Hoping that fresh air would help, he returned to the deck and leaned back against the window of the cabin, but his terrible lethargy remained. So this is what old age feels like, he told himself. Falling asleep as soon as you enter a warm room. Needing a wall to prop you up so you don't fall asleep. Longing to be home and in your bed.

He got off at San Silvestro and walked through the underpass, to the left and out to the main *calle*, and then down to the left and to the front door. As he put his key in the lock and thought of the five flights of steps he had to climb, he realized that moving to Palazzo Falier, when that happened, would be no better, not really, for it had just as many steps, even if the family seldom used the top two floors.

Three years ago, the Conte had asked an engineer to examine the possibility of putting in an elevator, and after a month during which the walls had been tapped and measured and dug into by pencil-thin drills, the engineer had told him that, no, there was no possibility that an elevator could be installed in the building. The Conte had inquired if the fact that he had been at school with the father of the current Soprintendente di Belle Arti would affect this decision in any way, only to have the engineer reply immediately that, though this relationship would have had a certain validity and force ten years before, it no longer had the same value, and thus there was no way to install the elevator.

The Conte, unable to contain his surprise, had asked why it was, then, that so many of the *palazzi* of the friends of his youth were now being transformed into hotels, all with elevators.

'Ah, Signor Conte,' the engineer had replied, 'those are commercial projects, so of course the permissions are granted.'

'And I'm nothing but an ageing citizen of Venice, I suppose?' the Conte had asked. 'So my convenience doesn't count?'

'Not in the face of that of wealthy tourists, it doesn't, Signore,' the engineer had said before leaving. Because he, too, was the son of a school friend of the Conte, he had not sent a bill, and the Conte, for the same reason, had sent him a dozen cases of wine.

By the time Brunetti recalled this story, he was at the door to the apartment. He let himself in, hung up his jacket, and went towards the living room, whence he heard the sound of voices. He entered and found his family on the sofa, facing the television, where people dressed in the fashion of the early part of the last century sat at a long table arrayed with what looked like a formal dinner. The fruit platter at the centre of the table appeared to be the height of a horse, and to wash and iron the tablecloth – should it ever have managed to dry sufficiently – would surely have taken members of the staff an entire day.

'*Downton Abbey*, I presume,' he said in English, a remark which was greeted by shushing noises from all three of them. On the screen a thickset and apparently thick-headed woman declared that she was not accustomed to such remarks, prompting the woman facing her to reply that there was no need to take it personally, for she had intended no offence.

'Nor do I intend any offence,' Brunetti said and turned and went into the kitchen to eat his dinner.

When he reached his office the following morning, he first checked his emails and found, among a number of official memos and reports he wished he could treat as spam, a mail from Signorina Elettra, telling him that the attachment was taken from a surveillance camera at the parking garage in Piazzale Roma for the hours before the attack on Federico d'Istria. His car was the seventh in the row, she added.

Brunetti opened it and found himself staring down a narrow strip of space between a grey cement wall and the front and back ends of the line of cars parked against it. He watched it for a few moments and saw, at 12.35, a car pull into a space towards the end of the row. A man got out, slammed the door of the car, and walked away. The tape then jumped ahead to the next sign of motion; the small clock in the top right corner of the screen told him that an hour and twenty-two minutes had elapsed. A different man approached another car, opened the door and got in. He backed out and drove away. Forty-two minutes later, something enormous came into the frame from the right-hand side, and then the scene went black.

Brunetti stopped the film and moved the cursor back a minute, then started it again. As soon as he saw motion, he stopped the film and studied the image on the screen. Giant flying white sticks? Something sickle-shaped and black? He tapped the cursor and played the scene again, still failing to grasp what he was seeing.

He picked up his phone and dialled Signorina Elettra's number. When she answered, he asked, 'What is it?'

'A black lens cover from a camera was placed over the lens of the video camera.'

'And the things that look like white sticks?'

'Fingers,' she said, though he had realized it as soon as he asked her the question.

'White because of gloves?'

'Yes.'

'Thanks,' Brunetti said. 'Anything else?'

'You can see that d'Istria's car is backed into his space. When he opened the boot, which was about fifteen minutes later, he was attacked. It was still open when the ambulance got there.'

'Any news from the hospital?' he asked.

'I called them at eight, but all they said was that he was resting quietly.'

'I'll wait until ten and call his wife,' Brunetti said, then asked, 'When was he attacked?'

'The call came at two minutes before three, about twenty minutes after the lens was covered.'

'What was he carrying?' Brunetti asked.

'What?'

'Was anything found by him? A briefcase or a suitcase?'

'Let me look,' Signorina Elettra said. He listened to silence and then she was back. 'A sports bag with two tennis rackets.'

'Thank you,' Brunetti said, then quickly added, 'See if you can find out if a taxi took a woman from Accademia to Piazzale Roma at about that time.'

'A woman?' she asked.

'Yes.'

'I see,' she said. 'I'll see what I can find out.' She was gone.

If Freddy's attacker had paid attention to his habits and had seen him leave the *calle* with a bag holding tennis rackets, they'd have had little doubt where he was going. People played tennis on the mainland: he'd be going to the garage at Piazzale Roma. Perhaps he had met a friend and stopped for something to drink, perhaps his boat had been late, perhaps he had decided to walk: anything could have delayed him long enough to allow someone else to get to the garage before him, provided that person knew his habits and knew how to move quickly in the city.

Brunetti dialled Signorina Elettra's number again. 'We need the videos from the garage, from that same camera and from whichever ones show the lanes the cars use to drive in and out. And from the elevators and stairway doors opening on that floor. We're probably looking for a woman who shows up there but doesn't go to one of the cars, who simply takes a look around and walks away. And who is there that same day, or – if we're lucky – around the time he was.'

After considering this for a moment, he added, 'What did the magistrate's order say?'

'"Video recordings",' she answered immediately. '"The ones showing the area in which is parked the car of the victim."' She paused, then added, 'I just love the language of the law.'

Brunetti ignored that and said, 'Good. Remind them at the garage and ask for the tapes for the last three weeks.'

'We need someone to look at them,' she said.

Hearing her use the plural, he suddenly remembered and asked, 'Aren't you on strike any more?'

She laughed. 'No, it ended this morning.'

'Why?'

'Some of the men who work with Alvise checked the witness statements – on their own time – that were taken at the protest and questioned the people who gave them.

As it turns out, one of them had made a video of the victim tripping over one of the poles their sign was attached to.' Brunetti, well aware of her rhythms, waited for the grand finale.

'In the background, Alvise can be seen, at least three metres from him. They also found two people who were with the man when he was filming, and they confirm that the victim tripped and fell and hit his head.'

'So much for police violence,' Brunetti said, and then asked, 'Does that mean Alvise has been reinstated?'

'As of today. Couldn't have been better timed.'

'Why?'

'Francesca Santello's aunt took her home yesterday. To Udine. And I didn't know what other work to invent for Alvise.'

'What about the father?' Brunetti asked.

'He called me after he put them on the train. He said he's heard rumours from people who work at the theatre – he didn't say what they were, but I think we know – and he wants to keep her out of the city until this is settled.'

Brunetti was relieved that the girl was, if not safe, at least far from Venice. 'Then Alvise can be the one to check the tapes from the parking garage.'

Signorina Elettra went silent, and he waited while she assessed the level of difficulty that task would pose for Alvise. After a moment, she said, 'All right. He should be able to do that.'

'Will they come to your computer or will someone bring them?' he asked.

Did he hear her sigh? 'They'll send them by computer, Commissario.'

'Can you find him a place where he can watch them?'

'Bocchese's assistant is on vacation: Bocchese would

probably let Alvise use his desk and computer. He likes him.'

'Bocchese likes Alvise, or his assistant does?' Brunetti asked automatically, always interested in any alliances in the Questura.

'Bocchese does.'

'Good. Why don't you ask Bocchese first, so he can start as soon as the tapes arrive?'

'Yes, Dottore. I'll call him now,' she said and broke the connection.

Brunetti remembered a time, at the beginning of his career, when, in order to find someone who was staying in the city, they had only to contact the hotels and *pensioni* with a description of the person and, if known, the nationality. There couldn't have been more than a hundred places to call. Now it was impossible to trace anyone through the warren of hotels, rental apartments, cruise ships, *pensioni*, bed and breakfasts, both legal and illegal. No one knew how many there were or where they were, who ran them, or how many guests they had. She could be anywhere, Brunetti reflected.

He lapsed into a long reverie, stretched back in his chair, hands behind his head, as he thought about desire and violence. Flavia had tried to explain the strange desires of fans, but they had sounded entirely passive to him: they wanted to be well thought of by the people they admired. And who did not? Perhaps life had been too generous to him, for the only woman he had ever desired to the point of pain at the thought of not having was Paola, the woman he had married and who was now part of himself. For her, and for his children with her, he willed the good: he couldn't remember which philosopher had defined love this way, but he thought it was as perfect a definition as he had ever heard.

What happened to passion when it wasn't returned or valued, or even acknowledged? What strange thing could it turn into? What happened when the desired object told you to get lost? What happened when all that ardour had no place to go?

A knock at his door pulled him free of these thoughts and caused the front feet of his chair to crash to the floor. '*Avanti*,' he called out. He looked up and saw Signorina Elettra, again dressed in her businesswoman costume of shirt and waistcoat, though today's shirt was black, while the waistcoat was golden silk brocade covered with what looked like hand-embroidered bees. Words made superfluous by the beauty of the brocade, Brunetti could do nothing more than nod approvingly.

He noticed that she carried papers in one hand.

She held them up. 'These just came.'

'And they are?' he asked.

'Information about the necklace.'

It took Brunetti a moment to recall the necklace left on Flavia's dressing table. 'Tell me,' he said.

'I sent photos around.'

'And?' Brunetti asked.

'I had an answer from a jeweller in Paris within a few hours, saying he made the necklace thirty-eight years ago for a certain Doctor Lemieux.' Before Brunetti could comment on the feat of memory, she added, 'He still remembers the stones.'

'What else did he tell you?'

'The doctor had it made as a gift. The jeweller thinks it was for his wife, although after all this time he's not sure. He did remember that the doctor told him he'd brought the stones back from Colombia a long time ago. Not the highest quality, but very good. That's what the jeweller said.'

'Did he tell you how much the doctor paid for it?'

'He said it took his best workman a month to make it. The gold and work would cost about twenty thousand euros today.'

'What?'

'Twenty thousand euros.'

'And the stones?'

She came across the room and set a photo on the desk in front of him. Green stones lay strewn about on a smooth beige background. The quality of the colour reproduction was such that they could have been dark green sweeties, for all he knew. Some were square, some rectangular, some larger, some smaller, but all had the bevelled edges of the stones in Bocchese's photo.

She tapped at it with her forefinger and said, 'The jeweller took a photo of the stones he was given.'

'Where's the necklace?'

'It's still in Bocchese's safe.' Before he could ask, she said, 'I called him and asked him to tell me their shapes and sizes.'

'They're the same stones?'

Brunetti had known her long enough to sense she was keeping something back, probably the best part. He thought about the satisfaction she was sure to take and so asked, 'And their value?'

'The jeweller said that, in today's market, they'd be worth about forty thousand euros.' She paused, smiled, and added, 'Each.'

24

'That makes it worth a half a million euros,' said the astonished Brunetti, thinking of how he had carried the necklace through the city in a shopping bag and left it on the kitchen table overnight. Half a million euros.

More practical of mind, Signorina Elettra asked, 'What now?'

Summoned from his reflections, he said, 'We should find who Doctor Lemieux had the necklace made for,' using the plural with her, as he always did, as if promising to float in the ether above her shoulder as she searched her computer for what he asked her to discover. 'And then we need to know who owns it now.' She glanced at him, saying nothing, and he asked, 'Where does he live?'

'Paris. At least he did when he had the necklace made.'

Accustomed as he was to playing fast and loose in his own country, Brunetti was punctilious when dealing with the police in others. 'Then we have no choice but to contact the police there and tell them . . .' he began, then stopped speaking as he thought what this would entail. 'We can tell them that a piece of jewellery found in the course of another investigation has been traced to him, and that we'd like . . .' Again, he failed to finish, stopped, and said, 'They won't give us this information, will they?'

She shrugged and asked, 'Would we give it to them?'

'Perhaps, but not for weeks,' Brunetti answered, then added, 'If then.' He stared at the wall of his office and saw only a wall.

After a long time, Signorina Elettra said, 'Someone there owes me a favour.' Perhaps to prevent the embarrassment of having to answer any detailed question he might ask, she added, 'I gave him some information a few years ago.' Brunetti prayed she would tell him no more.

Silence settled around them, protective and calm.

Confining himself to the necessary, Brunetti said, 'We'd need to know who owns it now and, if possible, where that person is.' He considered the blandness of what he had just said and added, 'No need to mention what we're working on: routine matter.' Few people were as good at making things sound routine as was she. 'You might try to find out if the necklace has ever been reported stolen.' In response to her sudden glance, he said only, 'You never know.'

Signorina Elettra returned to taking notes on the back of the photo of the stones. That finished, she looked at him and asked, making a vague gesture towards some other part of the building, 'What do we do with it now – leave it in Bocchese's safe?'

Now certain of its value, Brunetti was uneasy about leaving the necklace with Bocchese. In the past, seized drugs and weapons had gone missing from Bocchese's office, but the safe had – so far as Brunetti knew – never been robbed. But half a million euros?

Brunetti could think of no secure place where he could put it. They had no safe in their house: ordinary people didn't have safes because they didn't have things to put in safes.

His father-in-law had one, he knew, where he kept family papers and his wife's jewellery. 'Leave it there,' he said.

When Signorina Elettra left his office, Brunetti found himself at a loss for what to do until she called in her favour and got the information. To pass the time, he decided to find Vianello and explain *Tosca* to him. It seemed less arduous than the attempt to understand the workings of the mind that made their presence at tonight's performance necessary.

He explained the plot of the opera to Vianello at the bar at the bridge, standing at the counter with a glass of wine while he spoke. Bambola, the Senegalese barman, listened along with Vianello as Brunetti recounted the story: sexual blackmail, torture, murder, deceit, betrayal, all leading to and topped off by suicide. Vianello listened attentively to the end, then asked, 'How is it that the police have the power to execute a prisoner?'

Bambola took a long swipe at the counter, rinsed the cloth, and raised a hand to capture Vianello's attention. 'It's like that in my country, too, Ispettore. If you do something they don't like, they take you away and that's the end of it.' Then, perhaps disapprovingly, 'But nothing so public as the way you police do it here.'

Vianello and Brunetti exchanged a glance but said nothing. They went back to the Questura, but Brunetti, glancing at his watch, decided to go home for lunch and give Alvise enough time to watch the videos from the parking garage.

* * *

'But you've already seen it, *Papà*,' Chiara insisted, setting her fork down and taking her attention away from her gnocchi with *ragù*. 'Why do you want to see it again?'

'Because it'll probably be different,' Raffi interrupted and said, to the general surprise of everyone else at the table.

'Since when are you an expert?' Chiara asked. Brunetti, struck by the words, backed up to relisten to the tone and found it more weighted with curiosity than sarcasm.

Raffi set down his own fork and took a sip of water. 'It's common sense, isn't it? If I hear a band give two concerts, they're not going to be the same, are they? Even if they play the same songs. So why not opera?'

'But the story's always the same,' Chiara said. 'The same things always have to happen.'

Raffi shrugged. 'They're not machines, are they? They have good days; they have bad days. Just like other singers.'

Well, Brunetti thought, at least Raffi hadn't said 'real' singers. Perhaps there was hope.

Apparently satisfied with that explanation, Chiara turned to her mother and asked, 'Why aren't you going?'

Paola's smile was her most bland, which was often her most dangerous. 'You're going to Lucia's to study, and Raffi's helping Franco get his boat back into the water this afternoon and staying for dinner.' She got to her feet and took their plates as they handed them to her, put them in the sink and returned with an enormous platter of grilled vegetables.

'I'm not sure that's an answer, *Mamma*,' Chiara said.

'You'll understand some day when you're married and have kids, *stella*,' Brunetti told her.

Her attention swivelled to him.

'You get to be home alone, Chiara,' Brunetti said.

'What's so great about that?' Chiara asked.

Paola, who was facing her at the table, gave her a level, adult look. She tasted a thin wheel of zucchini, approved her own cooking, and took another bite. She set her elbow on the table and cupped her chin in her palm. 'It means I do not have to prepare dinner, or serve it, or wash the dishes after it, Chiara. It means I can have bread and cheese and a salad, or no salad, or no bread and cheese, and make myself whatever I want to eat. But more importantly, it means I can eat when I want to, and I can read while I'm eating, and then I can go back to my study and lie on the sofa and read all evening.' When she saw Chiara get ready to speak, Paola held up her hand and continued. 'And it means I can come in here and get myself a glass of wine or a glass of grappa or make myself a coffee or a cup of tea or just have a glass of water, and I don't have to talk to anyone or do anything for anyone. And then I can go back to my book, and when I'm tired, I'll go to bed and read there.'

'And that's what you want to do?' Chiara asked in a voice so small she could have been an ant standing under a leaf.

In a much warmer voice, Paola said, 'Yes, Chiara. Once in a while, that's what I want to do.'

With the back of her fork, Chiara mashed at a piece of carrot until it was an indistinguishable blob on her plate. Finally, in a voice that had grown a bit stronger, she asked, 'But not always?'

'No, not always.'

On the way back, Brunetti marvelled at the way Paola managed so successfully to teach her children the ways of the world with a grace and charity that often left him at a loss for words. As a child, it would never have occurred to him that his mother had a real life of her own. By definition, she was his mother. After all: that was her position and job in the cosmos, a planet circling the gravitational centre of her sons.

Chiara had just been forced into a new understanding of cosmology, where planets followed their own orbits and did not circle round at her convenience. Brunetti had read, just that week, an article reporting that 25 per cent of Americans did not know that the Earth circled the Sun: he wondered how many people ever realized that the world did not circle around them. 'Better that she learn it now,' he muttered to himself, then looked nervously around, hoping that no one had heard him.

He reached the Questura at three-thirty, just as Foa was pulling in to the dock. Vice-Questore Patta, coming up the stairs from the cabin, saw Brunetti and held up a restraining hand. He jumped, lithe and limber as an antelope, to the *riva* and walked away from the boat without bothering to thank the pilot, who tossed a cable around the stanchion and, when the boat was pulled up tight to the *riva*, took that day's *Gazzetta dello Sport* from behind the tiller.

Brunetti waited, holding the door, for his superior. Perhaps because he was a commissario, Brunetti got a nod of acknowledgement. 'Come up to my office in five minutes,' Patta said and walked away.

Clearly, Brunetti thought, he was not the sun around which Planet Patta orbited.

He decided to turn the five into ten and went to see what Alvise might have discovered on the tapes. He found the officer in a closet-sized room into which had been crowded a single chair, a desk, and a laptop. A snake-necked desk lamp illuminated the area around the computer; some natural light came in from the single oval window behind Alvise.

He stood when he saw Brunetti at the door but did not salute, perhaps not trusting himself to do so in so small a space. 'Good afternoon, Commissario,' he said in a serious voice. 'I think I have something.'

'What is it?' Brunetti asked, slipping around the desk to stand behind him, the better to see the screen.

'A woman who came into the garage,' Alvise said. He looked at some notes on his desk and continued. 'On the eighteenth – that's ten days ago – at three in the afternoon.' He moved the chair a bit closer to the desk and asked, 'Do you mind if I sit, Commissario? It makes it easier to use the computer.'

'No, of course not, Alvise,' Brunetti said and moved aside a bit to allow the officer to slide into the chair. Alvise put his forefinger on the pad and moved the cursor around on the screen. Brunetti bent over, the better to see, and a moment later Freddy emerged from the door to the stairs, walked directly towards the camera and quickly disappeared. Another moment passed, and a different camera showed him walking away from them, heading down a long line of cars. He stopped at one, moved around to the back, opened the boot and slung in his shoulder bag. He went to the driver's door, opened it and got in, pulled the car out into the aisle, and drove away.

Alvise moved the cursor again, and this time a woman emerged from the same door and moved quickly to one side, where she was half hidden by a cement pillar. Occasionally, part of her head emerged from behind the pillar, then as quickly disappeared. 'How many minutes later is this?' Brunetti asked, not having noted the time in the previous film.

'Thirty-four seconds, Commissario.'

The woman remained behind the pillar for two minutes

and seven seconds, then turned and moved awkwardly back to the door and disappeared.

'Did you see her again?' Brunetti asked.

'No, sir. The camera that shows the door stopped working two days later.'

'Stopped working or was stopped?'

'I called them at the garage, and they said it happens all the time.'

'Thanks for doing this, Alvise. It must be exhausting, when all you have as a point of orientation is a parked car.' Brunetti used the voice he had once used to praise the children's drawings.

'I checked all of the tapes twice. She's the only person who came in but who didn't go to a car and drive away.'

Brunetti stood upright and patted Alvise on the arm. 'Good work,' he said but then realized that Alvise might thank him for the praise. To avoid that, he said in a brisk voice, 'You can go back to the squad room now. You're back on the normal roster.' Alvise stood quickly, managing to knock his chair over backwards. Brunetti took this opportunity to leave the room.

He walked up to Signorina Elettra's workplace and, not seeing her at her desk, went and knocked at Patta's door.

'*Avanti*,' his superior shouted, reminding Brunetti that Tosca uses the same word after she stabs Scarpia. 'Get thee behind me, Satan,' he muttered to himself and opened the door.

'What's this about your using that fool, Alvise, to try to find a suspect?' Patta demanded as Brunetti entered his office.

Brunetti approached the desk and, without being asked to do so, took a seat facing the Vice-Questore. 'He's not a fool,' he said. 'And he's found her.'

'What?'

'He's found her,' Brunetti repeated.

'Her?' Patta asked. Brunetti watched his superior open his mouth to say more and then change his mind.

Calmly, Brunetti continued. 'He's studied the surveillance tapes from the garage and managed to spot the person who probably tried to kill the Marchese d'Istria,' he said, thinking this might be the first time in his life he had used Freddy's title.

'What tapes? Where'd they come from? How is it that Alvise saw them?'

Brunetti crossed his legs and explained calmly how they had requested and received the magistrate's order to examine the tapes, being careful, as was his habit whenever he employed official procedures to obtain information, to report the least important details conscientiously to his superior.

'You said "probably". Does this mean you're not sure?' Patta asked, as if he expected the suspect to have already signed a confession.

'One time he went to the garage, she came out of the same door he used, hid behind a column and watched him until he got into his car and drove away, then disappeared back through the door,' Brunetti said.

'Couldn't there be some other explanation of what she did?'

'I suppose so,' Brunetti said in a measured, friendly voice. 'She could have been looking for a place to plant a bomb, or perhaps she wanted to see how wide the parking spaces were, or maybe she was a tourist and mistook the parking garage for the Basilica di San Marco.'

Then, removing all jocularity from his voice, he said, 'She followed him, hid, watched him, and left. If you can find a better explanation for her behaviour, Dottore, I'll certainly consider it.'

215

'All right, all right,' Patta said, waving an exasperated hand at all these facts. 'Who is she?'

'We haven't got that far yet, Signore,' Brunetti answered. 'She might be French. We're checking on that.'

'Don't take so long about it that she stabs someone else,' Patta said.

'I'll do my best, Vice-Questore,' Brunetti said affably and got to his feet. 'I'll get on with it now.' Imitating Alvise's deference to superior rank, he raised his hand towards his forehead, turned and left the room.

Signorina Elettra was at her desk, speaking on the phone. She covered the mouthpiece with her hand and raised her chin in an inquisitive gesture. Brunetti pointed upwards, and she nodded her assent. She glanced towards Patta's office and returned her attention to the telephone.

It was more than half an hour before she appeared outside Brunetti's door. She closed it, sat in front of his desk, and placed some papers on her lap. She looked at the top one, at him, back at the paper, and said, 'Dottor Maurice Lemieux – who is a chemist – owns a company that supplies pharmaceuticals to the French national health system. He is a widower and has two daughters: Chantal, who is thirty-six, married to an engineer who works for Airbus, has three children, and lives in Toulouse. And Anne-Sophie, who is thirty-four, not married, and lived with her father until three years ago, has never worked but studied at the Conservatory and left without finishing her courses.'

'Studying what?' Brunetti asked, though he knew, really.

'Singing.'

Brunetti braced his left arm across his stomach and, resting his right elbow on it, rubbed at his face with his hand. He discovered a small patch just to the side of his mouth that he had missed while shaving that morning and continued to rub at it gently with the first two fingers of his hand.

'Tell me more,' he said.

She slid the first page from the others and laid it carefully face-down on his desk. Head lowered, she continued. 'Three years ago, Doctor Maurice Lemieux took out a restraining order against his daughter Anne-Sophie, who is now prohibited from coming within two hundred metres of him or of her sister Chantal, her husband, or their children.'

'Because?'

'Because Anne-Sophie accused her father of trying to steal her sister's affections from her.' Signorina Elettra looked at him, then back at the papers.

'Further, she accused her father of giving objects from his home – objects left by his wife to their two daughters equally but which Doctor Lemieux was allowed the possession of during his lifetime – to her sister, who supposedly moved them to her home in Toulouse.' Before Brunetti could ask, she supplied the answer: 'Paintings of great value, rare porcelain, furniture, their mother's jewellery, and other objects which were listed in the formal accusation and are listed in his late wife's will.'

'So she's the injured party?' Brunetti asked, keeping his voice level.

'That is not the way the police came to see it. Nor the judicial system.'

'What happened?'

Signorina Elettra slid the second page aside and consulted the third. 'She made phone calls to her father in which she accused him of betrayal and dishonesty. When Doctor Lemieux stopped answering her calls, Anne-Sophie began to send him emails which passed from accusation to threats. Finally, after more than a year of this, he consulted the police and filed a complaint after producing copies of the emails he had received from her.'

Signorina Elettra spoke as though she were reading aloud a fairy tale. 'After the police authenticated and studied the mails, and the Doctor provided an affidavit from a court-appointed lawyer declaring that all of the items listed in the plaintiff's accusation were still in Doctor Lemieux's possession and in his home, the case was passed to a magistrate, and a court case was opened.' Signorina Elettra lifted her eyes from the sheet of paper then placed it on top of the last.

'It took a year for the judgment to be reached,' she said, then added, in a more active voice, 'Sounds like something that could happen here, doesn't it?'

'Too fast,' Brunetti limited himself to saying.

She went on. 'This is the judgment that is now in effect: she has to stay away from all of them.'

'And has she?'

'So it would seem,' Signorina Elettra answered. 'She may have left the country. At any rate, she's had no contact with them for more than a year.'

'Do they know where she is?'

Signorina Elettra shook her head. 'I had no direct contact with them: all I saw were the police files.'

Brunetti thought of the flowers and the emeralds and the fact that Anne-Sophie had never worked, and asked, 'Is this a wealthy family?'

Rather than answer the question directly, Signorina Elettra said, 'One of the paintings she said her father gave to her sister is a Cézanne, and the other is a Manet.'

'Ah,' Brunetti answered. 'Did the mother leave money to her daughters?'

She glanced at the papers, but Brunetti was of a mind that this was unnecessary. 'Each received more than two million euros, and the person I spoke to in Paris said there was talk of Switzerland.'

With people who owned Cézannes, Brunetti knew, there was always talk of Switzerland.

'Is there a photo?' he asked.

Disconcertingly, because it made him wonder if she had somehow inserted a chip in his brain and could now read his thoughts, the next sheet she held was a photo, which she handed to him, saying, 'She's the third from the left in the second row.'

He looked and saw a class photo of girls in their teens, posed against a high bank of snow, all dressed for skiing and holding their skis upright, to the left of them. The third from the left in the second row was a tall teenaged girl with a happy smile plastered on her face. She could have been the sister of any of the other girls in the photo: in fact, most of them could have belonged to the same family.

'When and where?' he asked.

'St Moritz, about twenty years ago. School ski holiday.'

'What school?' he asked, remembering the cracked blackboards and battered seats and desks of his *liceo*.

'Swiss. Private. Expensive.'

'Other photos?'

'There used to be some family photos, but she took them all when she left her father's house.'

'And during all of this law case, which the press must have loved, no one managed to take a photo of her?' he asked.

'There are some, but from the side or from far away,' said Signorina Elettra apologetically, as if she were responsible for the lack. Then, in explanation, 'The French are more restrained about these things than we are. Not every trial turns into a circus.'

'Lucky people,' Brunetti said, then, seeing that she still had something important, he asked. 'Anything else?'

'She was in an automobile accident about five years ago, and spent more than two months in the hospital.'

'What happened?'

'She was driving through an intersection, and someone ran a red light and crashed into her car.' She looked up at Brunetti, pausing, then said, not bothering to consult the paper, 'Her mother was with her, and she was killed. So were the other driver and the person with him.'

Like a rat, he leaped. 'Who saw the red light, then?' His imagination was off: guilt, denial, responsibility for her mother's death, the deaths of two other people, months in the hospital to figure all this out, assess and accept her guilt, then deny it. Who could emerge untouched from such a thing?

'The people in the car behind her said their light was green,' Signorina Elettra said, putting an end to his wild scenario. 'Her right leg was broken in three places, and she was left with a limp.'

His memory flashed away, first to the way the woman on the tape from the garage moved so awkwardly when she walked to the door after watching Freddy get into his car, and then to something that didn't want to come back to him. He shifted his mind away from it, the way one does when trying to see an object in the dark. But nothing came.

He turned his attention to Signorina Elettra and saw that there were no papers left.

'Nothing else?'

'No. I'm trying to find her medical records, so I can have a look, but it's not easy to work in France.'

She seemed so distressed that Brunetti grew curious. 'Why?'

'They guard their records better,' she said, then, with a whiff of self-deprecation, 'or perhaps I'm just not very adept at their systems.'

'Perhaps your friend Giorgio at Telecom could help you look for her,' Brunetti suggested, remembering the name of the friend she had found so helpful in some of her researches.

'He's not with Telecom any more,' she said.

Brunetti's panic lasted only a moment, calmed by the realization that no friend of hers would ever name names. 'Has he changed jobs?' he asked, praying she would answer yes.

She nodded. 'He's set up his own cyber security company. In Liechtenstein. They're more friendly to business there, he tells me.'

'Has he been there long?' Brunetti inquired.

She gave him such an intent look that Brunetti went back to wondering about the computer chip and if she were checking to see if it was still in place.

'No,' she said after a longish pause. 'He hasn't moved there. The company's there, but he still lives where he always has, in Santa Croce, next door to his parents.'

'Ah,' Brunetti said. 'I thought you meant he'd moved there.'

'No, only the company. He's set up a proxy server, so he can run it from here, making it look like he's living there.'

Brunetti nodded, quite as if he understood both the reason for and the means of doing this. 'Perhaps he could give you a hand with this,' he suggested.

'He's already working on it,' she said and got to her feet.

25

Brunetti decided to try to do his part and, switching on his computer, went to Google and put in Doctor Lemieux's name. Most of the articles that came up were in French, and after reading his way slowly through some of them, he found one from *Il Sole 24 Ore*, dated five years before, explaining the planned merger of Lemieux Research with a pharmaceutical company in Monza. He found a subsequent article stating that the merger plans had been cancelled but found nothing else in Italian.

He read through the titles of the remaining articles in French until he found one about the automobile accident in which Anne-Sophie Lemieux had been injured and her mother killed but learned from it nothing that Signorina Elettra had not told him.

He did not know the name of the other sister's husband and so checked for Chantal Lemieux, finding nothing. For Anne-Sophie, aside from the report on the accident, there was only a brief mention that she had appeared in a minor role in a production of *Orfeo* at the Conservatory of Music in Paris. This was six years before.

Idly, recalling Signorina Elettra's perpetual admonition that you never knew what the internet had hidden in its cracks, he checked the date of the article and then, slowly and painstakingly, read through the schedules of the opera houses of Paris for the weeks before and after the date of Anne-Sophie's appearance in the student production.

Four days after it, Flavia Petrelli had sung in *La Traviata* at Palais Garnier. He felt the hair on his right arm move and rubbed at it roughly until the sensation was gone. Next, he'd be slaughtering chickens on the terrace and reading their entrails.

He opened another tab and keyed in 'stalkers' and was not at all surprised to find that the bulk of the articles listed were in English. More than a quarter stalked famous people; in cases where the stalker sought the love of the victim, the stalking lasted more than three years on average, and the majority of these stalkers were women. As to the victims, they suffered loss of sleep, often moved house in an attempt to elude the unwanted attentions, sometimes tried to change their job, and had the constant terror of dealing with a person who did not recognize the norms of human life.

When he'd last seen Flavia, she'd been unable to disguise the tension that filled her. He wondered how she could concentrate on singing with something like this hanging over her head. His impulse was to call, if only to ask . . . But what to ask? Had anyone else she'd spoken to been attacked? Had anyone tried to kill her? The best he could manage was to do what he had offered: go with Vianello to tonight's performance and then to the last one. And see what happened.

He called Vianello's number, and when he answered, Brunetti asked, 'Did you see Alvise yet?'

'You'd think he was a bridegroom,' Vianello said, as happily as if he had been a guest at the wedding. 'He had everything except a flower in the lapel of his uniform.'

'Where'd you assign him?' Brunetti asked, sure that the officer would want to return to his full responsibilities.

'He looked so good, I sent him on patrol between San Marco and Rialto.'

'Is there trouble there?' Brunetti asked.

Vianello laughed. 'No. But he's so decorative, I wanted the tourists to see him. Next year, at Carnevale, we'll probably have hundreds of tourists dressed as policemen.'

When he stopped laughing, Brunetti said, 'He really did do a good job with those videotapes,' hoping Vianello would mention it to the other officers.

'He told me you'd said that,' Vianello said but did not elaborate. Then he asked, 'What time tonight?'

'It starts at eight. I'll see you at the stage entrance at seven-thirty.'

'Can I get her autograph?' Vianello asked.

'No jokes, Lorenzo,' Brunetti said with false severity.

'I mean it. Nadia's niece is mad for opera, and when she heard I was going to see it tonight, she asked me to get an autograph.'

Concerned that Vianello might have said more than he should have, Brunetti asked, 'Nadia didn't think it strange you were going?'

'No, I told her I was assigned to a unit to accompany the Prefetto and a Russian diplomat. And I made it clear that I didn't want to do it.'

'That's not true, is it?' Brunetti asked.

'No,' Vianello said, and then confessed, 'Well, at first I didn't much like the idea, but I've been looking at some of it on YouTube, and I'd like to see what the real thing is like.'

Brunetti wasn't sure how much they'd be able, or allowed, to see from backstage, but still they'd get a look at the production the way few people saw it: less glamour, more truth.

He told Vianello he'd see him later, and hung up. His thoughts returned to Flavia and the paradox of what he did and did not know about her: he knew the names of her last three lovers, but he couldn't remember the names of her children; he knew she was frightened by the mad attentions of a violent fan, but he didn't know what her favourite books were, or food, or films, or anything. He had saved her from the accusation of murder and had saved her lover's life, years ago, but he didn't know why it was so important to him to help her.

He looked across his desk and saw the papers that had accumulated there in the last few days: abandoned, unread, of little interest. He slid the first pile towards him, found his glasses in his desk drawer, and forced himself to attend to them. Overcome by the dullness of the first three, he was turning to drop them in the wastepaper basket where non-sensitive documents could be placed when he shoved the pile away from him and got to his feet. He had been content to listen to messages about Freddy and not go and see him. Now he looked at his watch and saw there was still time to get to the hospital before going home to change for the opera.

Brunetti phoned the hospital from the police car, telling first the switchboard and then the surgery ward that he was Commissario Guido Brunetti and was on his way there to speak to the Marchese d'Istria about his attempted murder. Though neither his rank nor Freddy's title seemed to have the least effect on anyone he spoke to, the word 'murder' proved remarkably galvanizing, and as soon as he arrived at the Surgery Ward, he was led to the room without question or hesitation.

The Marchese Federico d'Istria seemed to be in good health. He looked tired and worn and was obviously in pain, but Brunetti had seen many people who had been attacked, and Freddy stood up well when compared to them. He was propped up on a snowbank of pillows, arms at his sides, each attached to a drip. A single plastic tube ran from under the covers and into a transparent plastic bag half filled with pink liquid.

Brunetti walked over to the bed and placed his hand on Freddy's arm, as far from the needle as possible, and said, 'I'm sorry about this, Freddy.'

'It's nothing,' Freddy whispered and made a dismissive clicking noise. Trouble, what trouble?

'Do you remember anything?' Brunetti asked.

'You the policeman?' Freddy asked, not managing to finish the last syllable of the final word.

'I'm always a policeman, Freddy,' he said, then added, 'Just as you're always a gentleman.'

Brunetti was glad to see Freddy grin at this. But he winced and closed his eyes, then pulled in a lot of air through clenched teeth. He made a kissing motion to push the air out, the motion Brunetti had seen countless people in pain make.

He looked at Brunetti and said, 'More than thirty stitches.' Brunetti wondered if Freddy, normally the most modest of men, were boasting. 'Punctures,' he said to explain the number.

'Nasty things,' Brunetti agreed. 'Explains all this.' He waved a finger at the drips and pointed at the tube that Freddy couldn't see. He began to feel like a character in the British war movies he'd watched as a boy. Should he tell Freddy to keep a stiff upper lip? Whatever it meant, Freddy seemed to be doing it naturally.

'You remember anything?' he asked again.

'I don't tell you, you pull out my drips?'

'Something like that,' Brunetti said, shaking his head. Then, voice serious, he insisted, 'Tell me.' When he saw Freddy close his eyes, he said, 'This person is going to hurt Flavia.'

Freddy's eyes snapped open.

'I'm not kidding. She's the target. It's the person who's been sending the flowers.'

'*Maria Santissima*,' Freddy whispered. He closed his eyes again and moved his shoulders on the pillows, wincing when he did. 'I put the bag in the boot. Behind me, someone. Thin. Then pain in my back. I saw her hand, and the knife. I elbowed her, but I fell.' He looked at Brunetti and his face went slack. 'Flavia,' he began and was suddenly not there any more. Brunetti stood over him and watched his chest rise and fall, rise and fall. He wanted to do something to help Freddy, but all he could think of was to pull his blanket higher up on his chest, but that might affect the needles. Instead, he placed his palm flat on the back of the hand lying closest to him and left it there for a long time. Then he squeezed it softly and left the room.

26

When they met at the theatre, Brunetti told Vianello only that Freddy had said it was a woman who had attacked him. His friend was in pain but not apparently in any danger; the rest of the meeting seemed too personal to be told, even to Vianello. What had Freddy wanted to say about Flavia, or what message did he want to send her? Freddy and Flavia had lived in Milano during the time of their affair, although Brunetti had met her only years later. In fact, that brief meeting on the Accademia Bridge was the only time he had ever seen them together, other than in photos. Vianello held the door open for him, and Brunetti abandoned his thoughts and entered the theatre.

The area around the porter's office seemed more confused than it had been the last time Brunetti was there and the volume of conversation higher. To Brunetti, the voices sounded more angry than excited, but he ignored them and, not bothering to show his warrant card to the porter, went upstairs to look for the stage manager, who had given him permission to come backstage to the last performances in response to Signora Petrelli's request.

They found his office, not without difficulty, and were met at the door by a harried-looking young man who held two *telefonini*, one pressed to his left ear, the other to his chest: '. . . many times do I have to tell you? I can't do anything,' he said roughly and switched phones. And voices. 'Of course, of course, we're doing all we can, Signore, and we're confident the general manager will have an answer by the end of the second act.' He held the phone away from himself for a moment and used it to make the sign of the Cross on his body. That done, he returned to listening for a moment, then said, 'I'll see you there,' and stuffed both phones into the pockets of his jacket.

Looking at the two men in front of him, he said, 'I live in the circus. I work in the circus. I'm surrounded by ravening beasts. How may I help you?'

'We're looking for the stage manager,' Brunetti said, making no attempt to introduce themselves.

'Isn't everyone, *tesoro*?' the young man asked and walked away.

'I once told my mother it must be wonderful to be a movie actor,' a straight-faced Vianello said.

'And?'

'And she said she'd burn herself alive if I ever said such a thing again.'

'Wise woman,' Brunetti observed. He looked at his watch. Quarter to eight.

'I suppose the best thing we can do is stand on opposite sides of the stage,' he told the Inspector. 'She told me two men from Security will bring her back and forth from her dressing room.'

A woman wearing jeans and a headset walked towards them, and Brunetti asked, 'Which way's the stage?'

'Follow me,' she answered, not bothering to ask who they were or why they were there. Apparently, once a person crossed the Styx, no one thought to question their right to be in Hell. She walked past them, and they followed her down the corridor, through a door, up a staircase, down another door-lined corridor, and then down a single flight of steps. '*Avanti*,' she said, pointing ahead, opened a door, and disappeared.

There was less light, but they heard noise from up ahead. They walked one behind the other, Brunetti leading. He thought of using the torch on his phone but instead stopped for a few moments to allow his eyes to adjust to the dimness. He started again, found a thick fire door, opened it and stepped into muffled sounds and bars of light.

It took him a moment to work it out: they had somehow arrived backstage, at the very farthest point from the orchestra pit, off on the right-hand side. Brunetti looked out on the stage and recognized the inside of the church of Sant'Andrea della Valle, with scaffolding leading up to a platform built in front of the unfinished portrait of a woman. Below the platform stood a double row of pews, an altar, an enormous crucifix hanging on the wall behind it. The heavy curtain separating this scene from the audience was closed.

Brunetti tried to remember whether Tosca arrived on stage from the left or the right, but failed to recall which. It would be some time before she appeared, at any rate, so they had a chance to place themselves to best advantage, if only he knew what that was. 'You stay on this side, and I'll go to the other.' Vianello was looking around as though he'd been asked to memorize the scene and write a report on it.

'Will I be able to see you over there?' the Inspector asked.

Brunetti studied the distance and thought about the opera. All of Act One took place in this setting, so all they had to do was select two points from which they would not lose sight of each other while still having a view of the stage. The next act took place in Scarpia's office and the third on the roof of Castel Sant'Angelo: steps, the wall against which Cavaradossi would be shot, and the low parapet over which Tosca would leap to her death. Brunetti had no idea where it would be best to stand: probably with the stage manager, if they ever found him, who would have to keep everything in view for the entire performance.

'We can send messages,' he said, feeling foolish, especially since he didn't know if this would be possible in the backstage area. 'Stay here, and I'll try to get under the scaffolding.'

'So we're looking for a woman?' Vianello asked.

'Freddy saw a woman's hand, and everything we've learned says it's a woman,' Brunetti answered. Before Vianello could ask, he added, 'The suspect is French, thirty-four, tall, and has a limp. Nothing else.'

'Do we know what she wants?'

'Only she and God know that,' Brunetti said. He patted Vianello on the arm twice and started across the stage. The instant he stepped forward, two people hissed at him, and another young woman wearing a headset ran at him and pulled him back beside Vianello.

'Police,' Brunetti said, giving no further explanation. 'I have to be on the other side.' He extricated his arm from her grip.

Without ceremony or question, she took him by the sleeve and led him, walking fast on tennis-shoed feet, to the left. She slipped behind the piece of plywood that formed the altar and back wall of the church and crossed back to the other side of the stage. She deposited him a metre from the back of the scaffolding, told him not to move, and walked away.

Brunetti slipped under the scaffolding, its stairs hiding him from both the audience and the stage. Through a space between the plywood boards, he looked across to where Vianello stood. His friend looked in his direction and raised a hand.

The voices of the audience came through the curtain, dull and low, like the ebb and flow of waves on a beach. A man wearing a microphone and earphones hurried across the stage and set a wicker picnic basket at the bottom of the steps leading to the portrait, turned, ran lightly across the stage, and disappeared through the metal grating of the *cappella* of the Attavanti family.

The audience noise slowly diminished, then stopped, and there came a round of tepid applause, followed by a long pause. Then they came, the five doom-filled notes that began the opera, then the swish of the curtain, followed immediately by the busy music that announced the arrival of the prisoner escaped from Scarpia's dungeons, and they were on their way.

Brunetti widened his stance in anticipation of being there for the entire act. He leaned back tentatively against a horizontal board that helped support the scaffolding. He looked in Vianello's direction, then at the singers onstage. Time passed, Brunetti lulled by the familiar music, however muffled the sound might be up here.

Flavia was right about the conductor: things did plod along, even the tenor's first aria. Every so often, Brunetti turned in a full arc, searching the stage and what he could see of the backstage area for anything or anyone looking as if it didn't belong there. The woman with the headset suddenly appeared next to Vianello, but neither acknowledged the presence of the other.

He was so occupied with looking around that he missed the musical build-up to Flavia's entrance and tuned back in only when he heard her calling out for 'Mario, Mario, Mario.'

The audience greeted her arrival with wild enthusiasm, even before she did much of anything, though Brunetti recalled that there really wasn't much of anything for her to do in the first act. She stood not more than six or seven metres away; from this distance, he could see the theatricality of her makeup and one or two places on her velvet gown that were rubbed smooth. The closeness, however, also increased the force field that surrounded her as she half spoke, half sang her jealous accusations to her lover. The tenor, who had been rigid and artificial in his first aria, came alive in her presence and sang his brief passages with an intensity that flooded over Brunetti and surely washed out into the audience. He'd questioned people who had killed for love, and in their confessions he had heard this same rapturous certainty.

The act proceeded. Flavia left, and in her absence everything slackened. Brunetti wanted to go back to her dressing room but decided not to, both because he did not want to distract her during a performance and because he feared being seen or heard if he tried to move from where he was.

He watched the action, saw how the tenor exaggerated his facial expressions to project them across the footlights. Scarpia seemed badder than bad and thus unconvincing, but as soon as Flavia returned and he could aim his lust at her, the mood tightened; even the music sounded worried.

She prowled the stage in search of her lover, body vibrating with jealousy. Scarpia turned from snake to spider and spun his web until she fell into it and, maddened by suspicion that had turned to certainty, fled the stage. Only the many-peopled majesty of the procession and Te Deum kept things from sliding downhill once she took her energy from the stage. Puccini was a showman, and the scene was powerful, ending with Scarpia's agonized admission that he had lost his soul.

The act ended, and the applause swept through and under and around the curtain. Brunetti watched the three principals walk to centre stage and, hand in hand, pass through the opening to take their applause.

The applause died down while Brunetti stood and debated whether to try to find her dressing room or not. The security guards, who had watched the first act from the wings, had flanked her as she left the stage. He chose not to add to her stress; instead, he decided to make a circuit of the backstage area in search of Vianello so they could try to find a someone who, like them, did not look as though they belonged there.

Twenty minutes later, he and Vianello stood just inside the fire door, watching the stagehands light and place the candelabra on Scarpia's table, fluff up the pillows on the sofa where the rape of Tosca was to take place, and set the knife carefully to the right of a bowl of fruit. A man came on to the stage, fussed with the fruit, slid the knife a centimetre to the right, stepped back to admire the new arrangement, and walked offstage.

Scarpia, smiling and talking on his *telefonino*, crossed the stage and took a seat at his desk. He stuffed the phone in the pocket of his brocade jacket and picked up his quill pen. Applause from beyond the curtain signalled the arrival of the conductor. And then the first notes.

Brunetti was struck by how calming this music was: one would never suspect that tragedy was to follow. The lightness disappeared, and soon enough Scarpia began his rapist's fantasies, words that troubled Brunetti deeply because he had often listened to arrested men say much the same thing. 'I prefer the smell of violent conquest to sweet consent.' 'God created varied pleasures, and I want to taste them all.'

Words quickly turned to action, and Brunetti found himself confronted by the sound and sight of violence. Cavaradossi threatened, Tosca welcomed, but only to be toyed with, her lover taken offstage to be tortured, crying out with pain. Horror piled on horror, until Cavaradossi, bloody and defeated, was dragged in and then as quickly offstage.

The music softened, grew definitely playful, strange prelude to the real horror of sexual blackmail. Brunetti turned his attention back to Tosca just in time to watch her discover the knife lying on the table, the delicate little fruit knife – a tiny blade, but long enough for what she saw instantly she could do with it. Her hand slapped down on the knife, and he almost saw her biceps expand with the force with which she grasped it. Had the weapon made her grow taller? Certainly, she stood straighter, and she had shaken off the air of hypnotic weakness.

Scarpia set down the pen, pushed himself up from his desk, the workman worthy of his hire and coming to collect, and walked towards her, taunting her with the safe conduct in his hand as though it were a sweetie and he were asking her to get into his car with him, please, little girl. As he lured her, she stabbed him in the guts, ripping the knife straight up to his breastbone and out. Brunetti had gasped when he saw her do it last week, and now, closer to her and even more fully convinced of the reality of what she was doing, he gasped again.

Scarpia turned from the audience, and Brunetti saw him squirt blood down his front from a tube in his hand, then turn to Tosca and grab at her. And she, face puffed up with rage, shouted at him that he'd had Tosca's kiss and that it was a woman who had killed him. 'Look at me, I am Tosca!' she screamed into the face of the dying man, and Brunetti felt the horror of her act at the same time as he marvelled that no woman in the audience stood up and cheered her.

She ripped the safe conduct from his dead hand, placed a candle by the other, dropped the crucifix on his chest and, as the music mimicked the dying away of Scarpia, she slipped out of the room to go and save her lover.

The curtain came down; applause flooded in from beyond it. Scarpia got to his knees and then to his feet, brushed himself off and stretched his hands to Flavia, who had been standing in the wings. Cavaradossi, face a bit less bloodied, came and joined hands with them, and the three passed through the opening in the curtain and found themselves engulfed in applause.

'My God, I had no idea,' he heard Vianello say from beside him. 'It's magic, isn't it?'

A convert, Brunetti thought, but said, 'Yes, it is, or it can be. When they're good, there are few things like it.'

'And when it's not?' Vianello asked, though he sounded as if he could not conceive of that.

'There are few things like that, either,' Brunetti said.

The applause died down, and when they looked to the other side of the stage, they saw Flavia flanked by the two security men. Brunetti waved, but she didn't see him and left the stage with the two guards. Tired of standing for so long, they asked a passing stagehand where the bar was and followed his instructions. They took two wrong turns, but eventually they found it, had a coffee, and listened to the comments that were being passed back and forth. Brunetti heard nothing he thought worth remembering, but Vianello listened attentively, as if there were something to learn from what people said.

They got back to their respective sides a few minutes before the curtain. The scaffolding behind which Brunetti had hidden had been restructured into the stairs leading to the rooftop of Castel Sant'Angelo, so he was left with nowhere to hide. He moved slowly through the darkness in the wings until he found a place that afforded him a view of the rooftop where the events of the third act would unfold.

A moment later, the two guards accompanied Flavia to the steps that led to the ramparts and waited while she climbed them, then retreated to their places at the sides of the stage.

Although there was only death to come, the scene opened with soft flutes and horns and church bells and the utter tranquillity of night's slow mellowing into day. Brunetti detached himself from watching the shifting of light on the stage and studied the people on the other side, who stood still with their heads tilted back to allow them to follow the action on the ramparts above them.

Brunetti, far off to one side, saw most of the area where the act would take place; above it rose the towering figure of the sword-carrying Archangel after whom the castle was named. His perspective also allowed him to see through the wooden frame that supported the ramparts, behind which stood the platform, raised on a hydraulic lift to about a metre below the ramparts, which held the cushioned Styrofoam panels that would catch the falling Tosca. Both the mechanism and the platform were invisible from the amphitheatre; indeed, from the ramparts themselves. A ladder led from the platform to the stage and would allow the resurrected Tosca to climb down in time to take her bows.

He watched the events unfold, heard the tenor sing his aria, saw Tosca rush on to the scene, but then he lowered his eyes and swept the backstage area, looking for any sign of anything or anyone out of place. Shots rang out from above him: Mario was a goner, although Tosca didn't know it yet. Calmly, calmly, she waited until the bad guys were gone, and then she told Mario to get up, but Mario was dead. The music grew wild, she panicked and screamed. The music screamed some more. When she ran over to the left, Brunetti could see her high above, standing at the edge of the wall, looking backwards, one hand raised ahead of her, the other flung out behind. '*O Scarpia, avanti a Dio,*' she sang. And then she leaped forward to her death.

The applause from behind the closing curtain drowned Brunetti's footsteps, and the curtain hid him from the audience as he moved around behind the painted scenery to the bottom of the ladder leading down from the platform. He heard some thumping from above, and then he saw a foot and leg appear over the side of the platform. Her foot kicked the hem of her dress out of the way, and she began to climb down.

Brunetti moved over to stand at the side and called up to her loudly enough to be heard above the applause that still came towards them from the theatre. 'Flavia, it's me, Guido.'

She turned and looked down, stopped suddenly, gripped the sides of the ladder and pressed her forehead against the rung in front of her.

'What's wrong?' he asked. 'What is it?'

She pulled her head back and, very slowly, started down again. When she got to the bottom, she stepped on to the stage and turned to him, eyes closed, one hand still clutching the side of the ladder. She opened her eyes and said, 'I'm afraid of heights.' She let go of the side of the ladder. 'Jumping on to that thing is worse than singing the entire opera. It terrifies me.'

Before he could respond, a young man carrying a bag of tools appeared between her and the mechanism that raised the platform to the ramparts. Though he was at least a generation younger, he gave her an appreciative smile and said, 'I know you hate it, Signora. So let's take it down and get it out of the way, eh?' He raised a metal ring that held a number of keys and turned his attention to the machinery.

Brunetti watched her as she notched up her smile and said, moving away from the young man and towards the curtain, 'Ah, how very kind of you.'

Brunetti shook his head at the raw charm of it and said, 'Well, you're down here now, safe and sound.' She forgot about her smile, and it disappeared, leaving her face tense and tired. 'It was wonderful,' he added and pointed at the curtain, whence still rolled the sound of applause and shouts. 'They want you,' he said.

'I'd better go, then,' she answered and turned towards the noise. She placed a hand on his shoulder and said, 'Thank you, Guido.'

27

He and Vianello stood together on the left of the stage while the cast took their bows. Baritone, tenor, soprano, and as their voice range rose, so too did the volume of the applause they received as they went out to take their solo bows. Flavia swept the board, as Brunetti thought only right and understandable. He watched her first solo bow through the opening in the curtain. No roses fell, an absence which filled him with great relief.

The applause went on and on, filtering back to the stage to mix with the sound of hammers and heavy footsteps. The hammering stopped well before the applause did, and when that began to die down, the stage manager, who turned out to be the young man with the *telefonini* they had met earlier, appeared and waved to the singers and conductor to take no more bows. He congratulated them on a successful performance and ended by saying, 'You were lovely, boys and girls. Thank you all and see you at the final performance, I hope.' He clapped his hands and said, 'Now, off you all go to dinner.'

When the young man noticed Brunetti and Vianello, he stopped and said, 'Excuse my rudeness earlier, *signori*, but I was trying to stop a disaster and had no time to talk.'

'Did you stop it?' Brunetti inquired. Beyond them, the applause faded and then disappeared.

He grimaced. 'I thought I did, until five minutes ago, when I received a text message that has led me to abandon all hope.'

'I'm sorry,' Brunetti said, unable not to like this peculiar character.

'Thank you for the thought,' he said, 'but, as I told you earlier, I work in the circus and am surrounded by ravening beasts.' He gave a polite half-bow and moved off to speak to the tenor, who had not yet left the stage.

Glancing around, Brunetti saw that the stage manager, the tenor, and he and Vianello were alone there, nor was there the loud bustle of a production being taken down. The crew had probably begun its strike.

Flavia had reappeared and was now talking to the stage manager. The young man waved a hand towards the back of the stage, opened his arms wide, and then shrugged with exaggerated emphasis. She patted his cheek and smiled at him, and he went away looking better for it.

She turned and, when she saw Brunetti, came over, and he took the chance to introduce her to Vianello. The Inspector was strangely awkward and could do no more than say thank you a few times and then go mute.

'We'll walk you home,' Brunetti said.

'I hardly think that's . . .' she started to say, but Brunetti cut her short.

'We'll walk you home, Flavia, and go up to the apartment with you.'

'And give me hot chocolate and cookies?' she asked, but with a warm voice and a small laugh.

'No, but we could stop on the way if we pass a restaurant that's still open.'

'Didn't you eat already?' she asked.

'Real men are always hungry,' Vianello said in the deep voice of a real man, and this time she laughed more easily.

'All right. But I have to phone my children. I try to call them after every performance: if I don't do it, they'll get grumpy.'

She reached out quite naturally and grabbed Brunetti's wrist, but it was only to turn it so that she could see his watch. Just finding out what time it was made her look tired. 'I'd rather be singing Lauretta,' she said. When she saw that Brunetti didn't understand, she added, 'In *Gianni Schicchi*.'

'Because she doesn't have to jump?' Brunetti asked.

She smiled, glad that he remembered her fear. 'That, of course, but also because she has only one aria.'

'Ah, artists,' Brunetti said.

She laughed again, relieved that his evening's performance was over. 'I might be some time. It takes forever to get out of this,' she said, sweeping her hands down the front of her dress.

Looking around and failing to see the two guards, Brunetti asked, 'Where are your gorillas?'

'Ah,' she said, 'I told them the police would be here for the curtain calls and would take me back to my dressing room.'

Like Ariadne, she knew the way, turned left and right without hesitation and took them, in a matter of minutes, to the door of her dressing room. A woman sitting outside got to her feet when Flavia approached. 'I'm not on strike,

Signora,' she said with restrained anger. 'Just those lazy slobs in the stage crew.'

Brunetti made no remark about the solidarity of the working class. Instead, he asked, 'When did that start?'

'Oh, about twenty minutes ago. They've been threatening it for weeks, but tonight their union voted for it.'

'But you don't agree?'

'In the middle of a financial crisis, those fools go on strike,' she said, with no attempt to disguise her irritation. 'Of course we're not joining them. They're crazy.'

'So what happens?' Brunetti asked.

'Everything stays put, and the people at the concert tomorrow afternoon can look at the roof of Castel Sant'Angelo while they're listening to Brahms.'

So that's what the phone call had been about, Brunetti realized. And that was the disaster that had made the stage manager uncertain about seeing everyone at the last performance.

Perhaps the woman heard the rancour in her own voice, for she added, 'I understand they haven't had a new contract in six years, but neither have we. We've got to work. We have families.'

Years ago, Brunetti had vowed never to engage strangers in discussions of politics or social behaviour, aware that it was the safest way to avoid armed conflict. 'Then the performance won't . . .' he began when Flavia interrupted to say, 'I'm going to change and make those calls. Come back in twenty minutes.' Brunetti and Vianello started off down the corridor, aiming to take a slow walk around that floor of the theatre.

When they disappeared, Flavia said, pulling at the skirt of her costume, 'I'll hang it up and leave it. You can go home, Marina. You have a key, don't you, to get in tomorrow?'

'Yes, Signora.' And then, 'I'll be at work,' she said, with heavy emphasis on the pronoun.

Flavia opened the door to the dressing room, switched on the lights above the dressing table, and turned and locked the door from inside.

'Good evening, Signora,' a woman's voice said softly from behind her. Flavia gasped, regretting her hurry to make those calls, her eagerness to rebuff Brunetti's caution.

'Your performance tonight was glorious.'

Flavia willed herself to remain calm, forced a smile on to her face, and turned to see a woman standing to the side of her dressing table. In one hand she held a bouquet of yellow roses. In the other she held a knife. Was it the knife she'd used to stab Freddy? was Flavia's first thought, but then she saw that the blade was longer than the one she had been told had been used on him.

As Flavia watched her, the woman went in and out of focus, or at least Flavia saw different parts of her but failed to make out the whole. Try as she might to see her face, at first all she could see were the eyes and then the nose and then the mouth, but no matter how she concentrated, she could not bring them together to tell what the woman looked like. The same thing happened when she looked at the body. Was she tall? What was she wearing?

Flavia softened her expression and kept facing in the direction of the shifting form near her dressing table. Dogs smell fear, she had once been told; they attack when they sense weakness.

She recalled an old saying of her grandmother's: '*Da brigante uno; a brigante, uno e mezzo.*' If a brigand gives you one, give him back one and a half. But first you had to calm the *brigante*; you had to lull the monster into sleep.

The knife had never gone out of focus, but Flavia ignored

it to the degree that she could, pointed to the flowers and said, 'Then it's you who's sent me those roses. I'm glad, finally, to be able to thank you for them. I've no idea where you managed to find them at this time of year. And so many.' She was a prattling fool, utterly transparent but unable to come up with better lines. The woman would sense her fear; soon she would smell it, too.

The woman, however, behaved as if she found Flavia's comments perfectly normal, as in a sense they were, and said in response, 'I didn't know what colour you'd like, but then I remembered you wore a yellow dress to dinner in Paris a few years ago, and I thought it might be right.'

'Oh, that old thing,' Flavia said in her most dismissive girls-all-together voice. 'I found it in the sales and bought it on impulse – you know how it is – and, well, I've never been sure it really suited me.'

'I thought it looked lovely,' the woman said, sounding wounded, as if she had given Flavia the dress, only to have it rejected.

'Thank you,' Flavia said, then walked very slowly and naturally to the dressing table, pulled out the chair in front of the mirror and sat. She waved to the sofa and said, 'Why don't you have a seat?'

'No, I'll stand.'

'Do you mind if I take off my makeup?' Flavia asked, reaching for the box of tissues.

'I like you with it,' the woman answered in a voice so astrally cold that Flavia's hand stopped above the box and refused to move, either to take a tissue or to move back to her lap, where the other one was. She stared at it, willed it to move, to come home to her. And after a moment it did, fleeing to her lap, where it wrapped itself around its mate and curled up into a ball.

'You're lying,' the woman said calmly.

'About what?' Flavia asked, managing to sound curious and not at all defensive.

'About the flowers.'

'But they *are* beautiful.'

'But that man, the one you had the affair with, he brought them out and threw them on the street, the same night I gave them to you,' she said heatedly. And then, in a voice grown icy, she added, 'I saw him.'

'Freddy?' Flavia asked with an easy laugh. 'He's terrified of his wife, and he was so afraid she'd think he'd sent them to me that, the instant he saw them, he panicked and said he had to get them out of the house.'

'But it didn't stop him from having you in the same house with him, did it?' she asked, voice suddenly heavy with insinuation.

'That was his wife's idea,' Flavia said easily. 'That way, she said, it would be easier for her to keep an eye on us.' She was about to make some slighting remark about jealous women when one look at the expression on the woman's face led her to abandon the idea. 'Besides, in her heart she knows there's nothing between us any more.' Then, as if the thought had just come to her, she added, 'Hasn't been for twenty years, really.'

The woman, whose reflection Flavia now saw in the mirror in front of her, did not respond, and she was tempted to let herself grow slack and stop this mad play, but the mirror had cleared her vision, and the sight of the reflected knife was enough to prod her spirits and make her say, 'Why is it you're here?' She had once sung Manon with a tenor who had spat on her during a rehearsal, and she put the same warmth into her question that she had put into the duets with him, and the same skill.

'I saw you before, you know,' the woman said.

Flavia was about to say that, if the woman knew she

had worn a yellow dress in Paris, that was no surprise, but she said, instead, 'And I suppose you've heard me sing.'

'And I wrote to you,' she said with fierce energy.

'I hope I answered,' Flavia said and smiled at their joint reflections.

'You did. But you said no.'

'About what?' Flavia asked with curiosity she did not have to fabricate.

'Music lessons. I wrote to you three years ago about taking music lessons from you, but you wouldn't do it.' Flavia watched as the woman bent down to place the flowers on the floor. But only the flowers.

'I'm sorry, but I don't remember doing that.'

'You refused,' she insisted.

'I'm sorry if I offended you,' Flavia said, 'but I don't give singing lessons.' Then, to make it sound like a principle, she added, 'It's not my talent.'

'But you talked to that student,' the woman said, her voice veering up towards rage.

'That girl?' Flavia asked with convincing disdain. 'Her father's the best of the *ripetitori* here, the best one to work with. What else could I say to her?' she asked, making it sound like an entreaty for a friend's understanding of a moment of human weakness.

'Would you have given her a lesson if *she'd* asked?' the woman demanded.

Thinking of the first act of *Traviata*, Flavia repeated the scornful tinkle of descending notes she'd used when Alfredo had first declared his love. 'Please don't make me laugh. If I were to give a singing lesson, it wouldn't be to a young thing like that: she doesn't know a solfeggio from a shoe.'

For the first time since this nightmare began, the hand

holding the knife lowered slightly, to mid-thigh. The woman leaned forward, and Flavia began to make sense of her face. She might have been in her mid-thirties, but there was a dry, tired look around her eyes that made her look older. Her nose was small and straight, her eyes disproportionately large in relation to her other features, as if she'd lost weight suddenly in a severe illness.

She held her mouth tight as if in habitual disapproval, or perhaps pain, though it came to Flavia that, in the end, they did pretty much the same thing to a person. She wore a simple black woollen coat, open over a dark grey dress that fell to her knees.

'Would you ever give a lesson?' she asked.

Flavia saw a tiny flash of light from the keyhole of the prison in which this woman had trapped her. Would she give a lesson?

There came a tapping at the door. 'Flavia, are you there?' she heard Brunetti ask.

'Ciao, Guido,' she said with effortful ease. 'Yes, I'm here, but I'm not done. My daughter's on Skype with her boyfriend and told me to call back in five minutes. And I still haven't called my son.' This much, at least, was true. 'I've decided not to bother with dinner, so why don't you and your wife go home, and I'll see you tomorrow?' As she finished speaking, she looked down and saw that the nails of her right hand had torn two strips from the velvet of her gown.

Brunetti's voice came back, casual and light. 'You must be beat. I understand. We'll go around to Antico Martini. If you feel like joining us on your way home, we'll be there. Otherwise I'll see you tomorrow morning; eleven or so. Ciao, and thanks for the performance.'

As if the voices had not interfered with them, the woman repeated her question, 'Would you ever give a lesson?'

Flavia forced an easy smile on to her face and said, 'Not while wearing this thing, I wouldn't. People have no idea how hard it is to sing wearing all this stuff.' She ran tired hands across the bodice of the dress and down the thick folds of the skirt.

'If you could change, would you give a lesson?' the woman asked with monomaniacal insistence.

Flavia upped the wattage of her smile and said, 'If I could change, I'd give a lesson in tap dancing.' She stopped herself from laughing, and left it to the woman to get the joke. But she seemed not to find it funny. As Flavia thought back over their conversation, she realized that the woman had taken everything she'd said with dead earnestness and was deaf to anything other than the literal meaning of words. Best not to play with this woman, then.

'Well, if I could be comfortable, I suppose I could think about it,' she said.

'Then change,' the woman said, gesturing towards her with the hand that held the knife. Seeing it, the point aimed at her face or her breast or her stomach – did it matter *where* it was aimed, for God's sake? – Flavia froze. She could not move; she could not speak, she could barely breathe. She stared into the mirror, aware neither of herself nor of the woman standing near the door, and thought, not for the first time, of the things she had left undone in her life, the people she had hurt, the stupid things she had cared about.

'I said you can change,' the woman said unpleasantly, the voice of someone who did not like to be ignored.

Flavia forced herself to her feet, and turned towards the bathroom door. 'My clothes are in there,' she said.

The woman took an uneven step towards her and said, 'You can bring them out here.' There was no questioning or bargaining with that voice.

Flavia went into the tiny room and grabbed her slacks, sweater, and shoes. Keeping her head down, she glanced in the mirror to see if there was any chance that she could swing around and slam the door, but the woman was already standing in the doorway, watching her, so Flavia abandoned the idea. This is how they break your will, she told herself. They stop you from doing the little things, and then there's no chance you'll try to do the big things.

Favouring her right leg, the woman backed away from the opening but stood with her body blocking the door. Flavia walked in front of her and dumped her clothing on the back of the chair. She reached behind her head and searched with nervous fingers for the clasp of the zipper at the back of the dress. She had it, lost it, grabbed it again, and pulled it down halfway, then pulled her arms around to her back and finished pulling it down. She let the dress fall to the ground and kicked off the always-too-tight velvet slippers she had worn with it.

Standing there in her underwear, she avoided looking at herself in the mirror and picked up the old pair of blue woollen slacks she often wore to the theatre, refusing to let herself believe that this had anything to do with superstition. She kept her head down while she pulled up the zipper at the side but managed, through the hair of her wig that fell across her face, to catch a glimpse of the woman. Her expression reminded Flavia of what she had seen on the faces of some of the nuns when she was in *liceo*: very theatrical boredom painted over a look of hungry intensity that was as unsettling as it was confusing to young girls.

Not bothering to remove the ridiculous tiara from it, she peeled off the wig and tossed it on to the table, then looked in the mirror to strip off the rubber cap. She tugged her sweater over her sweat-soaked hair and felt a flash of security as she pulled it down over her breasts. She slid her feet into her shoes and tied them, glad that they were tight and rubber-soled.

Still bent over her shoes, she practised smiling and thought for a moment that her face – or her heart – would break into pieces at the effort. When her mouth felt right, she sat up and asked, 'Is it you who'd like the lesson?'

'Yes, please,' the woman said politely. She sounded childlike in her pleasure, and Flavia feared she would not be able to keep herself from screaming.

Flavia tried to remember what her own teacher had asked her the day she took her first private class. Memory supplied it. 'Are you working on anything at the moment?'

The woman looked down at her shoes, brought her hands close to one another but could not grip them together because of the knife, and said something Flavia could not hear.

'Excuse me?'

'*Tosca*,' the woman said, and Flavia took a very deep breath and then another. I will ask her. I will ask her. I will sound normal and ask her. 'Which act?'

'Three. The final scene.'

'Yes, it's difficult, isn't it, because her emotions are all over the place. What do you think those emotions are?' Flavia asked in what she hoped was a dispassionate, pedantic voice.

'I never thought about that,' the woman said, her face blank with confusion. 'I just thought about the music and how to sing the notes.'

'But that depends on her emotions; that determines everything.' The last act of *Tosca*, and she'd never thought about the emotions? She'd stick that knife into me without a second thought. Flavia put a serious expression on to her face. 'She comes up on to the roof and finds Mario. She's holding the safe conduct she's killed Scarpia to get. So there's joy, but she's just killed a man. Then she has to tell Mario to pretend to die when they shoot him, and when they do, she thinks they've won everything and praises him for his acting. And when they're alone, and he's dead, she realizes she's lost everything. Then they come to get her, and she knows the only escape is death. That's a roller coaster of emotions, don't you think?'

The woman's face was impassive. 'I know it's difficult to sing, especially the duet that comes before all that.'

Best to agree with her, best to let her think she knows everything there is to know about this opera. 'Yes, that's true,' Flavia said sagely. 'You're certainly right about that.'

'And then she dies,' the woman said, and Flavia stopped breathing for a long time. She tried to think of what to say, but her brain, her imagination, wit, all of the things that made her herself, had ceased to function. She looked down and saw her shoelace and thought of how beautiful it was, how perfect, what a wonderful way to tie a shoe, and how efficient shoes were, to keep your feet safe. Safe.

She sat up and asked, 'Would you like to try the last part of it?'

'Yes.'

Here was a way out of this room. 'But we certainly can't do it here,' Flavia said. 'In so small a space, I can't tell anything about your voice.' She had to let her think of it. 'It's really the most dramatic moment in opera, don't you think?' she asked in a normal voice while her musician's mind thought of the cheap, shouting vulgarity of it. 'Maybe we could find one of the rehearsal rooms?' She made herself sound unconvinced, left unasked the question of where else they could try to practise it.

'They're all too small,' the woman said, and Flavia wondered how she knew that.

'Then we have no choice but to stay here,' Flavia said, moving with evident reluctance towards the upright piano that stood against the other wall.

'Why not the stage?' the woman asked and Flavia, prepared for it, hoping for it, lusting with every shred of life in her for it, asked, 'Excuse me?'

'The stage. Why can't we do it onstage?'

'Because . . .' Flavia began. 'But it's not . . .' And then she let surprise win and she said, as at a great revelation, 'Of course. Of course. No one's there. There's no reason we can't use it.' She turned to the woman with a smile that she immediately tried to hide, as if unwilling to treat this woman in a friendly fashion. After all, how could an amateur come up with such a clever idea when she, familiar with every inch of the theatre, had not thought of it?

'I know the way,' the woman said, taking two steps towards the door. She stepped aside and took Flavia's right arm in her left, and Flavia felt the solid muscle of it, realized that the woman was almost a head taller than she. To feel the woman's hand on her arm, even through the wool of her sweater, was to feel her flesh creep, an expression she had always thought utterly ridiculous. How could flesh creep? The answer was simplicity itself: by giving the sense of moving away involuntarily from contact with a disgusting substance.

The woman's touch was not light; and though it was in no way painful, it was revolting. Flavia kept pace with her, conscious of the faint irregularity of the woman's gait, wondering where Brunetti was, or his colleague whose name she couldn't remember. Were they ahead or behind? How could they stay hidden if neither of them knew the theatre? Talk, you fool, talk and talk and talk.

'Have you worked on "Vissi d'arte"?' she asked with what she made sound like real interest. Every time she'd sung it, from the very first time as a student until earlier tonight – and how long ago had that been, dear God? – Flavia had hated the aria. She didn't like the whining slowness of the music, Tosca's endless, whingeing list of complaints, the bargain she tried to make with God: I gave You that, so You owe me this. 'It's one of the most beautiful arias he wrote.'

'I had trouble with the slow tempo,' she answered.

'Yes,' Flavia said thoughtfully, 'it's one of the problems with it, especially if you're working with a conductor who tries to drag it out and make it last longer.' Just as she was trying to drag out her own every word and make them last longer, the better to warn Brunetti that they were coming towards him or moving away from him. 'On the stage,' she said with added volume, 'it's easier, I think, and it usually works.'

The woman stopped and wheeled Flavia around to face her. 'I told you I want to work on the last scene, not "Vissi d'arte".' She gave Flavia a close look, and Flavia saw her eyes for the first time. 'There's too much emotion.'

Stunned into silence by the woman's remark, Flavia nodded and was unable to stop herself from taking a half-step backwards.

A vice closed on her arm, pressing a nerve against the bone, either intentionally or accidentally, but that really didn't matter, did it? Does she want to see my pain? she wondered, or is it safer for me to ignore it?

'The third act,' Flavia asked thoughtfully. 'From where?'

'From when they come up the steps,' she answered.

'Hmmm,' Flavia said. 'There's a great deal of shouting, and the music is very intense, so you've got to be careful to pitch your voice above all of that.' She thought she'd risk it and began just as the soldiers came rushing up the stairs to the roof. 'All she says, really, is "*Morto, morto, o Mario, morto tu, così*".' It was a trick she often used at dinners or parties, to jump into a part and go from talking in a normal voice to singing at full voice.

The vice clamped down again, and the woman yanked her close. Like a mouse watching the cat draw near, Flavia could do nothing but stare at her, then down at her own imprisoned hand. She watched another hand, this one with a knife, approach her own, and she watched as the woman drew the blade very slowly over the back of her prisoner's hand, lightly, a steel caress that left a small red line behind when she lifted the blade from the skin. 'Don't make so much noise,' she said. 'Not until we're on the stage.'

Flavia nodded and watched as the tiny droplets bubbled to the surface of her skin and joined together like raindrops on the window of a train. Which one would drop off first? she caught herself wondering.

The woman pulled back a red fire door, and they were on the stage.

28

Brunetti and Vianello, standing just outside the main stage curtain and hidden by it, could not be seen from the stage, although the small opening between the ends of the curtain allowed them a view of the area illuminated by the safety lights. The ramparts of Castel Sant'Angelo, its wall cut back and open in part to allow the audience to see the surface, were visible to them both, as they had not been while they were standing at the sides. They saw Flavia plunge through the fire door on to the stage and come up short as the woman behind her yanked her by the arm. The dimness made it impossible to read their expressions, but Flavia's terror was evident in her awkwardness and in the way she flinched from the woman's every move.

Neither man moved, neither breathed as the taller woman led Flavia across the stage and to the bottom of the steps leading to the roof and ramparts. The sword-bearing Archangel Michael flew above them; Brunetti whispered a hope to him that he would help defeat the enemy.

Brunetti watched the woman with the knife shove a resistant Flavia to the first step, where she balked and shook her head defiantly. The woman yanked Flavia around to face her, put the knife on the centre of her stomach, then leaned forward to whisper something he could not hear. Flavia's face froze with raw terror, and he thought he could hear her whispered 'No. Please.' She lowered her head and went limp for a few seconds, as if stabbed, then nodded weakly two or three times and turned back towards the stairs. She put one foot on the bottom step and, hauling herself up with her left hand, walked slowly to the top, the woman with the knife on her right.

Flavia stopped short on the last step, for the staircase brought her out only metres from the place from which she had leaped to her death less than an hour before. No attempt had been made to disassemble the stage setting, he saw, and someone had forgotten to pick up the blue soldier's cloak that had been tossed over Mario's corpse. A rifle was carelessly propped against the wall by the top of the staircase. The strike had brought work to a stop, and the ramparts would stand there until it was settled.

He saw Flavia approach the cloak; the woman, still attached to her arm like a limpet, stopped her and said something to her.

Brunetti tapped Vianello on the shoulder and pointed to the staircase, then to his own chest and made tiny walking motions with two fingers. He started off to the right: if he entered the stage from that side, neither woman would be able to see him, just as he would lose sight of them. When he slipped around the edge of the curtain into the wings he heard their voices, but it was not until he reached the bottom of the steps that he could distinguish the words.

'This is the place where you sing from, so you have to be sure to be facing out when you sing, or your voice won't reach the audience,' he heard Flavia say in a strained voice. 'If I turn away,' she began, her voice growing smaller, 'they don't hear me as well as they do when I turn back to them,' she finished, her voice now back to full volume. 'Remember how big the orchestra is: more than seventy musicians. If you don't sing loud enough, they'll cover you and block you out.'

'Should I move to the other side of his body?' the woman asked.

'Yes. Good. That way you're naturally facing the audience, and you're also keeping an eye on the stairway because it's the only way up to the roof, and that's where Scarpia's men will have to come from to get you.' Brunetti took this for a message sent out like a note in a bottle.

From above him, Brunetti heard footsteps and used their sound to cover the noise he made starting up the steps. When the noise of their footsteps stopped, he froze, halfway up.

'Let me stand between you and the steps so I'll hear if your voice will carry above all that competition.' Then, a second later, 'I'm *not* moving away. I want some perspective in watching you, and I have to have some idea of how your voice is projecting.' With exhaustion, not irony, Flavia said, 'Besides, there's nowhere I can go up here, is there?' If the woman gave an answer, Brunetti didn't hear it.

'All right, start from, "*Andiamo. Su*",' he heard Flavia say in the commanding voice of a teacher. Good for her to assert some authority this way, though he had doubts about her chance of success.

258

'No, lower, right down to his face. You have to bend down as if he's alive, and when you sing, "*Presto. Su*", you have to sound happy, and the "*su*" really has to sing. You've just played a tremendous joke on them all, and now the two of you are going to escape and go to Civitavecchia and sail away, and you'll live happily ever after.' Flavia stopped and Brunetti could sense her thinking about that. People can live happily, many do, and certainly she had spent great portions of her life living happily, but no one lived happily ever after. No one lived ever after.

He climbed up another two steps until his head was two stairs from the top, then backed down one and sat, hunched down to keep his head well hidden.

A woman's voice that was not Flavia's cried out, '"*Presto! Su, Mario. Andiamo*"' – rough, entirely without emotion or beauty – but she had no sooner sung the words than Flavia cried out, 'No, not like that. You have to be *happy*. You're bringing him good news. He's alive, and you're both safe. You're going to live.' Had Flavia's voice not cracked on the last word, Brunetti would have judged it a perfect performance.

To cover it, Flavia said, voice louder, 'Now try the "*Morto, morto*", but you have to throw your heart into it. She knows he's dead now, and she's intelligent enough to know she's going to die next, and soon.'

'Show me how it should sound,' the woman said evenly. 'I don't understand how it should sound.'

'"*Morto, morto*",' came Flavia's choked response, and then, '"*Finire così. Così? Povera Flavia.*"' It was chilling. It was the voice of someone who knew that she was going to die, and soon. The good times were over. Mario was dead, and she was next.

Brunetti had brought his gun, but he knew he was as likely to hit one of them as the other. He had always treated practice as a useless bother, and this was the result: to be this close to someone about to commit a murder and not to be able to stop them. If he stood up suddenly, she was as likely to stab Flavia as to attack him.

'Her name is Floria, not Flavia,' the woman corrected her.

'Yes, of course,' he heard Flavia say, and then she made a noise, half sob, half hiccup.

'That's when she sees them, isn't it?' the woman asked.

'Yes. They come up the steps.'

Was that a signal, a request, or only what happened in the opera? Flavia's voice gave no sign.

'And that's when she goes up on the wall?'

'Yes. Over here. It's a low wall. They always make it that way so you have no trouble stepping up on it, and, besides, it looks higher to the people in the audience.'

'But what about jumping?'

'There's a giant mattress on a platform behind. The worst thing that can happen to you is that you bounce up, and the people in the galleries see part of you.' Flavia's voice was calm again, easy and almost chatty. 'It happened to me in Paris once, years ago. A few people laughed, but nothing else. This one is made of about ten layers of rubber and plastic mattresses. It's lovely to fall on it.' But then Flavia pulled the woman's – and Brunetti's – attention away by saying, 'You have to be careful when you call out Scarpia's name and say that you'll see him in front of God. She's killing herself, and she'll be judged for that, but she's sure she'll be forgiven. And she's reminding Scarpia's soul that he will be judged at the same time and there'll be no forgiveness for him.'

'But he loved her,' the woman said, her confusion audible.

'But she didn't love him,' Flavia said, and he heard the

resignation in her voice, as if she knew these words might kill her but didn't care any longer.

He heard nothing for a long time and decided to risk taking a look. He raised his head above the level of the floor and turned in the direction of the voices. He saw Flavia looking towards the absent spectators, the woman standing next to her but turned away and showing Brunetti her back. Flavia, dressed casually in sweater and slacks, still wore the full makeup of Tosca, though the tiara and the wig were gone. Her features were exaggerated and, this near to her, with the makeup rubbed around in places and sweated off in others, grotesque.

Flavia stepped on to the rampart and, looking past the woman, who was still below her, saw Brunetti. Her expression changed not in the least. She reached down to help the woman on to the low wall, but she ignored Flavia's outstretched hand, as she ignored the blood on the back of it, and stepped, not without difficulty, up beside her. She stretched out her arms to maintain her balance, the knife coming so close to Flavia's face that she had to pull her head back quickly to avoid it.

Brunetti ducked his head down and looked back at the curtain. Vianello's ghost-face was visible in the small opening. Brunetti signalled to him, and Vianello held up a single finger and waved it back and forth in a quick negative. Brunetti kept his head down and listened.

'Yes, he did love her,' Flavia said with fierce agreement. 'But Tosca didn't love him and wants him damned. That's what you have to convey if you want the scene to work.' No sooner had Brunetti registered the anger in her tone than Flavia removed it and said with warm encouragement, 'Just give it a try. Your voice can be ragged if you want it to be, so long as you convey her hatred. It might even help.'

'My voice is never ragged,' the other woman objected.

'Of course not,' Flavia said hastily, as if she wanted to waste no time commenting on the self-evident. 'What I meant is that you can force it to sound ragged for the effect of it. Like this.' And she showed her what to do, stopping after, 'O, Scarpia'.

'What do you think?' Flavia asked. 'The raw quality makes her anger real. After all, she has reason to be angry.' Hearing the way she said that, Brunetti pushed his head up to see what the source of such rage could be. Had the woman menaced her with the knife?

No, she still stood there, facing Flavia, hanging on her every word. And Flavia said, 'Put your arms out, raise them up to Heaven, where you think God is waiting for you, and call Scarpia's name.' The woman remained motionless, facing Flavia, speechless.

'Go ahead, try it. It's scenes like this that liberate singers,' Flavia said.

From behind her, Brunetti watched first the woman's left arm rise and then, the knife still in her hand, the right. She stood like that, cried out, 'O, Scarpia, avanti a Dio', and turned away from what was meant to be her audience, arms reaching forward. Brunetti trembled with pity at the raw ugliness of the voice. Three years at the Conservatory, and this the result? Dear God, the pathos of it, and the terrible, terrible waste.

He closed his eyes at this thought, and when he opened them again he saw Flavia lurching to the side of the moving woman in what looked like an attempt to avoid the knife. Panicked feet seeking purchase on the narrow rampart, Flavia appeared to lose her balance, her arm passing dangerously close to the other woman's face. Stunned, she let go of the knife, and when she saw it fall, leaned forward to catch it; the thrust of her movement, added to her weight, sent her to the edge of the false wall. Her foot tripped over it and she toppled over. Brunetti stood up, listening for the sound of her flopping on to the mattresses into which Flavia had been falling for two weeks.

Instead, after what seemed a long silence but could have been no more than a few seconds, he heard a heavy thud from well below where he could see Flavia.

Flavia stood on the wall, staring straight ahead, and then she lowered herself to the edge of the parapet and put her head between her knees. He heard footsteps running across the stage, but he ignored them and climbed the remaining steps.

He ran across the platform to her and went down on one knee. 'Flavia, Flavia,' he said, careful not to touch her. 'Flavia, are you all right?' Her shoulders heaved as she dragged breath into her lungs and shoved it out, her hands crossed over and pushing at her chest. He saw the blood running down the back of her right hand. The cut looked deep enough to leave a scar, he thought, then marvelled that he could think of such a thing at such a time.

'Flavia, are you all right?' – hoping there were no other cuts. 'Flavia, I'm going to put my hand on your shoulder. All right?'

He thought she nodded. He placed his hand on her, held it there, as if to give her some contact with the rest of the world. She nodded again, and gradually her breathing slowed, but still she did not look up.

Hearing Vianello come up to them he said, 'Call them, then go down and take a look at her.'

'I already did,' the Inspector said. 'She's dead.'

When she heard that, Flavia raised her head and looked at Brunetti. It was only then that he remembered the young man with the key, smiling at Flavia and saying he'd lower the platform with the Styrofoam panels because she hated it so much.

Behind him, he heard Vianello move off and start to make a phone call.

He removed his hand from her shoulder, and he saw her register the gesture. 'She told me she knew where my children live,' Flavia said.

He got to his feet and stood looking down at her. Then he put his hands under her arm and helped her to her feet.

'Come on, we'll walk you home,' Brunetti said.

THE WATERS
OF ETERNAL
YOUTH

Read on for an exciting extract from the new
Commissario Brunetti novel by Donna Leon.

1

He had always hated formal dinners, and he hated being at this one. It made no difference to Brunetti that he knew some of the people at the long table, nor was his irritation lessened by the fact that the dinner was being held in the home of his parents-in-law and, because of that, in one of the most beautiful *palazzi* in the city. He had been dragooned into coming by his wife and his mother-in-law, who had claimed that his position in the city would add lustre to the evening.

Brunetti had insisted that his 'position' as a commissario di polizia was hardly one that would add lustre to a dinner held for wealthy foreigners. His mother-in-law, however, using the Border Collie tactics he had observed in her for a quarter of a century, had circled his heels, yipping and yapping, until she had finally herded him to the place where she wanted him to be. Then, sensing his weakness, she had added, 'Besides, Demetriana wants to see you, and it would be a great favour to me if you'd talk to her, Guido.'

Brunetti had conceded and thus found himself at dinner with Contessa Demetriana Lando-Continui, who sat perfectly at ease at the end of a long table that was not her own. Facing her at the other end was the friend of her heart, Contessa Donatella Falier, the use of whose home she had requested in order to host this dinner. A burst pipe in the room above her own dining room, which had managed to bring down a good portion of the ceiling, had rendered the room unusable for the foreseeable future, and she had turned to her friend for help. Contessa Falier, although not involved in the foundation for which this benefit dinner was being given, was happy to oblige her friend, and thus they sat, two contessas, a bit like bookends, at either end of the table at which were seated eight other people.

A small woman, Contessa Lando-Continui spoke lightly accented English in a voice she had to strain to make carry down the entire table but seemed at ease speaking in public. She had taken care with her appearance: her hair was a cap of dull gold curls, cut short in a youthful style that seemed entirely natural to someone as small as she. She wore a dark green dress with long sleeves that allowed attention to be paid to her hands, long-fingered and thin and entirely unblemished by the spots of age. Her eyes were almost the same colour as the dress and complemented her choice of hair colour. As he studied her, Brunetti renewed his conviction that she must have been a very attractive woman a half-century before.

Tuning back into her conversation, Brunetti heard her say, 'I had the good fortune to grow up in a different Venice, not this stage set that's been created for tourists to remind them of a city where, in a certain sense, they've never been.' Brunetti nodded and continued eating his spaghetti with shellfish, thinking of how much like Paola's it was, probably because the cook who had prepared it was the same woman who had helped Paola learn to cook.

'It is a cause of great sadness that the city administration does everything it can to bring more and more of them here. At the same time,' the Contessa began and raised her eyes in a quick sweep of the faces before her, 'Venetian families, especially young ones, are driven out because they cannot afford to rent or buy a home.' Her distress was so palpable that Brunetti glanced across the table at his wife, Paola, and met her eyes. She nodded.

To the Contessa's left sat a pale-haired young Englishman who had been introduced as Lord Something or Other. On his other side sat a famous English historian whose book about the Savoia family Brunetti had read, and liked. Professor Moore's invitation had perhaps been prompted by her having made no mention in her book of the involvement of her hostess' late husband's family, the Lando-Continui, with Mussolini's regime. On her left sat another Englishman who had been introduced to Brunetti as a banker and then, just opposite Brunetti, his own wife, sitting at her mother's right hand.

Brunetti thus sat next to his mother-in-law and opposite his wife. He suspected this placement was somehow in violation of the rules of etiquette, but his relief at being near them put paid to his concern for *politesse*. On his left sat the banker's companion, a woman who turned out to be a Professor of Law at Oxford, then a man Brunetti had seen on the streets over the years, and last, a German journalist who had lived in the city for years and who had arrived at a point of such cynicism as almost to make him an Italian.

Brunetti glanced back and forth between the two contessas and was struck, as he ever was when seeing them together, by what odd pairings life makes for us. Contessa Falier had inherited the other Contessa when the latter became a widow. Although they had been friends for years, the bond between them had grown stronger upon the death of Conte Lando-Continui, and they had passed from being fast friends to being true friends, a fact Brunetti pondered each time he met the second Contessa, so different was the sobriety of her person from that of his mother-in-law. Contessa Lando-Continui had always been polite to him, at times even warm, but he had always wondered if he were being treated as an appendage of his wife and mother-in-law. Did most wives feel this way? he wondered.

'I repeat,' Contessa Lando-Continui resumed, and Brunetti returned his full attention to her. While she was gathering her breath to fulfil that promise, she was interrupted by a flourish of the hand of the second man to her right, the one Brunetti had vaguely recognized. Dark-haired, somewhere close to forty, and with a beard and moustache much influenced by the style of the last Russian Tsar, he interjected, speaking loudly into the pause his gesture had created.

'My dear Contessa,' he said, getting slowly to his feet, 'we're all guilty of encouraging the tourists to come, even you.' The Contessa turned towards him, apparently confused by this rare conjunction of the words 'guilty' and 'you', and perhaps nervous that this person might know some way they might legitimately be conjoined. She placed both hands, palms down and beginning to tighten, on either side of her plate, as if prepared to pull the tablecloth to the floor should the conversation veer towards that conjunction.

A confused hush fell on the table. The man smiled in her direction and entered the gap created by her silence. He was speaking in English in deference to the majority of the people at the table, over whom he swept his eyes. 'For, as you all know, the *largesse* of our hostess in aiding the restoration of many monuments in the city has preserved much of the beauty of Venice and thus added without measure to its desirability as a destination for those who love it and appreciate its wonders.' He looked around and smiled at his audience.

Because he was standing near to her and spoke clearly, the Contessa could not have missed the word '*largesse*', at the sound of which her expression softened and she released her death grip on the tablecloth. She raised one hand, palm forward, in his direction, as if hoping to stop all and any praise. But, Brunetti reflected, the voice of truth was not to be gainsaid, and so the man took his glass and raised it in the air. Had he memorized his speech, Brunetti wondered, so easily had it flowed.

Then, leaning forward and seeing that the man was thick of body, Brunetti remembered he'd been introduced to him at a meeting of the Circolo Italo-Britannico some years ago. That would explain his ease with English. A small photo of his bearded face had appeared in an article in the *Gazzettino* a few weeks ago, reporting that he'd been appointed by the Fine Arts Commission to lead a survey of the carved marble wall plaques in the city. Brunetti had read the article because there were five such plaques over the door of Palazzo Falier.

'My friends, and friends of La Serenissima,' he went on, his smile growing warmer, 'I would like to take the liberty to toast our hostess, Contessa Demetriana Lando-Continui, and I would like to thank her, personally as a Venetian and professionally as someone working to preserve the city, for what she has done to protect the future of my city.' He looked towards the Contessa, smiled and added, 'Our city.' Then, raising his free hand to encompass the others and forestall any feeling that he had excluded the non-Venetians, he broadened his smile. 'Your city. For you have taken Venice into your hearts and into your dreams and thus have become, along with us, *Veneziani*.' This last was followed by applause that went on so long he finally had to set down his glass in order to raise both hands to push back the fervour of their response.

Brunetti wished he'd been seated beside Paola, for he wanted to ask her if they were in danger of being propelled into charm-shock; a quick glance in her direction showed him that she shared his concern.

When silence returned, the man went on, now speaking directly to the Contessa, 'Please know that we members of Salva Serenissima are deeply grateful for your leadership in our efforts to see that the living fabric of this city that we love can remain an integral, inspiring part of our lives and hopes.' He raised his glass again, but this time he waved it in an all-inclusive circle of praise.

The banker and his companion rose to their feet, as at the end of a particularly moving performance, but when they noticed that the others at the table remained in their chairs, the banker smoothed out a wrinkle in the knee of his trousers and sat down, while she carefully tucked her skirt under her, as if that were why she had risen to her feet.

Salva Serenissima, Brunetti thought, understanding the man's connection to the Contessa. But before he could try to work out just what the speaker might be doing for the organization, a deep male voice boomed out in English, 'Hear, hear,' quite as if this were the House of Lords and His Lordship needed to express his approval. Brunetti put on a smile and joined the others in toasting, though he did not follow through by drinking. His eyes went back to

Paola, now in three-quarter profile as she stared down the table to her mother's friend. As if sensing his attention, Paola turned her head towards him and allowed her eyes to close and then open slowly, as though she'd been told that the Crucifixion had only just begun and there still remained a number of nails.

The man who had spoken, apparently having exhausted his store of praise, sat down and returned to his now-cold dinner. Contessa Lando-Continui did the same. The others attempted to resume their varied conversations. Within minutes the dinner continued to the tinkle of silver voices and silver cutlery.

Brunetti turned to his mother-in-law and found that the Border Collie had been called off, leaving behind a somnolent poodle, highly decorative but bored and inattentive. Contessa Falier, seeing that Paola was busy talking to the banker, set down her fork and moved back in her chair. Brunetti noticed that the woman on his left was busy speaking to the man who had proposed a toast to Contessa Lando-Continui, so he returned his attention to his mother-in-law, a woman whose opinions often surprised him, as did the far-flung sources she consulted in forming them.

Their talk veered to that week's stories about the vast MOSE engineering project that was meant to protect the city from the danger of the advancing tides. Like many residents of the city, both of them had thought from the very beginning that the whole thing stank: everything that had happened in the last three decades had only increased the odour. Brunetti had heard and read too much to have any hope that the elaborate and pharaonically expensive system of enormous metal barriers intended to block the waters of the sea from entering the *laguna* would ever actually work. The only certainty was that the maintenance costs would increase every year. The ongoing investigation of the missing millions, perhaps wildly more, was chiefly in the hands of the Guardia di Finanza: the local police knew little more than what was printed in the papers.

At the first revelations of the depth and breadth of the pillaging of European money, the city authorities had grown red-faced with outrage that quickly turned to embarrassment as one high official first claimed his innocence, only to concede that perhaps some of the money intended for the MOSE project had indeed found its way to his election campaign. But, he insisted, he had never touched a euro of it for his personal use, apparently of the belief that buying an election was less reprehensible than buying a Brioni suit.

After a brief flirtation with indignation, Brunetti's native good sense had asserted itself and he had dismissed disgust as an inappropriate response. Better to think like a Neapolitan and view it all as theatre, as farce, as our leaders at play, doing what they do best.

He felt the moment when both of them tired of the subject. 'You've known her for ever, haven't you?' Brunetti asked, giving a quick glance to the head of the table, where Contessa Lando-Continui was speaking to the German journalist.

'Since I got to Venice,' she said. 'Years ago.' Brunetti wasn't sure how pleased she sounded at that; she had never, in all these years, revealed very much about her feelings for the city for which she had left her native Florence, beyond her love of her family.

'She can be the worst sort of battleaxe, I know, but she can also be generous and kind.' Contessa Falier nodded in affirmation of what she had just said and added, 'I'm afraid most people don't see it. But then, poor thing, she doesn't see many people.'

Contessa Falier glanced around the table before adding, in a quiet voice, 'This is an exception. She'll host these dinners with potential sponsors, but she doesn't like to do it.'

'Then why do it? Surely they must have an office for fund-raising.'

'Because everyone loves a lord,' she answered, lapsing into English.

'Meaning?'

'She's a contessa, so people want to say they've eaten at her table.'

'In this case,' he said, glancing around the familiar dining room, 'it's not even her table, is it?'

The Contessa laughed.

'So she invites them here and you feed them, and in return they contribute to Salva Serenissima?' Brunetti asked.

'Something like that,' the Contessa admitted. 'She's dedicated to the work they do, and as she's grown older, she's become more and more intent on seeing that young Venetians can continue to live here and raise their families here. No one else bothers with that.' She glanced around the table, then at Brunetti, and finally said, 'I'm not sure the work Salva Serenissima did on the smaller mosaics on Torcello was all that good. In places, you can see which are the new *tesserae*. But they did some structural work, too, so it's more good than bad.'

Because he had not been inside the church in years and had no more than a vague memory of sinners being sent to Hell and a great deal of pink flesh, Brunetti could only shrug and sigh, something he had taken to doing often in recent years.

Lowering his voice and moving away from the thought of sinners going to Hell, Brunetti asked, 'The man who spoke? Who is he?'

Before she replied, Contessa Falier picked up her napkin and wiped at her lips, replaced it and took a sip of water. Both of them glanced at the man near the end of the table and saw that he was now speaking across the table to the historian, who appeared to be taking notes on a small piece of paper as she listened to him. Contessa Lando-Continui and the English lord were engaged in amiable conversation, he speaking in loud, heavily accented Italian.

Apparently feeling protected by the deep boom of his voice, his mother-in-law leaned towards Brunetti and said, 'Sandro Vittori-Ricciardi. He's a protégé of Demetriana's.'

'And he does what?'

'He's an interior designer and a restorer of stone and marble; he works for her foundation.'

'So he's involved in the things she's doing for the city?' Brunetti asked.

Her tone sharpened. 'These *things* save the city about three million euros a year, please remember, Guido. As well as the money to restore the apartments that are rented to young families.' Then, to emphasize the importance, she added, 'It replaces money the government won't give any more.'

Brunetti sensed a presence behind him and sat up straighter to allow a waiter to remove his plate. He paused until the Contessa's had been removed, and said in a conciliatory voice, 'Of course, you're right.'

He knew that tonight's dinner was meant to bring together potential foreign donors and native Venetians – he was one of those on offer. Come to the zoo and meet the animals that your donations help survive in their native habitat. Come at feeding time. Brunetti was not fond of the part of himself that entertained such thoughts, but he knew too much to stifle them.

Contessa Lando-Continui had been trying for years, he

knew, to get her hand into Count Falier's pocket. He had been both gracious and adamant in deflecting her every attempt. 'If so much weren't stolen, Demetriana, the city could pay for restorations, and if politicians' families and friends didn't get public housing, you wouldn't have to ask people to help you restore the apartments,' Brunetti had once heard the Conte tell her.

Unrebuffed by Count Falier's remarks, she continued to invite him to her dinners – she had even invited him to this one in his own home – and each time she did, the Conte remembered a last-minute meeting in Cairo or a dinner in Milano; once he had begged off by mentioning the Prime Minister; tonight, for all Brunetti knew, it had been an appointment with a Russian arms dealer. Brunetti thought the Conte didn't much care how believable his excuses were, so long as he could amuse himself by inventing stories that would agitate the Contessa.

So there they were in his absence, he and Paola and his mother-in-law, offered as a sop to the insistence of the Contessa and, perhaps, as a treat to the visitors: not only Contessa Lando-Continui but Contessa Falier, two real aristocrats for the price of one. And the next generation tossed in as lagniappe.

The dessert came, a *ciambella con zucca e uvetta* that delighted Brunetti, as did the sweet wine served with it. When the maid came around again to offer a second help-ing, Paola caught her husband's eye. He smiled back and shook his head at the maid's offer as if he had meant to do it, failing to persuade Paola but managing to convince himself.

That done, he felt entirely justified in accepting a small glass of grappa. He pushed his chair back a bit, stretched out his legs, and lifted his glass.

Contessa Falier, as if there had been no interruption, returned to their former subject and asked, 'Are you curious because he works for her?' She moved to one side the glass of grappa the waiter had left in front of her.

'I'm curious about why he thinks it necessary to flatter her so,' was the best answer Brunetti could provide.

The Contessa smiled and asked, 'Is it being a policeman that makes you suspicious of human motives?' She spoke naturally now that the conversation was more general and individual voices were covered by the others.

Before Brunetti could answer, Contessa Lando-Continui set down her spoon and, glancing at her friend at the other end of the table as if for permission, announced, 'I think coffee will be served in the *salone*.' Sando Vittori-Ricciardi got immediately to his feet and moved around behind her chair to pull it back for her. The Contessa stood and nodded her thanks, allowed him to take her arm, and moved off towards the *salone*. She passed through the door that led from the dining room towards the front of the *palazzo*, the guests falling into a disorderly line behind her.